"Jackie Pilossoph is the kind of author who epitc
next door,' and this translates into the well-rounded, warm-hearted and
inspiring novel, *Free Gift With Purchase*. Ms. Pilossoph allows her characters
to simply be who they are, without judgment, which results in the reader
being able to appreciate them for their imperfections. At the heart of this
wonderfully written novel is a story about the powerful relationships women
develop with their female family and friends. What I truly loved about this
novel is the inspiring message. I simply could not put the book down."

–KATHRYN HAMILTON, CHICK LIT CENTRAL

"This is a novel that anyone with a sister or mother should read. It shows how
a family, even when being put through trials, can and should stick together.
The laughs and tears shared are truly uplifting."

–CHARLOTTE LYNN, A NOVEL REVIEW

Free Gift
With Purchase

A novel by

Jackie Pilossoph

Hello Number 3!

Free Gift With Purchase is my third novel and I can't even begin to tell you how much I enjoyed writing this book!

Getting back into the dating scene at 41 years old was a trip, and that's where the idea for this novel came from. *Free Gift With Purchase* is fiction, but it is VERY LOOSELY based on events that happened to myself and my friends as we struggled through the nightmare world of dating in our forties. So, the first people I would like to thank are the men who gave me the material needed to light the fire and make this book laugh out loud hilarious, sexy, heartfelt and meaningful. More specifically, thank you to the guys who inspired me to create Preston, Luke, Denny and all the Matts!

I'd also like to thank my sister, Sue, (the smart one). Although Laura is very different from Sue, and again, all of the events in this book are fictitious, bits and pieces of my sister can be seen through sweet, kind, generous Laura, and her caring, selfless nature when it comes to her sister, Emma, just like my sister is always there for me when things get rough.

Other people I'd like to thank include those who gave me feedback and helped make *Free Gift With Purchase* a better book: My LA based manager for Jackpot!, Kathy Muraviov, (and her sister Karen!), Wendy Sherman, Christine Salah, Lynn Bruno, Liz Becker, Rachel Rosenberg, Jackie Langas, Marcy Pettersen, Dina Silver, Kristin Portolese, Melissa Uhlig, Susan Freund, Monni McCleary, Michell Galin, Erin Niumata and Jennifer Devine.

Thank you to all the women who gave me your salsa recipes! Thank you to Mia McNary, who created my fleuron (the little makeup brush that begins each chapter.) So cute! I would also like to thank my editor, Marc Alberts from the Pioneer Press, and all of my clients/editors who have included my work in their publications. And thank you to Beth Engelman for getting me the job at the Pioneer Press! Thank you to all of the women who support me every day, including all the members of EPWNG, and all the women who had me at their book clubs this year. Thanks for reading my books, offering to help in any way you can, and giving me words that motivate me to keep working and striving to be the best author and writer I can be.

I'd also like to mention my dear, sweet friend Susan Palkovic, who had a really really rough year this year (to say the least) and handled it with courage, immense strength, grace and lots of humor. Love you lots Susan! You inspire me to no end.

As always, thank you to my mom, Frieda and my dad, Zack, who call me every day to find out my book numbers (and other exciting news I might have), my siblings, Billy, Vicki, Sue, Robin, Andrew, my nieces and nephews, Ali, Zack, Sara, Jamie, Gena, and Jada, and my boyfriend, Mark. Thanks for being such a great family! And last but definitely not least, to my angels, Isaac and Anna, I love you more and more each and every day as you grow, and I'm so proud of you.

I am truly blessed with all my Free Gifts!

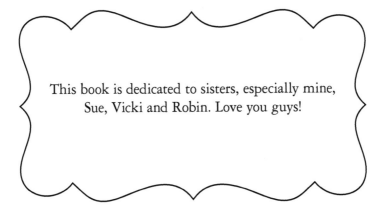

This book is dedicated to sisters, especially mine,
Sue, Vicki and Robin. Love you guys!

Free Gift
With Purchase

Chapter 1

"**B**e there in 5," I texted Laura when I got to the intersection of Willow Road and the Eden's expressway, which was approximately that many minutes away from her posh Wilmette brick colonial, a home for which I believe she paid $2.4 million, fifteen years earlier.

Laura didn't text back, which wasn't surprising. That wasn't my older sister's style. The way she lived her life, she couldn't find time to go to the bathroom, let alone answer a text with a quick response like "ok."

The woman was an orthopedic surgeon, mother to my eighteen year-old niece, Audrey, and wife to my extremely high-maintenance brother-in-law, who just to give you an example, liked freshly squeezed orange juice, meaning he requested that Laura squeeze actual oranges every morning. Then there was the endless volunteering, not to mention the dozens of committees on which my sister served. To say she had limited free time was putting it mildly.

Today was a rare occasion. Laura decided to forego her yoga class and instead use the one free hour she had in her day to let me take her to lunch for her birthday. This wasn't the actual day. Laura had turned forty-four almost three weeks earlier, but this was her first available time slot to celebrate, and if it was up to her, just like her husband and her daughter, she would have done nothing to acknowledge it, which is why I pushed her into having lunch.

I pulled up to the mansion and texted, "I'm here." Then I turned up the Bruce Springsteen CD that was playing in my Lexus RX 350 and sang *Glory Days* at the top of my lungs. And I waited. And waited some more. When the song was over, I shut the ignition off, got out of the car and entered the house through the unlocked front door. Wilmette was so high-class and so upscale that Laura often left her front door unlocked. To be fearful of a burglar in her neighborhood was borderline ridiculous.

I was convinced that the reason my sister didn't respond to my second text was that she was upstairs, standing in front of the mirror in her huge walk-in closet, talking herself out of the fourth shirt she tried on. My sister, who had been labeled as a genius by our parents at age five, had absolutely zero self-confidence when it came to the way she perceived her physical appearance. I think because she had been told by our mom and dad, along with everyone else in the community how smart she was all her life, she assumed she had nothing to offer when it came to her looks.

Ironically, her petite figure was close to perfect, and her face was beautiful. Still, no matter how many compliments she received from people, and no matter how much she was constantly hearing she looked exactly like Eva Longoria, Laura refused to let herself see how physically attractive she really was.

I walked into the house and headed for the stairs. What's so strange about what happened next is that for some odd reason, I never even thought to call out her name. It never occurred to me to let her know I was in her home. If I had shouted, "Laura? It's me. Are you upstairs?" the course of events that took place would have happened quite a bit differently. But I didn't shout out my sister's name. I stayed silent. And no one in the house knew I was there.

My right foot was on the first step of the wooden staircase and my hand was on the banister when I heard a sound that made my heart stop and made me cringe at the same time. A woman was moaning.

"Oh Alan, you're so hot," I heard next. Confusion set in. I instantly knew someone was having sex, but did Laura actually sound like this? My gut said no way, given the fact that my sister would never say Alan was hot (nor would anyone else I knew, for that matter) which is why I tiptoed off the step and made my way to the entryway of the kitchen. When my eyes made contact with the sight that would change many lives forever, I gasped so loudly I was shocked the couple didn't hear me.

There was Alan, my brother-in-law of twenty-two years, butt naked, leaning over the kitchen counter, his big white butt staring me in the face like a deer in headlights. Yup, there was my brother-in-law, the guy who I'd always treated just like my own brother, the nice young lawyer who called me for my sister's ring size before buying her engagement ring, the caring son-in-law who sat at the hospital with us when my father had hip surgery, and the friend who offered his shoulder for me to cry on so many times.

My brother-in-law was now the guy whose ass was currently staring me in the face, traumatizing me not only by seeing someone in the act of sex, but by unknowingly revealing his slimy indiscretions. In front of the cheater was a woman, and the only things I could see were her humungous knockers bouncing around, and big pieces of her bleached blonde hair swaying from side to side. It was almost surreal. How could this be happening? Why wasn't this jerk where he was supposed to be right now, working in his downtown law office?

And where was Laura, his faithful, loyal wife who had a work ethic like none I'd ever seen before, not to mention a heart of gold? Where was my dear, sweet sister, who wanted and wished only for a happy, peaceful family life? 'Poor Laura,' was all I could think. My innocent, naïve sister would die if she saw this.

I wanted to shout, "Hey! What do you think you're doing?" at the top of my lungs, but I didn't. Instead, I fled Laura's house, got back into my car, and drove off as fast as I could. When I got a few streets away, I pulled the car over and stopped. Then I sat there literally shaking, the reality of the cheating hitting me even harder than it had when I saw my naked brother-in-law and his flat pancake butt just two minutes earlier.

I looked down at my Blackberry and noticed I had a text from Laura. "Got called into work. Pick me up in front of hospital, 12:15. Hope that's okay. Sorry." I took a deep breath and headed for St. Francis hospital. What on earth was I going to do? Tell my sister during her birthday lunch that I just walked in on her husband having sex with a girl on their kitchen counter, where Laura cuts up vegetables how he likes them, (in bite-size pieces) for his salads? I decided right then that lunch was going to be difficult, and that it was probably going to have to involve alcohol.

Chapter 2

"I'm not drinking at lunch and you shouldn't either," said Laura, just after I ordered a glass of Pinot Noir at *The Sushi Palace*, our pick for her birthday celebration, the event that was about to turn into my nightmare.

I of course ignored my sister and turned back to the waiter. "She'll have one also." Then I looked at Laura and asked, "What's the big deal? You're done working, aren't you?"

She smiled, "I guess."

Laura began telling me about a patient who came into the E.R. with a broken spine and two broken legs. I wasn't getting much of the story, as the only legs I was thinking of were the two sets of naked ones that I'd just seen in my sister's kitchen.

"Hello? Are you even listening to me?" Laura asked, "I feel like I'm talking to a wall."

"Sorry," I said.

"You seem really weird today. What's wrong?"

"Nothing."

"Tell me."

"It's nothing, really."

"Tell me!"

The wine arrived at that moment, and I couldn't remember ever feeling more grateful that we had a good waiter. I took a big chug.

"Aren't you even going to make a toast?" Laura asked.

"Sure," I replied. Then I held up the glass and with sincerity I said, "Best wishes for a healthy, happy, forty-fourth birthday." I looked right into my sister's eyes and finished, "You deserve it, Laura." Then I took another huge gulp.

"Emma, if you don't tell me what's wrong, I'm going to kill you!"

"I'm fine, seriously."

"Bull. You're acting really strange, and you're chugging wine on a Monday afternoon!"

I literally had to stop drinking to respond. "I am not!"

"Look at your drink."

I looked down at my now almost empty wine glass. At this moment the waiter came back and asked, "Would you like another?"

"Yes, please," I responded. Then I looked at Laura. "What?"

"I'm waiting," she said.

I took a long deep breath and then blurted out, "Do you like this lipstick?" I pointed to my mouth. "It was a free gift with purchase from Lancome."

"It's pretty."

"Yeah, there was also a waterproof mascara and four eye shadows in the gift. You should go get it."

"Emmie," she said, "Please tell me what's wrong."

"Please don't call me that. It makes me feel like I'm five years old."

"Okay," she said with sarcasm, "*Emma!* What's wrong?"

I looked her right in the eyes and said softly, "Take a sip of wine."

Laura giggled nervously and did as she was told.

"Take another one."

She did it.

"Take another one," I said again.

"Emma!"

My second wine arrived at this moment and I took a big sip. Then I said, "Laura, I went to your house to pick you up for lunch..."

"Oh, I'm so sorry. I was just really busy with patients and I didn't have time to text."

"It's okay," I interrupted, "but I walked into your house and Alan was having sex with a woman in your kitchen." Another big chug.

"Are you two ready to order?" said our waiter, suddenly appearing and having the worst timing in the world.

Laura was frozen, her face white as a ghost.

"Could you give us a minute?" I asked the waiter.

"Of course," he said.

"Actually, I'm ready to order," Laura said in a fake, cheery voice. Then she turned to me and asked, "Can I order for both of us?"

"Uh...sure,"

Laura proceeded to order five or six items, saying things like, "that looks delicious," and "definitely need one of those," after each selection. I knew my sister better than anyone in this world and I knew that on the inside she was dying, and on the outside she was maintaining her persona of controlled, courteous, well-mannered, pleasant professional while ordering raw fish. "We may order more later," she finished with a sugary smile, "May I have another wine?"

"Coming right up," said the waiter.

Laura then chugged what was left in her glass.

"So, how's Izzie?" she asked.

"Laura, say something."

"I am," she said happily, "I'm saying I want to know how my niece is."

"I mean say something about Alan."

"Something about Alan...hmm...let me think..."

Now I was frightened because even though I'd never really seen Laura lose it, I thought she might actually go ballistic for the first time in her life. Her calm, fake tone was unnerving.

"Let's see," she continued, "the woman in the kitchen must have been Maggie, his personal trainer." Laura's wine arrived at this moment and she took a big sip. "He's also fucking Kellie, a paralegal in his office, and I believe Joannie, who owns the new dry cleaners in our neighborhood. Those are all of Alan's girls right now, I think. There might be a couple more. I'm not sure."

"Okay, Laura, your tone is extremely scary on several levels, the main one being that you know your husband's cheating on you right and left and you've never mentioned this to me?" I practically shouted, "How can you be living like this?"

"Please lower your voice, Miss Drama Queen," she answered.

"You know Alan is sleeping around and you're not doing anything about it?"

"What do you expect me to do?" she asked, her eyes now brimming with tears.

"Anything but put up with it!"

"What? Get a divorce?"

"Yes!"

"No thanks."

"So it's okay for your husband to nail three other women. You're just going to live with it. Are you sleeping with him?"

Laura let out a huge laugh and answered, "Uh...that would be a firm NO."

"Look Laura, I'm so sorry. I feel sick. What can I do to help you?"

A tear rolled down her cheek. "Nothing. You and I are very different people, Emma. I'm not strong like you."

"Huh! You think I'm strong?"

"Yes," she said with a gentle smile, "At least you used to be. You're temporarily...how should I say it...not you? When you stop feeling sorry for yourself, you'll be strong again. When's that happening, by the way?"

"Umm...never?" I giggled.

"You know, I wish you would channel all the vigor and drive and guts you have for MY situation and invoke it on yourself. I feel like you have no fight left in you."

"Things can turn upside down so fast," I said with the sadness I so often had in my voice these days.

"Where's that built-in courage that I used to be so envious of?"

"On a long vacation?"

Laura smiled, "Time for it to come home."

"And time for you to face up to the fact that you have a shitty marriage." I looked at my sister and she looked really hurt, so I added, "No offense," which made her smile.

"Things with Alan aren't that bad," she said, "We're friends. It's been that way for years, for most of our marriage, in fact. So if he wants to live his life this way, I have two choices. Put up with it or get a divorce. And I choose number one. I have no interest in Alan romantically anymore. But I don't want to meet anyone else either. So I just make it work."

"Look, I'm not that surprised by what you're telling me. I never really felt like you and Alan wanted to rip each other's clothes off or anything."

"Em!"

"What? I'm just being honest. But the cheating, that truly was a shock."

"Why? Men cheat."

"Yeah, but not men like Alan."

"Why not?"

"Because who would want to sleep with that dork?!"

It really was funny, and we both burst out laughing, but I could tell that Laura was really affected. It was one thing when she suspected her husband of infidelity, but having confirmation that someone actually caught him in the act must have been pretty brutal.

I was so protective of Laura, constantly telling people (in front of her) that she was "the good sister, the one who dedicated her life to helping people, the angel, the good mom, the good wife." I could tell that this ultimate betrayal was like a knife in her back, and it was frustrating because I couldn't protect her.

"You know, with Audrey leaving for college in the fall, you could actually have a really nice life," I said, "You could have lots of freedom, lots of peace, and lots of time to do fun things without a loser who cheats on you."

Laura nodded.

"I want to kill him," I said angrily.

"Don't say that. You don't mean it."

"Yes, I do. I want to go back to your house right now and kick box the crap out of him."

"What?!"

"Yeah, I've been taking kick boxing classes on Tuesdays and Fridays." I demonstrated as I spoke, "Right hooks, left hooks, uppercuts, cross punches... I could give him some much deserved bruises. Say the word."

"No thanks," she giggled.

All of a sudden, at this very moment, I burst into tears. Laura tried to comfort me, which was totally ironic.

"I'm so sorry," I said, while semi-hyperventilating, "I just want you to be happy, Laura, and I thought you were."

"I have a beautiful daughter, a job I love, no financial worries, two healthy parents, an adorable niece, and a crazy but wonderful sister. I have a lot to be happy about."

Through tears, I asked, "How do we have the same blood pumping through our veins? If I were you, I would NEVER EVER compromise and sleep in the same bed with a cheater like Alan. If I were you, I'd rid myself of the screwed up baggage holding me down. If I were you, I'd file for divorce and milk the guy for every cent I could."

"And if I were YOU, I'd get over what happened, stop blaming myself, stop feeling guilty and move on. It's been over a year since Sam died, and it's okay to still be grieving his death. But this guilt you have over it, it's enough already. Let it go and try to start moving on. Could you maybe try to date a little bit, dip your toe in the water?"

"No thanks."

"I'm not saying you should dive into a relationship, but you haven't even gone out with one guy. In fact, have you had any interaction with a man in the past year, other than dad?"

"Yes, actually."

"Who?"

"The guy who works in the wine section at Trader Joe's. He really knows his Pinot Noirs."

Laura took a deep breath. "You better watch it or you're going to get some right and left hooks from *me*. I've taken kick box classes, too."

"Ooh, I'm scared."

"What about a job?" Laura asked, "Have you thought any more about going back to work?"

"What's the point?" I asked bitterly, "I don't need the money thanks to Sam's insurance policy."

"Fuck the insurance policy!"

"Laura!" I said with a laugh. I always found it so funny when Miss Prim and Proper used a four-letter word, which wasn't often, trust me.

"Not for the money, Emma. Work would give you self-worth, satisfaction, and the feeling of productivity."

"I know. You're right," I said, "But I'm not ready. Besides, I like staying home with Isabelle."

"Who's in school most of the day," she answered.

I didn't say anything for a few moments. I just sat there with my head down. Then, I looked at my sister. "Did I ever tell you my last words to Sam?"

"Why are you bringing this up again?" she answered, exasperation in her tone.

"I hate you," I said coldly, "Those were my last words. I hate you."

"Oh my God! Are you going to blame yourself for the rest of your life?"

"I don't know."

Laura took my hand across the table and with tears in her eyes, my dear, sweet, gentle sister said softly, "There's a light that shines on your face. You're a beautiful woman. And yes, I'm sure it will be years that you will grieve Sam's death. I think that's okay. But you're wasting good years lamenting about what you think your role was in Sam's death. Emmie, you didn't have a role in his death. Do you understand that? How many times do I have to say it? You didn't kill Sam. Come to terms with it. Please."

"Thanks," I smiled, letting those words roll right off of me, as I usually did. At that moment, Laura had a look of defeat on her face.

Our conversation shifted and for the rest of our lunch we talked about fun things such as celebrity gossip, real people gossip, and Izzie, and by the time we finished eating, my sister and I found ourselves laughing and giggling and in pretty good moods, given the circumstances. Of course, both of us were pretty buzzed.

"Well, at least we managed to forget about our problems for a little while, right?" Laura said.

"Yup. We celebrated your birthday, Laura. We celebrated your life." I held up my wine glass and with tears in my eyes I said, "Cheers to your forty-four years of life."

Laura held up her glass. "To life," she said with a smile, "To BOTH of our lives."

Upon hearing my sister toast my life, pain and guilt enveloped me as it so often did now, as if I didn't deserve to have a life, since my husband didn't have one anymore.

As if my sister could read my mind, she said, "Stop it right now."

Over coffee, Laura said to me, "I'll make you a deal. I'll consider getting divorced if you agree to go on a date."

"Tell you what. If Bradley Cooper calls me, I'll go out with him."

"That's not an option. You need to go out with a guy. A real guy."

"Bradley Cooper's not a real guy?"

"Em, please?"

"I'll think about it," I giggled, pulling out my Blackberry, "Right now, I'm calling us a cab."

Laura took a sip of her coffee, motioned to my lips and declared, "I have to go get that lipstick."

I smiled and gave her a wink. "Lancome counter... Bloomingdales...free gift with purchase."

Chapter 3

Early the next morning, Izzie was sitting on the kitchen counter playing chef's assistant like she always did when I made salsa. This was becoming an almost daily ritual now. For some odd reason, experimenting with different salsa recipes was therapeutic for me, and whenever I felt sad or depressed or bad about myself (which was most of the time), I did one of two things. I either planted new flowers in my garden or I made (and ate with vegetables or chips) some kind of salsa. After yesterday's visit to my sister's house, my garden had several new flowers in it and my refrigerator was stocked with salsa. And still I was making more!

"What should we call this one?" Izzie asked me, referring to the salsa I was concocting.

"Well," I answered while adding a touch more lime juice to the mixture, "Tell me what's in it and then we'll figure out a name."

My six year-old started naming the ingredients. "Lime juice, tomatoes, onions..."

I nodded my head and added some more garlic.

"Garlic," she continued.

"Beans..."

"I know!" she exclaimed, "Let's call it *Try not to fart salsa!*"

I burst out laughing and then, just to be a good mommy I added, "That's not nice. Don't say that."

"Then why are you laughing?" she giggled.

"Because it's funny," I answered.

"Hey, mom?"

"Yeah?"

"Did dad like salsa?"

I thought about the question and honestly, I couldn't really remember Sam having a strong opinion either way about salsa. "You know what dad loved?" I answered.

Izzie's eyes lit up, just as they did every time we talked about her father. "What??"

"He loved Taco Bell," I said with a smile.

"He did?" she asked excitedly, "What did he get there?"

"Everything! He'd order at least five things."

"Cool," she smiled.

And that was the end of the conversation. And I was pleased, because I thought it was healthy for Izzie to ask about her dad, which she was doing more and more lately.

Just then the phone rang. It happened to be Stacy McGowan, who was confirming our kids' play date for after camp. It was mid July, and so typical for this time of year in Chicago, the weather was sticky and extremely warm. So, the plan was to head over to Stacy's at 3:30 and let our kids play in the sprinklers in her backyard.

Stacy and John McGowan had boy girl twins the same age as Isabelle, and the three had clicked since we'd met them years earlier. Because they'd gotten along so well for so long, I had spent a lot of time at their house for play dates and get-togethers, and I'd become pretty good friends with their mother.

Just as Izzie did, I had always looked forward to going over to the McGowan's or having them over at our house because talking to Stacy was fun, unlike the forced conversations I'd endured with so many other parents of Isabelle's friends. Some of them, although kind and decent people, were strange or hard to connect with, and I would find it stressful to sit there and make small talk while our kids were playing. Stacy was different. We had connected right away so our get-togethers became more about *all* of us, not just the children.

Now that Izzie was a little older, most of her play dates were drop offs. So today, I could easily have dropped my daughter off at Stacy's house but I chose to come along.

The only awkwardness between Stacy and I was the same awkwardness I had with everyone in my life, which was that the subject of Sam was constantly being danced around. Like all my other friends and acquaintances, Stacy had tried to talk about his death a few times, asking me how I was doing and if I needed anything. I would quickly brush it off, telling her I was fine. Then I'd change the subject. Eventually, just like everyone else, she stopped asking.

The only people who had never stopped trying armchair psychotherapy on me were Laura and my mother. They would plead with me to open up. They would tell me it was unhealthy to bottle up my feelings. And I would tell them that not only were my feelings bottled, but that the lid was on so tight, not even one of those bottle-opening gadgets from *Bed, Bath and Beyond* would help get the lid off.

So here we sat, Stacy and I, in our bikinis, lounging and soaking up the sun, peacefully watching our kids play in the distance, and definitely not talking about Sam. I'll never forget, we were discussing the Jennifer Lopez and Marc Anthony break up.

All of a sudden, up walked two men, Stacy's husband, John, and some other guy whose looks literally made my jaw drop. Both men were dressed in business suits, and I immediately surmised that this hot hot hot stranger, who looked a bit younger than me was one of John's co-workers from *Winchester Foods,* which was one of the largest food manufacturers in the U.S., second only to *Kraft* and *Sara Lee.*

Upon the sight of this man, I felt as if I'd just woken up from a deep sleep. Maybe Laura had planted the seed in my head the day before, or maybe it took seeing the most absolutely drop dead gorgeous man on earth, I'm not sure. All I know is that suddenly, one look at my friend's husband's co-worker had just given me the first sexual impulse I'd had in years. John's friend was literally causing me to have trouble breathing. And it was very scary, but amazingly appealing.

"Hey, honey!" exclaimed Stacy as she got up to hug her hubby. "Hi, Preston!" she then said as she hugged Mr. Perfect.

Preston?! That was his name? 'Oy Vey!' was all I could think. Emma Jane Bricker, nice Jewish girl who married nice Jewish guy (nice during most of the marriage, that is), was now struggling for air at the sight of a guy named Preston, who's ethnic and religious background were both unknown at this point, the only certainty being that he wasn't of the Jewish faith.

15

"Hi, Emma!" said John, leaning down to give me a hug, probably trying to ignore the fact that my mouth was hanging wide open, my eyes were glazed, and my body was trembling harder than the recent earthquake in San Francisco.

The twins began to swarm their dad, and my heart sank while I watched my sweet daughter watching them closely, probably wondering why it was so unfair that she didn't have a daddy to hug.

"Emma, this is Preston Christiansen," said Stacy, "He works at Winchester with John."

Now I almost burst out laughing. This was too much. Christiansen was his last name? How much more non-Jewish could he get?!

"John's my boss, actually," said Preston with a wide grin, "Nice to meet you."

"You, too," I said to Jesus Christ's son.

I wasn't sure if I was imagining it or just wishing it, but Preston held his gaze a little longer than someone would normally, and I wondered if it was because he could sense my attraction to him. Yet, I wouldn't have been surprised if someone told me that every girl acted like she was in a trance-like state when introduced to him.

"And this is her little girl, Isabelle," said Stacy.

Preston leaned down and shook my daughter's hand and at that moment, watching him treat her like an adult, I knew he didn't have kids. I also knew with certainty that he was single. "Nice to meet you," he said with a smile.

"Nice to meet you," she said in her sweet, little voice.

"Preston had to take his car in for service and it won't be ready for another hour so we thought we'd hang out here while we wait," John explained.

"Want a drink?" Stacy asked the guys, "Coke, Diet Coke?"

"I'm good, honey," answered John.

Preston responded, "I'll have a Coke if you don't mind."

"I'll have *you!*" I felt like saying. But I didn't. I just sat there dazed.

Stacy headed into the house to get the drink while John went to swing the three kids on the tire swing.

"So, how do you know Stacy?" Preston asked me.

"Our kids go to the same camp," I answered.

"I see," he nodded.

His big brown eyes were haunting, almost, and his dark skin seemed so soft and perfect, not to mention the six pack abs I knew without a doubt were hiding under his white business shirt and tie. I had a strong desire at this moment to rip off his clothes right then and there and put my hands all over his chest. 'What was happening to me?' I wondered. For so long, not one thought of sex. Now I was bursting with sexual energy.

Just as Stacy came out with the Coke, Izzie came over to me and sat on my lap. "Mom," she said, "I'm thirsty."

"I have apple juice in the fridge," Stacy answered, "Let me go get it."

"Don't be silly," I said, lifting my daughter off my lap and standing up, "I'll go." Then I headed into the house to get the drink, holding my stomach in so tight that it was actually painful.

Once in the kitchen, I opened the refrigerator door and got a very annoying surprise. The big plastic container of apple juice practically jumped out at me and fell out onto the floor. It was obvious that one of the kids had put it in the fridge just halfway onto the shelf.

I quickly grabbed a roll of paper towels that was lying on the counter and then got on my knees and began to clean up the spill. As I was wiping up the puddle I heard the screen door open and figured it was Stacy. I was very wrong.

"What happened?" I heard Preston ask me with a chuckle.

I was both frightened and electrifyingly excited when I looked up and saw him standing over me. My heart began to pound literally outside my chest. "Oh, it's fine," I managed with a nervous smile, "Just a little spill."

Mr. Major Christian Person then did something I couldn't believe. He got down on his knees beside me. "Let me help you," he said softly, taking the paper towel roll out of my hand. He never took his eyes off of mine. Slowly he began to wipe the wood floor.

"Thanks," I said. Then I had to look away. This was just too much for me. I was afraid he could see right through me, and see how much I wanted him to grab me, take me to a bed (any bed) and throw me down on it.

"No problem," he smiled.

"So, you work with John?" I asked in an attempt to make casual conversation.

"Yup."

"I see." Now I was looking at the floor, feeling majorly self-conscious due to the fact I was in a bathing suit on my knees.

"Can I say something to you?" Preston asked.

I stopped cleaning and looked up at him. "Okay."

"I know this sounds really strange, and don't think I'm a complete weirdo or anything, but I'd love to see you naked," he said with a shy grin.

My gut reaction to this unbelievable statement was to burst out laughing.

"I'm being completely serious," he went on, "I've never said that to anyone before, I swear to God." Now he was almost stuttering, as if he just realized he may have crossed the line and regretted his bombshell declaration. "You're just really, really pretty, and there's something about you... Oh, God, I'm really sorry. You must be offended." He put his head down and continued cleaning up.

"What about my husband?" I asked him, "Don't you care about him?"

"Actually, I asked John what your deal was before I came in here. He told me you're single."

"So you think because I'm not married, you can just come in here and tell me you want to see me naked and I'm going to sleep with you?"

"No, not at all. Actually, I'd like to go out with you. On a date."

"Why?"

"Why wouldn't I? You're hot," he grinned.

I just sat there, unable to speak.

"So, are you offended?" he asked.

"Actually, if you want to know the truth, I think you're genuine."

"I'm usually not this blunt."

"You verbalized what most guys only have the guts to think. I like that," I smiled, "a lot."

He gave me a grin that literally melted me. It was strange. Two people with a fairly large age gap and vastly different lifestyles had met, and within seconds had connected on a sexual level. In my forty-two years of life, this was a first for me. Preston and I had skipped the courtesy period. We'd omitted any polite exchanges and gone right to what was real, what was the truth. It wasn't complicated and it wasn't sugar coated. We were attracted to each other and we were honest about it. And it seemed right.

"So, do you want to get together sometime?"

"I think so."

Preston then proceeded to do something unbelievable. He leaned over and kissed me, and I don't mean he gave me a light peck. The kiss was intense, and done with determination and purpose. My lips hadn't touched a guy's lips in over a year, but I can say with certainty, that wasn't the reason Preston's kiss was so remarkably extraordinary. There was a kind of passion in it that I was pretty sure I'd never experienced. And kissing him back came so natural it was frightening. I now understood the meaning of infatuation. Or maybe I didn't. Maybe infatuation was too mild of a word.

"What's going on in here?" I then heard John say with a nervous chuckle. I quickly stood up and said, "Nothing," while Preston cleared his throat. "Didn't mean to interrupt, but Isabelle really wants her drink."

"Sure," I said. Then I quickly poured a glass of water and dashed out the door, leaving the two guys standing in the kitchen. To say I was completely horrified is putting it mildly. My friend's husband had just walked in on me and his work buddy on our knees, sucking face, while my young, innocent child sat outside, fifteen feet away. What could Preston possibly say to his boss about that? I had no clue, but what I did know, was that it was time for us to pack up and head home.

I was barely able to look anyone in the eye when saying good-bye. To Preston, I managed, "Nice meeting you," a polite smile on my face, the thrill still bottled up inside me.

"You too," he said with a grin.

I turned away and we headed for the car.

"Thanks for the salsa!" Stacy shouted, "It was delicious!"

"Anytime!" I responded, "Thanks again for having us over!" I wanted to thank Preston, as well. I wanted to let him know how much I appreciated the life-altering kiss he planted on me. I wanted to tell him that I would undoubtedly never forget what had happened to me on my friend's kitchen floor, how a splendid, almost magical kiss had taken me to a place I'd never imagined I'd go.

Lying in bed that night, I tossed and turned for awhile, unable to think about anything else but Preston Christiansen, the Christian. He wanted to see me naked. Would it happen? I asked myself. I wasn't sure, but the thought of it was making me dizzy.

Chapter 4

Thanks to one of my best friends, Xanax, I was in the deepest sleep I'd been in for weeks. I was dreaming, and in a tranquil, almost zombie-like state of mind. Unfortunately, my dear mother would put an abrupt end to the peaceful slumber at around midnight.

With its loud ring, the phone that sat on the nightstand next to my bed and inches from my head woke me abruptly. After my brain registered what was happening, I instantly surmised that someone I knew was dead. I figured that if a person was calling me in the middle of the night, death had to be the only explanation.

"Hello," I managed, my heart pounding and my voice a quivering whisper.

"Emma? Is that you?" said my mom so loudly, I jumped.

"Who else would answer my phone, Mom?" I asked.

"Did you hear?" were her next words.

"No. Who died?"

"No one, thank God."

"Oh, well that's good."

"I just got off the phone with Laura," my mother said, "I guess you haven't heard."

"What?"

"Alan's leaving her."

"What?!"

"For some aerobics whore."

"Helene!" I heard my dad say. I assumed he was right next to her. "Helene!"

"What? She is. She's a whore."

Just then, I heard call waiting. "Mom, hold on. This must be Laura calling me." I clicked over. "Hello?"

All I heard was sobbing. My sister couldn't even speak. She just cried. After about two and a half seconds I said, "Laura, it's going to be okay. Don't worry. I promise."

More weeping and blubbering.

"Seriously, you're going to be fine. I swear." I remembered my mother on the other line. "Hold on. Let me hang up with Mom." I clicked back over. "Mom, this is Laura. Let me go talk to her."

"I'm coming over to your house," said my mother, "Tell Laura I'll pick her up on my way."

"What? You're coming over? Now?"

"I'll be there in twenty minutes. Tell your sister I'll be at her house in ten." I could hear my dad objecting in the background. "Shhh! I'm going," she said to him. "Emma, we'll see you soon." Then she hung up.

I clicked back to my sister, who I knew was still on the line because I could still hear the crying. "Laura, listen. Mom's picking you up in ten minutes and bringing you here."

"Okay."

The fact that she was able to utter the word okay made me feel a lot better.

I stumbled out of bed, now regretting the Xanax. I checked on Izzie and then made my way downstairs and into the kitchen. The obvious choice of food for anyone who was hungry was staring me in the face when I opened the refrigerator. The question was, which salsa was more appropriate for Laura's time of need? Would she feel comforted by Hot Banana Salsa? Or would Tomato Celery salsa be more soothing?

I took out both containers, along with some celery and a jug of orange juice. Just as I headed to the pantry for some tortilla chips, I got a text. I figured it was Laura telling me they were on their way.

It was from a number I didn't recognize and it read, "Can't stop thinking about the kitchen floor." I gasped and put my hand over my mouth.

There was only one person who could possibly be the sender of this text: the gorgeous creature who made my heart stop with his huge biceps, his dark, seductive eyes, and his bold innuendo.

I started to laugh. Standing in my kitchen in the middle of the night, I felt so happy and so giddy that I wanted to dance and sing and do cartwheels around the house. I felt a little bit guilty for feeling so great. After all, my sister was probably in such pain, and this was most likely the low point in her life. How could I be so elated at a time like this? Simple. This wasn't about Laura. This was about me, and the fact that a guy named Preston Christiansen, just like Prince Charming, had kissed my lips and had woken me from a deep, deep sleep.

I decided I had to hide my euphoria right now and get into supportive sister mode. I knew Laura would be thrilled for me, but this wasn't the time to start sharing the beginning of my new love life. So, I decided I'd hide it from her. Just for tonight.

I cut up some celery, and then I began putting everything on the kitchen table. After reading the text from Preston about eight more times, I sat down and texted back. "The kitchen floor was really nice."

Then I waited. I waited for Mom and Laura, and I waited for another text. I dipped a chip into the Hot Banana Salsa and ate it. It tasted sweet and hot and surprising, just like Preston.

Just then, another text. "When can we get together?" it read. Before I could respond he texted again. "How about dinner Friday night?"

"How old are you?" I texted.

"Does it matter?" Preston texted.

"Yes."

"35."

Just then, I heard a light knock at the back door that led into the kitchen. My heart was pounding furiously and I was energized beyond belief, with a warm and happy feeling all through my skin. A thirty-five year old, whose looks were right up there with those of a movie star, and whose demeanor made me shiver with delight had just asked me, forty-two year old Emma Bloom, single mother with major baggage, out for dinner. I was immensely flattered and I suddenly felt like a major cougar. And I was beyond happy about it!

But for now, I had to act sad, somber, and concerned. Not that I would be acting. I really felt all those things for Laura. But Preston was making

23

me crazy! It was frightening to think about someone in a sexual way after everything that had happened to me, but it was unbelievably alluring, too.

I opened the door, taking deep breaths to calm myself down. "Hi," I said with a sad smile, hugging my mom and then Laura.

My sister hugged me back tighter than I can ever remember, and we stood there and embraced for a long time. My mother sat at the table for a moment. Then she stood up and I'm pretty sure she was watching the grip Laura had on me, because at that moment she blurted out, "We may need some wine."

Laura and I turned to her, both of us with looks of surprise on our faces. No one in my family has ever been a big drinker, so for my mother to feel like we needed alcohol right now was a big indication of how serious she thought Laura's situation was, and how little of a clue she had as to how to handle it.

"What?" my mom said defensively, as she perceived our looks of shock to be judgmental.

"Nothing, Mom," said Laura, "I think you're right."

I went over to my wine rack and pulled out a bottle of Pinot Noir. "So tell me everything," I said to Laura as I got the wine glasses out of the cabinet.

My mother answered for her. "Alan has been sleeping with that slut for over a year and he says he's in love with her," she said as she dipped a chip into the banana salsa, "He said he's probably going to marry her!" She ate the chip and then said, "This has a very weird taste, but it's good."

Laura couldn't help but giggle.

"Try it," said Mom.

"Marry her?" I said, while uncorking the wine, "There's no way."

Laura nodded, "That's what he said." Then she put a chip and salsa in her mouth and exclaimed, "This is great!"

"Back up," I said, "Tell me the whole story."

My sister took the wine glass I handed her and began, "Alan came home a couple hours ago and told me we needed to talk..."

I sat there sipping my wine and listening to Laura tell the story of the official end of her twenty year marriage. All I could think was, 'How could this have happened to my kind, gentle sister? It was so undeserving. Where was the justice? On the other hand, after seeing my soon-to-be ex asshole brother-in-law getting down and dirty with his new girlfriend, who I'd be willing to bet was only in the relationship for the cash, a big part of me realized he was most likely doing Laura an enormous favor in the long run. Still, I found myself furious, the picture of his disgusting, big white butt still fresh in my mind. Would that image remain etched in my brain forever? If so, I decided I'd definitely be throwing up a lot in the future.

"He actually told me he's been looking at engagement rings!" exclaimed Laura, tears welling up in her eyes.

"I never liked him," said our mother.

"Mom!" said Laura and I in unison.

"What? I didn't. But I kept it to myself all these years."

Right then, I got a text. Everyone heard it because my phone was still sitting on the kitchen table.

"Who's texting you right now?" asked Laura.

"I don't know," I lied. I was trying to stay calm, but my insides were bursting with excitement.

"Well, look and see," said my sister.

"No, it's okay."

Laura gasped. "You're hiding something! Is it from a guy?"

"No," I lied.

"Yes!" Laura exclaimed, "It is! Come on, tell me!"

Our mom sat there eating salsa, half amused and half confused.

I smiled and looked at the text. "I'm waiting," it read, "Friday night?" I let out a laugh.

"Well?" asked Laura.

Taking a deep breath I said, "I met someone."

Both women were now wide-eyed, and as excited as Isabelle gets in the *American Girl* Store.

"Is he Jewish?" was instinctively my mother's first question.

"Mom, is that important at this point?" Laura asked.

I put my hands over my face, too embarrassed, almost too ashamed to go on, as if my family members could read my dirty mind and see how much I was considering the possibility of being the next suburban Cougar on the loose.

"Just tell us," said my mom.

"Whatever it is, it's okay," said Laura, "I'm thrilled by this. It's wonderful."

I looked up at them and blurted out, "He's tall, and dark, and gorgeous, and..." I took a deep breath in an attempt to get up the courage to finish, "and thirty-five."

Laura let out a scream of excitement.

"One more thing," I said.

"What?" asked my sister.

I looked right at my mother, who had just put a chip with salsa in her mouth, and declared, "His name is Preston. Preston Christiansen."

My mom almost choked on her food and Laura burst out laughing. So, I did too. After a moment, my mother cracked a smile and began to accept reality, which was that her daughter wasn't looking for a nice Jewish boy as a second husband. In fact, her daughter wasn't looking for a second husband period. The last thing I wanted or needed was a serious relationship, so wasn't Preston the perfect guy for me at this stage in the game? That was the thought that caused me to pick up my phone and text him back.

"Friday night sounds great," I texted. Then I declared to my family, "I have a date on Friday night."

Laura started clapping and my mom nodded her head in approval and said, "I'll babysit."

"Thanks, Mom," I said with a smile.

"Sure. So, how did you meet him?" she asked, "I mean, do we know anything about him? Is he a stranger?"

"Actually, he works for *Winchester Foods*. He works for Stacy McGowan's husband."

My mom looked pleased. "Good."

"So, do you want Izzie to sleep over my house?" Mom asked.

"No!" I said.

"Don't be so defensive. I was just thinking, you may want to...you know, have some privacy."

"Mom!" exclaimed Laura, "She's not going to sleep with him!"

"How do you know?" said Mom, "It's possible."

It was funny. When it came to sex, my sister was actually more conservative than our mother.

"Thanks for the offer, Mom," I said, "Let me think about it." Mom gave me a wink and Laura still had a look of disapproval on her face.

"Look, Laura," I said, "I actually met someone I want to have dinner with. I have no clue what's going to happen *after* the meal, but this is a really big deal to me. Aren't you happy that I'm at least interested in someone? I mean, I wasn't sure that would ever happen again."

Laura's judgmental attitude seemed to disappear at this moment, her face turning soft and light and happy. "Yes, I'm happy for you, Em. And whatever you decide after dinner, I won't judge you."

"Thanks," I smiled. And at that moment, I was thinking that I already knew what was going to happen after dinner. The writing was on the wall. It had been there since the second Preston and I met. It was so crystal clear, it was frightening. And appealing...

Preston texted back, "Sounds great. I'll get your address from Stacy. Be at your house at 7:00?"

"Ok," I texted.

"Looking forward to it," was his last text.

I looked at my mother. "Yes," I said, trying not to laugh, "I think I will have Izzie sleep over, if that's okay."

My mom and sister and I ended up sitting at the kitchen table drinking wine and eating chips and celery and salsa until 4:30. Laura cried at times, but mostly we talked and laughed and reminisced. And as sad as the circumstances were, I couldn't remember the last time I had so much fun. And in the worst time of her life, my sister seemed to feel the same way, putting aside her miserable situation and just simply enjoying sisterly and motherly bonding. As for my mother, who now had the burden of dealing with yet another daughter's tragedy, I knew she would never forget this night either.

At around 7:00, Isabelle came downstairs to find both her aunt and her grandmother sleeping soundly on the sectional in our family room. Grandma was covered with a wool blanket and Aunt Laura with the afghan that had been given to me by my father's mother several years earlier. As for Izzie's mother, I was sprawled out on the rug in a sleeping bag, a couch pillow under my head.

"Mommy, what are you doing?" my daughter whispered to me.

"Mommy had a little slumber party," I answered with tired eyes and a smile.

"Come to Grandma!" said my mother, waking up and sitting up.

Izzie quickly obliged and hugged her grandmother.

The next person to wake up was the slumber party guest of honor. "What about Aunt Laura?" she asked.

Isabelle leapt over and hugged her.

I was a bit hung over, extremely groggy, and my eyes were half-massed. The next words I heard, however, would wake me up in an instant.

"I have a great idea," my mother declared with conviction, "I think Laura should move in here for a little while."

"Where?" I asked.

"Here...in your house, Emma."

Izzie started cheering and clapping.

"The thing is," Laura responded, "Alan said he won't move out. He wants the house."

"Which means the case could take years," added my mother.

"And the thought of living in the house with that..." Laura looked at Isabelle, who was paying full attention to her. My sister realized she couldn't call her estranged husband the names she so wanted to call him, so she finished her sentence with, "man..."

"Right," said my mother, "You absolutely can't stay there with him!"

I looked at my sister and said with sincerity, "You're always welcome here."

Izzie screamed with excitement and hugged Laura, which made my sister's face light up.

I looked at my daughter. "We're going to have so much fun!"

While Isabelle jumped up and down, shouting, "Yay!!" I looked at Laura. She mouthed, "Thank you." Then I glanced over at my mother. She smiled and blew me a kiss.

Chapter 5

M ajor anxiety in anticipation of my date began just after I dropped Isabelle off at my parents' house late Friday afternoon. I kissed them all good-bye and headed for the door quickly, in order to avoid a certain person who I knew was going to try to grab me on the way out. Sure enough, my mother succeeded, catching me on the sly, when she knew my daughter wouldn't be listening, since she was instead enjoying cookies and milk in the kitchen.

"Make sure you use a condom, Emma," she preached, "Sexually transmitted diseases are a very serious concern."

"Will do," was all I said, smiling appreciatively and pretty much wanting to die, knowing there was a possibility that my dad heard.

My mother kissed my forehead and then said, "Oy vey." With a smile, I was out the door. That's when the torture officially began, the scary feeling of the unknown night ahead. And as I drove back home, I actually had to concentrate on taking long, deep breaths to calm myself down. "He's only a guy," I told myself, "He's only a guy." But he was the hottest guy, and he was the first guy, and he was the guy who had unearthed me, the guy who had perhaps brought red blood back into my cold, jaded veins.

I decided the best way to soothe my nerves was to go for a run. So when I got home, I threw on some shorts and a t-shirt and drove to a tranquil jogging path that was right by my house. Lined with beautiful landscaped trees, and bushes with flower buds, the trail wrapped around a small, scenic lake. The path was my favorite place to escape and exercise at the same time. It made me feel like I was in a remote forest, yet through the green, I could see the crystal clear lake glistening from the sun beating down on it.

There weren't too many people on the path during this early evening, which was nice since it made things even more peaceful. As I jogged along, I decided to pick out my outfit for the evening. This was not an easy task. What was the appropriate clothing to wear for a night out with a man who had made the daring statement that he wanted to see me without *any* clothes on? How much skin did I want to show?

Then, just as I mentally put on my little black sundress, something unbelievable (and awful and horrifying, I might add) happened. I fell. I don't know exactly how, but I think I tripped, and in an instant I was lying face down on the pavement.

I lay there for a second, my brain trying to figure out what, if any, body parts I'd injured. The only things I felt throbbing were both of my knees, and my gut reaction was to be thankful because I realized I could move all of my limbs, no problem.

The next thing that happened is bizarre. I heard a man's voice. "Are you okay?"

I sat up, still in shock from the fall, and looked up. Kneeling over me was a really nice looking guy. He had salt and pepper hair that was mostly salt, and I was guessing he was about my age or a little older. "Um…I think so," I said softly, while I looked into his kind, comforting blue eyes.

"Let me help you up," he said, taking my hands and lifting me to my feet, making me feel like some superhero was rescuing me. Although, who was I kidding? There were no superheroes living in my neighborhood, and even if there were, they were undoubtedly married.

When I stood up, I noticed the guy's body. It was nice. Not perfect, like Preston's, but strong and defined. He had a little belly, but it was obvious he made an effort when it came to his physique.

The next thing I noticed was blood on the ground. Panic set in, as I wondered what part of my body was dripping blood.

"Wow, you fell pretty hard," the guy said. He was looking at my knees. When I looked down, I was relieved that the extent of my injuries were scrapes on my knee caps that looked like the ones Izzie got when she fell off her bike the prior summer. That being said, they hurt like hell. I now understood the thirty minute crying episode my daughter had at the time. But even more concerning than the stinging and throbbing and burning pain and blood gushing, was the fact that I'd have to go out tonight with band-aids on my knees. 'Real sexy...' I thought to myself. Maybe I'd wear jeans instead of the little black dress.

"Really, are you okay?" the guy asked with a nervous chuckle.

"Yeah," I replied. Then I burst out laughing.

The guy started laughing a little bit, but mostly he was just watching me, waiting for me to finish laughing, I think.

"I'm sorry," I said in between giggles, "I can't believe that just happened."

Now the guy started laughing a little, but it was more out of obligation, in other words if he laughed, he'd be agreeing with me.

"I'm horrified," I said, my chuckling subsiding, "I mean, what a klutz!"

"Please," the guy said, "I've taken worse spills than that."

"Sober?"

The guy laughed. "No," he said. And we both smiled.

This whole thing seemed so strange. I had just fallen on my face, my knees were bloody, and I was standing here laughing about it with a very attractive married guy with kids (I assumed he was married even though I didn't spot a ring) who I instantly liked. I mean, really liked. He was good looking. Not hot, like Preston, but it wasn't really his looks that were causing instant adoration. There was something else. Something more. Something strangely comfortable, and this air he had about him that was putting me at ease. I felt like he'd been my friend for years.

"Look, I'm Luke Sullivan," he said, extending his hand.

I shook it. "Emma. Emma Bloom."

Luke smiled. "See that house?" he asked, pointing into the distance, "That's where I live. Let's walk over there and I'll treat your bruises." I must have looked at him like he had three heads, because he gave me a wide grin and added, "I'm not a psycho killer. I'm a trader. I work downtown at the Board of Trade. I'm a good guy, I promise. I have two kids and a wife who decided last year she doesn't want me anymore. Technically, I'm still married, just because getting divorced takes forever. I don't date. I work a lot. I spend time with my boys, and when I'm not with them, I watch sports with my guy friends...the ones whose wives let them go out with me...and sometimes I drink a lot." His grin got wider and he said, "I'm not drunk right now, though."

I realized I had a huge smile on my face. I liked this guy. He was charming. Not strikingly handsome like Preston Christiansen, but personality plus! He had this really nice mouth, very attractive, that looked even better when he smiled, and he had a way about him of self-confidence, combined with self-deprecation that I could tell was somewhat of a shtick. I liked the combo, a little bit conceited and a little bit modest, almost vulnerable.

"Okay, sure," I said with a smile.

It took about four minutes to walk to Luke's mansion, and during that time, I felt like I was on a first date.

"So, do you live in the area?" Luke asked.

"Yes, I live on Spruce."

"That's a nice street."

"Yes, it is."

"Do you have kids?"

"I have a daughter. She's six."

"Cute age."

"Did you say you have two kids?"

"Yeah. Nine year-old twin boys."

"Wow, that must be a lot."

Luke chuckled, "Yeah, they're a handful. It's weird being a single dad. I wasn't a very hands-on father when they were little, but now, with the divorce, I don't have a choice. And in a way, I'm lucky. I do a lot of things that moms ordinarily do, just because when they're with me, I have to deal with everything. I can no longer hand them over to their mother when things get rough."

I smiled, "Same with me, I guess. I do a lot of things a dad would normally do, since..."

"What?"

"Well..." I took a deep breath and then, for the first time in over a year, I actually shared my past with a stranger. "My husband died last year."

"Oh my God, really? How?"

I nodded, "He was in a car accident."

"I'm so sorry."

"Thanks," I answered with a sad smile, feeling guilty that I was overjoyed because I'd just actually said it out loud. Telling a person that Sam died was like letting a huge cat out of the bag. It made it real, and it made me feel like I was taking a huge step forward.

We entered Luke's big, huge, stone house from the back porch. Once inside, I was standing in his kitchen, looking around in awe, and realizing that he must be a really good trader. "So, was this your house when you were married?"

Luke chuckled as he rummaged through one of the kitchen drawers, "No. My wife lives about four blocks from here in our original house. I bought this place to be close to my kids."

I tried not to gasp, and instead replied casually, "Oh." Luke wasn't just a really good trader, I thought to myself. Luke was a really, really, really, really, really good trader. From appearances, he was completely loaded and raking in the cash.

"Here we go," said Luke, pulling out gauze bandages, antiseptic cloths, anti-biotic cream and band-aids. He brought them over and put them down on the granite-top kitchen table. Then he pulled out one of the chairs and told me to sit down.

"So, can I ask you a really personal question?" he asked, sitting in a chair across from me, reaching under my calves, lifting them up till my running shoes meet his knees.

"I can do it," I said, horrified once again because I was sure Luke noticed my unshaven legs (of which I was minutes away from shaving for Preston.)

"No. I take pride in being chivalrous. It builds up my badly bruised ego and makes me feel good about myself."

"Okay," I giggled.

Luke ripped open an antiseptic cloth packet and began wiping one of my knees.

"Ouch!" I shouted.

He chuckled, "Sorry, but I have to clean it."

"So, what's the question?"

"Well, what do you do after your husband dies? I mean, how the hell do you get through that?"

"I'm not sure what's more painful. The antiseptic or having to answer that question."

"Then never mind. Don't answer it. I'm sorry. I don't want to upset you."

"Actually, it's really strange. I don't even know you, but I want to answer it."

Luke nodded and began putting cream on my knees. It was so weird. It hurt, but I liked being touched by him. It wasn't sexual, but it wasn't platonic either. There was something about him that made me feel safe, secure, and very protected.

"The truth is, I haven't dealt with it at all. I don't date. I don't work. I don't do anything."

"Come on, you have to do something. What about your daughter?"

"Actually, yes, I take care of my daughter."

"That's something. That's everything."

"I also make salsa frequently and compulsively, and I work in my garden."

"Your garden?"

"Yeah. I love planting things. Flowers, plants, vegetables… There's something very therapeutic about taking care of plant life. Watering it, feeding it and watching things grow. My garden's awesome. You should come see it sometime."

"I should come see your garden?" he joked, "That sounds like a pick up line."

I burst out laughing, and then Luke laughed too, and there was a moment of familiarity and friendship that was odd, but very pleasing. For me to talk to a complete stranger about my dead husband was saying something about the complete stranger. Or maybe this whole thing was timing. Or maybe I felt safe with Luke because he was bandaging my physical wounds. I wasn't sure how the hell I'd just gotten here, to a magical place, ironically, again in someone else's kitchen, but here I was.

I liked Luke. I liked him a lot. Did I want to rip his clothes off and attack him like I did with Preston? No. But I sensed the potential for something deep, something meaningful, the start of a friendship, perhaps?

How my life had changed so much in just a matter of a few days was amazing. The widow, who for a year felt sadness, not to mention guilt beyond belief, who felt unworthy of any kind of pleasure in life, had met two people all of a sudden, two guys who had awakened her in very different ways. One, an attraction so powerful, causing a sexual desire like none I'd ever experienced, and the other, a safety net, someone who I almost instantly valued as a respected friend. Both men made me feel good about myself but in very dissimilar ways. They had one thing in common, though. Both of them infatuated me.

At this moment, I heard a dog barking. "Excuse me, I'll be right back," said Luke, standing up and leaving the room. A minute later, probably the cutest little beagle puppy I'd ever seen appeared, frantically running through the kitchen doorway, attacking me.

"Emma, meet Lucky, the newest member of my family. Lucky, this is Emma." As I made a huge, genuine fuss over Lucky, I instantly fell in love with her. She was white with big, floppy, light brown ears and black and brown patches all over her back.

A few seconds after Lucky showered me with kisses and smelled me, she went over to Luke and nestled her head into his rib cage. "This dog is so attached to me," said Luke with a chuckle, "She won't leave me alone. She's touching me like twenty-four seven!"

I could understand how Lucky felt. Like me, this pooch had instantly seen something in Luke that she liked, something she desperately wanted to hold onto. I felt like asking Luke to leave, so Lucky and I could have a private chat. I wanted to say to this furry little creature, "I really like your owner." I wanted to ask her, "Is he a good guy? Does he bring girls here? What have you seen? Is he genuine?"

"I'm so rude. I didn't even ask you if you wanted anything to drink," said Luke, "How about a bottled water?"

I looked at my watch and saw it was 5:30. "Actually, I have to go."

"Late for a big date or something?" he joked.

"Actually, I am."

"Oh," he replied, seeming a little surprised. This was the first awkward moment we'd had yet.

"It's my first date since my husband died."

Luke smiled, "I think that's really great. I mean it."

At this very moment, part of me wanted him to say, "No! Don't go on your date. Stay here with me and we'll order Chinese." If he would have said that, I probably would have said okay. Yet, who was I kidding? The man picking me up in an hour and a half was gorgeous and young, and his presence tended to stop my heart. Why wouldn't I want to go out with him? Because I was scared shitless. In Luke's house, I wasn't scared. Don't get me wrong, I wasn't bored either. And this wasn't purely platonic for me. But there was something oddly relaxing about being in Luke's big, quiet house, and I wanted to stay. Forever!

"Thanks, Luke," I smiled, "I appreciate the support."

"Can I have your phone number? Maybe we could do coffee sometime or go running together."

Score! He asked for my number! Yet, coffee and/or exercising together seemed very platonic. Still, as he programmed my number into his cell phone, I was very happy that he wanted to see me again, no matter what we would do together.

Luke walked me back to my car and per my request, we brought Lucky with us. I shut my car door, started the engine, and rolled down the window.

"Make sure you look beautiful tonight," said Luke, "I know you will. I wish I could see you all dressed up for your date."

"Thanks," I smiled, glancing down at Lucky, who was panting and wagging her tail. "Thanks for everything, Luke. Bye, Lucky!" I said.

I drove off, and in my rear view mirror I watched Luke and his dog turn around and start walking. He was adorable. Luke, that is. And Lucky... What a great name. It was funny. *I* was the one who felt Lucky. Luke liked me. I could tell.

Chapter 6

My doorbell rang at 7:04, and ironically, Preston could have gotten his wish if I'd have answered the door at that moment. That's because I was still wearing just my bra and underwear thanks to Laura, who called me fifteen minutes earlier, hysterically crying upon hearing the news that Alan bought his girlfriend a three-carat diamond ring.

"Audrey was the one who told me about it! Can you believe that? I had to find out through my daughter, that my *husband* is getting married!" she said, barely audible since she was sobbing while she spoke.

"What a jerk," I said sadly, "I'm so sorry, Laura. It'll be okay. I promise."

"I don't think so," she sobbed, "I mean, I'm forty four years old!" She sobbed more and then went on, "In two weeks, Audrey will be off to Europe and then college, and now, when I'm supposed to start enjoying life, I'm going to end up a lonely old woman with no one." She continued to cry and hyperventilate.

"Laura, first of all, you'll never end up alone. You'll always have me. And secondly, you *are* going to start enjoying your life more. It's just going to be different than what you pictured. You may actually meet someone you really love, now that Alan will be out of the picture."

"Meet someone? Are you crazy? I'll never ever go near another man, ever again! I find them all to be disgusting, selfish pigs who serve no purpose in life other than to bring strong women down and ruin everything!" She began sobbing again and I realized just how much Laura was about to go through.

Although death and divorce are very different situations, I could relate to my sister's feelings, and I was literally getting nauseous as I remembered how I felt in the months and weeks following my husband's sudden death. The thought of meeting, dating, touching, and/or opening up to another man in the slightest had been repulsive to me.

I also realized, however that Laura's outlook was temporary, and that all it would probably take for her to change her mindset was time, or let's be honest, a Preston or a Luke. All that being said, there was no reason to tell Laura any of this right now. I just had to allow her to vent and feel this way until something within her changed. And that time was undoubtedly down the road.

"Listen, Laura, I totally get how you feel and I know that in time you'll come to terms with all of this."

"Thanks."

"I love you and I'm really looking forward to having you move in."

"Can I start bringing stuff over tomorrow?" she asked, her voice filled with hope.

"Of course!" I said. I took a deep breath and hesitated before telling Laura I really had to get going.

"Oh my God!" she exclaimed, "I'm so sorry! I had no idea what time it was! I'll let you go. Call me in the morning?"

"Okay," I said, "Call me on my cell if you need me. I'll pick up, I promise."

"No, I'll be okay," she said, "You go have fun!"

"Thanks," I said, "I'm really nervous."

"Don't be, you cougar, you!"

I burst out laughing. "Actually, I'd prefer M.I.L.F.!"

We hung up and a moment later I heard the doorbell. I quickly slipped my little black dress over my head, giggling as I saw that the length of the dress wouldn't hide the band-aids. I didn't care, though. If there were no knee scrapes, there would be no Luke.

The bell rang again. Time to focus. I grabbed a pair of big silver hoop earrings and put them in my ears while running downstairs to get the door, all this while praying that my bold, confident, sexy, young guy was as cute as I'd remembered. When I opened the door and saw him standing there dressed in khaki shorts and a short-sleeve white pullover that accented his dark skin, eyes and hair, I realized that my prayers were more than answered.

Preston Christiansen was hot! He smiled, and I noticed that his white teeth identically matched his shirt.

"Hi," he said casually, seeming nervous, which I liked because I was a wreck.

"Hi," I said with a smile, "Come in."

"Thanks."

After a moment of the worst awkward silence I could remember in years, I suggested we have a glass of wine. Preston liked the idea, so I opened a bottle of Pinot, while he sat at my kitchen table, literally silent. 'Why is he so tense?' I wondered. What happened to the brave, self-assured guy on his knees in the McGowan's kitchen?

As if he read my mind he stood up, walked over to me, took the bottle out of my hand and began pouring the wine. "I'm really nervous," he said with a chuckle.

"Me too," I said.

Preston put the wine glasses on the kitchen table and then looked me right in the eyes and said softly, "You look really pretty." He never said a word about the band-aids.

His skills in the area of seduction were top notch and looking back, I think I was ready to go to bed with him right then and there. That's what I think now. But at that moment, I was focused on my trembling body. I calmed myself down by taking multiple little sips of red wine, which I think Preston thought was funny because he kept chuckling.

After the wine at my place, we headed to *Donatella's*, a little Italian restaurant in the next town over, which was cozy and intimate, the perfect place for a romantic first date. Another plus about the restaurant, I was sure I wouldn't run into anyone I knew. Not that I was embarrassed by Preston, I actually felt proud to be seen with such a gorgeous guy. But my community was very small and gossipy, and I didn't think that strutting around like a major cougar was that great of an idea. It would no doubt lead to lots of talk, and I was trying to avoid that since Isabelle now understood grown-up conversations.

Over more red wine, bruschetta, and grilled calamari, we talked about Preston's position at *Winchester Foods,* and I realized he was extremely smart, which gave me a newfound respect for him and added a new dimension to the guy. I learned he went to College at Northwestern, and had a Masters degree in finance from Harvard. Hearing him talk business made him sexier than he already was, which I didn't think was possible.

"So, when did you get divorced?" he asked halfway through dinner. This was the question that made me start taking bigger sips of wine. I realized right then that John and Stacy hadn't told him I was a widow. They'd probably just said I was single.

"About a year ago," I lied. I wondered what the hell I was doing, but figured it was too late now. I would tell him the truth later.

"What happened, if you don't mind me asking?"

"Actually, let's not get into that," I said with a polite smile.

"That's fine," he smiled back.

Preston was young. He was no doubt a womanizer, but he seemed wholesome as well. From what I could see, through his skin he emitted goodness, and his heart was pure and untainted. To start telling him about the circumstances surrounding Sam's death, and how everything had gone down seemed wrong. Very wrong. Other than my immediate family, no one knew the details of what happened the night Sam died.

My neighbors and people in my town had an idea. It had been in the newspaper. *Willow Ridge Man Dies in Head-on Collision...the autopsy showed a blood alcohol level of .14...* the article read. But no one knew what had taken place at my home just minutes before. No one knew. No one. And I wanted to keep it that way.

It was strange. Earlier in the evening, sitting at Luke's kitchen table getting my wounds cleaned was the first time I actually considered telling the story to someone. I had chickened out, though, deciding to wait and see if Luke and I would become friends before I aired my dirty laundry. With Preston, however, divulging this kind of scandalous information was out of the question.

"So no questions about your divorce, except one. Where does your ex-husband live now?"

"He doesn't live," I wanted to say, "His body is lying in the ground in a cemetery in the city."

"Chicago," I said curtly.

"Fair enough. New subject."

I smiled, "Sorry. I just want to have fun tonight, not drudge up the past."

"I understand," he said, holding up his wine glass, "Cheers."

"To what?"

"Having fun."

"Cheers," I said with a smile that was pure relief.

We took sips of our wines and then Preston said, "So, Isabelle's adorable."

"Thanks," I grinned.

"I totally want to have kids," he said.

"Really?"

"Yeah. I'd have a baby in a heartbeat."

"What's holding you back?"

"Well, this may come as a shock to you," he teased, leaning in toward me and lowering his voice, "I don't want to get married."

"Haven't met the right girl?" I joked.

Preston laughed and then said, "I'm not the right guy."

"You could be if you tried."

He smiled and replied, "Look, I know what I am. I'm the fun guy. I like being single and not having any responsibilities outside my job. I think I'd be a good dad. It's the commitment thing that I suck at."

I smiled at him, "You know something? It's nice to be with someone who knows himself, who isn't trying to be someone else, and who isn't afraid or ashamed to admit it. I respect that."

"I don't lie. Everything with me is upfront." He smiled shyly and added, "Like the kitchen floor."

"Ahh…the kitchen floor…" I flirted, "Let's talk about the kitchen floor."

Preston smiled.

"Have you told many women you'd like to see them naked?" I asked.

"No!"

"Then why me?"

"It was the way you looked at me when I first met you. I sensed a connection right away. It was strange. And very sexy, I might add." I was sure I was blushing at this point, but I kept listening. "I just knew I could put it out there and you'd be okay with it. Just like you were okay with me kissing you." He finished in almost a whisper, "which by the way, was really, really amazing."

Now he was looking right into my eyes. My heart began to pound and my body started to shake. "Yes! The kissing was amazing! Over-the-top!" I wanted to shout, "I WANT MORE!" I felt like I was losing control. I had to get a grip and gain some composure, so I excused myself and sought refuge in the ladies room.

In a stall, I put the toilet seat cover down and sat on it, and with my face buried in my hands, I had a silent argument with myself. One of me told myself to take deep breaths and get through the night without being a total slut and sleeping with a guy on the first date. The other one of me came back with, "Why not? You're 42 years old. You don't have to play games. Go for it. He just told you he's non-committal. What's the difference?"

My spat was interrupted by the sound of the bathroom door opening. Now I knew there was another woman in here and since there was only one stall, I had to wrap up the dispute with myself and get back to my date. I stood up and walked out of the stall, and when I saw who was standing there, I gasped. There was Preston, leaning against the counter with a big grin on his face.

"What are you doing?" I asked him, barely able to breathe, let alone speak.

He took my arms and then pushed me up against a wall and began to kiss me hard. Within thirty seconds his hand was up my dress. I lifted my legs and wrapped them around his waist, my body completely consumed and my core focused on nothing but how much I wanted to be as close as possible to this person I barely knew. I could never remember craving someone so much in my entire life.

A few moments later, there was a knock on the door.

"Oh my God!" I whispered.

Preston chuckled and put me down, and then I composed myself by going to sink and washing my hands. "Unlock the door," I said calmly and casually, clearing my throat and then taking a deep breath in an attempt to stop the pounding still going on in my chest.

When Preston opened the door, an older woman with curly gray hair and a big huge purse stood there with her mouth hanging open.

"I'm sorry," I said to her, while pulling my lipstick out of my purse, "We just had to straighten something out."

Preston added, "Yes, we had a misunderstanding and we had to talk about it." Then he turned to me and asked, "Do you feel okay about this, Baby?"

The woman stood there waiting for my reply.

I was a little taken aback by my date referring to me as "Baby" but I managed to answer, "Yes, honey," as if Preston was my significant other. "I'm so glad we cleared that up."

I reapplied my lipstick, both my date and the woman watching me intently. Then I turned to the woman and said, "You know, if you don't communicate, no one really knows what the other one is thinking."

The woman's face suddenly lit up and she changed from being judgmental to being our comrade. I wasn't surprised by how easily we won her over, though, because like most women, I knew she believed in talking things through.

"You're so right, dear," she exclaimed with a smile, "How long have you two been married?"

I was dumbfounded, but the Harvard grad was quick on his feet. "Nine years." He put his arm around me and added, "Nine years today!"

"That's wonderful!" she gushed, "Love the lipstick, by the way."

"Oh, it was a free gift with purchase from Lancome."

"I'll have to go get that!"

Preston was trying not to crack up while I bid farewell to our new friend. Awhile later, while a hot and bothered couple sat at the table waiting for our check, our waiter came over and told us the lady wanted to buy us dessert. We gracefully declined her offer and got the hell out of there almost immediately, both knowing exactly what needed to happen next.

What was it about this person who was bringing out every sexual impulse I ever had? It wasn't just because Preston was strikingly good-looking, although let's be honest, that did play a huge role. But clearly there was something else, a physical chemistry and a deep, inherent, unexplainable understanding between the two of us from the second we met, that we intensely desired each other.

The car ride back to my place was literally silent the entire time, with Preston using his left hand to drive and his right hand to hold my hand. The fact that we didn't exchange one word of conversation for the eight minute drive was extremely seductive, almost as if we were using the silence as foreplay to the noise we both knew we'd be making in my bed.

We walked into the house through the kitchen, where my black dress was lifted over my head after no more than two minutes of kissing that was so passionate I could barely breathe. Slowly we made our way up the stairs, items of clothing coming off each of us every couple of steps. Eventually, we landed on my bed.

Then, I proceeded to have, I have to say, hands down, the best sex of my entire life, which was a bit confusing in and of itself, since my divine pleasure was being somewhat invaded with guilt. Wasn't Sam, my husband, supposed to be the best sex I'd ever had? Wasn't Sam, love of my life, whose life had been unfairly cut short supposed to have rocked my world way more than Preston?

It was unfair. Unjust. Here I was, having an out of the ballpark, amazing romp. And Sam, he would never have sex again. He would never have *any* fun again. He would never get to see his daughter grow up. He would miss everything. And I *had* everything. So, while my body was being touched, and while I was experiencing physical bliss I never even knew existed, Sam remained buried in the ground. And it was messing with my head, until the ecstasy of what was going on got so intense, I let it overpower the shame and the guilt trip. Temporarily, anyway.

Hours went by as the two of us made love again and again. "Preston… Preston…" I whispered, as his kisses made their way from my collar bone downward. His name alone was a huge attraction. For some reason, the thought of the nice Jewish girl in bed with Preston Christiansen, (keyword Christian) seemed sacrilegious, which put the fear of God in me and turned me on immensely at the same time.

"Baby…" he whispered back to me.

Baby seemed to be my new name, and each time he addressed me that way I loved it more and more. The Christian faith and his baby whispered things to each other that were so personal and so intimate, it made me realize how little I knew myself. It was as if a stranger was in my bed, saying things and doing things that would have shocked Emma Bloom. Or maybe Emma Bloom had just discovered a part of Emma Bloom who had always been hidden deep within her. And maybe it took a man with magic to find it. Or maybe I just needed sex. I wasn't sure.

Preston and I laughed and scratched each other's backs and told each other funny stories. And he asked me about the band-aids on my knees and kissed them over and over again. I merely told Preston that I fell. I loved keeping the secret of meeting Luke to myself.

My gorgeous younger man and I had sex and more sex and more sex. And we cuddled. Yes, I suspected that tonight I was the envy of every woman alive when I realized what a cuddler I was with. He wanted to be held in my arms for hours, even while he slept, and I loved loved loved it!

When the last condom I had in my dresser drawer was gone, Preston and I decided to go to sleep for the night. "Sleep well, Baby," he whispered to me.

Then I fell asleep, my lover's perfect biceps wrapped tightly around me, and just as I was dozing off I had the strangest thought. I was sure that the flame, now fully lit between myself and this adorable guy, who most people would call my boy toy, was about to change my life. I couldn't really put my finger on specifically how, but I was sure something special was going to happen as a result of this person whose body was pressed close against mine and whose soft snores were rhythmically going into my ear. I couldn't have known at the time how right on my gut instinct really was.

Chapter 7

I've always believed that one of the most fun parts about being in a new relationship is talking about it with your best friend, or in my case, my sister. So the next morning, as I sat on the bed in my guest room watching Laura unpack some of her clothes and hang them in the closet, I exploded. Enthusiasm was gushing out of me as I told my completely innocent, sexually inexperienced sister all about my amazing night.

"I can't believe you almost had sex in *Donatella's* bathroom," she said, her tone both disapproving and filled with intrigue.

"Trust me, neither can I."

"So what's it like?" she asked me, "Sleeping with someone you barely know."

"Fun, Laura!" I shouted. Then I stood up on the bed and began jumping. "Fun! Fun! Fun!"

She gave me a look like I was nuts.

"Please don't judge me," I said, still jumping.

"I'm trying not to," she said, "It just seems…"

"What?"

"Don't you feel even the least bit slutty?" she asked.

I shouted even louder and jumped higher, "Yes! Yes I do!" Then I began laughing, and as much as she tried to hide it, Laura couldn't help but laugh too. My episode on the bed was interrupted by the ringing of Laura's cell phone, which was a hilarious shock in and of itself.

"Touch me in the morning...then just walk away..." I heard Diana Ross belt out. It took a couple seconds for my mind to register that my sister had changed her ring tone from one of the generic rings that came with her phone to Diana Ross's 1970 something mega-hit, "Touch Me in the Morning."

Immediately I burst out laughing.

"What's so funny?" she asked me as she walked over to the night stand where her phone was sitting, "I happen to love that song."

I giggled, thinking about how humorous it really was. My sister, Miss Prim and Proper, workaholic, mother of the year for eighteen years was now being the drama queen she'd accused me of being my whole life by going to the extreme of changing her ringtone to one of the most depressing (but beautiful) love songs of all time. But although really funny in a way, the reality of Laura being in so much pain that she went to this extreme was incredibly sad.

Laura answered, "Hi Mom. I'm at Em's, unpacking some of my stuff and hearing about her date." After a few moments of what I assumed was my mother complaining that I hadn't gone into enough detail when I came to pick up Isabelle, Laura said, "Okay, well how about lunch this week? Wednesdays are the best day for me...uh huh...okay Mom, I'll tell her. Okay, bye."

She hung up and then said, "Mom wants to talk to us about something."

"Is it me or is something going on with her?" I asked.

"Something's weird and I can't put my finger on it."

"I hope dad's okay," I said.

"I know. I actually asked her that and she said he was. You don't think she would lie, do you?"

"I don't, but something's definitely not right."

"Well, I guess we'll find out Wednesday. Can you go to lunch?"

I looked at Laura, my giddy mood turning a bit somber, "Am I free? Is that what you're asking? Because if it is, of course I'm free. I have no professional life, no job to go to, no aspirations. I'm just a middle-aged woman who's having amazing sex. That's it."

Laura smiled, "Can I ask you something?"

"Sure."

"Is he a good guy?"

"I don't know. My gut says yes, but is that really important right now? I mean, I'm not even sure if I'm ever going to see him again."

As those words came out of my mouth, I got a text. It was as if Preston was listening to our conversation and decided he had to set me straight. I read it aloud. "I want more."

Laura gasped.

While giggling, I texted back my gut instinct of a reply, "Yes u do and u will have it!" I couldn't believe how bold I was. Then again, I couldn't believe anything about myself, starting at the point where I was on my knees (pre-scraped) on my friend's kitchen floor kissing a complete stranger. But there was something about Preston that caused me to be the definitions of daring and uninhibited.

"When am I seeing you next? How about Wednesday?" his next text read.

My fingers seemed to be on autopilot. "Yes."

I burst out laughing and then sent another text, "Yes Yes Yes!"

Trying to hide her smile, Laura warned, "Just don't forget about lunch."

When Wednesday came around however, there was a head-on collision on the Eden's Expressway and four of the victims were brought to Laura's hospital, forcing my sent-from-God sister to kick it into overdrive and cancel lunch. So I never saw my family that day (with the exception of my parents for five minutes when I dropped Izzie off.)

This time my dad walked me to the door. "So who is this fella?" he asked.

"Just a guy dad," I smiled, "He's really nice and we're having fun."

Dad took a deep breath that said it all right there. He was trying to learn to adapt and accept the reality of his widowed daughter's new life.

"Don't worry, Dad," I said, putting my arms around him and hugging him tight, "I'm just having fun. I'm just..." I pulled away and finished, "Actually, I don't really know what I'm doing."

Dad gave me a big grin. "You're living, Em. Enjoy yourself. It's okay."

"Thanks for understanding."

"I understand more than you think," he replied.

"What does that mean?"

At this moment I heard shouting from the kitchen, "Stan? Is she gone?"

"No mom, I'm still here!" I shouted back with a laugh, "If you wait a few more seconds I'll be out the door and then you can talk about me as much as you want!"

My dad and I laughed and I hugged him again.

"I love you, Stan."

"Me too, sweetie."

Exactly two hours later, a hot babe appeared outside my window. I watched him peruse my garden before he knocked on the door. So nervous for the date (but in a good way), I cracked open a bottle of Pinot and had a glass before Preston even got to my place. And since the bottle was open, I offered him a glass when he walked in.

"Sure," he said with his dashing smile, "Let's have it on the patio so I can check out your garden more."

Now I was truly in heaven. My newly updated, enhanced, renovated, fixed up, whatever you want to call it garden was of interest to my new man, and I had the luxury of showing off all my recent hard work, the same work I'd offered to show Luke, my new friend, who had texted me a couple days earlier.

"Hi Emma, it's Luke. It was great meeting you. Now you have my cell phone number. Call if you ever want to go for a run. Hope your knee caps are healing. How was your date?" That was the first text.

I'd texted back, "The date was good." Ha! If he only knew! I continued, "Thank you for taking care of me. I would love to run with you sometime. Say hello to Lucky."

"Lucky's all over me. It's the most action I've gotten in awhile. If Lucky was a woman I'd tell her she needs to learn how to play hard to get. That being said, I'm not into dogs. More into girls. We'll talk soon. Glad your date was good, by the way."

I was very happy to hear from Luke, and thought he was sweet for being happy for me. Yet, part of me was disappointed because I wanted him to be jealous, not happy. His texts did seem a little flirty, though, and that was a good thing. I was getting mixed signals. Did Luke want to be my buddy? Or did he dig me? Maybe he had a girlfriend he didn't want to tell me about. Maybe he just didn't want to date. Or maybe he wasn't attracted to me in that way. I wasn't sure, but something seemed odd. Without sounding completely arrogant and conceited, my gut instinct was telling me Luke liked me. So why he was asking me to jog with him instead of have a meal was puzzling.

Would I go out with him if he asked? Probably. Although at this point, I wasn't thinking about it too much. I was having a hard time focusing on anything or anyone other than the man who'd led me out of Egypt and into the Promised Land, the man who deserved a humanitarian award for saving my soul, and the man who I now craved more than *Carol's Cookies* with vanilla ice-cream when I was pregnant.

I poured the wines and then led Preston out to the patio.

"I just planted those two white centennial rose bushes," I said with pride, pointing to the flowers.

"I like the white. Very pure..."

"Unlike what we did in my bed a few nights ago?" I wanted to ask. Instead, I smiled and said nothing, my cheeks turning as red as my potted Hydrangeas.

If I had to estimate, not fifteen minutes went by before we were passionately kissing on the patio and making our way into the house and up to my bedroom. Who needed food? Who needed to go out? The two of us had only one necessity: each other. That's why we spent the next couple hours naked.

I didn't think the sex could get any better than it was the first time we were together. I was very wrong. Tonight was even more intense, and I wondered if this was a fluke, or if Preston loved all his women the same way he loved me.

"Do you feel okay?" he asked me at one point.

"Yes, Preston, I feel okay," I whispered as I lie there, my naked body being showered with kisses. I wanted to tell him I felt more than okay. I wanted to tell him I felt physical bliss that was amazing, the best I'd ever felt in my life. And it was surreal, because I never knew this kind of pleasure existed. It was strange, but acceptingly inexplicable.

"I have to tell you something," said Preston. Now resting and lying naked, Preston's head was on my stomach and his arms were wrapped tightly around the outsides of my thighs.

"What?"

Preston sat up. "Well, I know about your husband. John told me what happened. I've actually known since the day after our date at *Donatella's*."

Not wanting to face him, I rolled over and covered myself with the comforter. "Oh."

Preston jumped over to the other side of me so I'd look at him. "Why didn't you tell me the truth?"

"I don't know. I guess I just wanted to be divorced like everyone else. I didn't want you to see me as the sad widow."

"You should have told me, Emma."

"I was going to."

"When?"

"I don't know. This is only our second date." I started giggling, "And it's not really even a date."

"Sure it is," he smiled.

"No, it's more of a hookup."

"I have a great idea," he exclaimed, "Let's go have a dinner date in your kitchen. I'm starving."

"Me too," I responded, relieved that the subject had just changed. I got up, went to my dresser drawer and pulled out a t-shirt. I put my arms in it and was just about to pull it over my head when I felt him pull it up and off of me.

"What are you doing?" I asked.

Preston took my arms and said, "You should have told me, Emma."

"I'm sorry."

"Don't hide anything from me, okay?"

I nodded and went to grab my t-shirt again, but Preston just took my hand and led me out of the room and down the stairs.

"Um, can I put some clothes on?" I asked.

"No," he said softly, "I want you to be naked for our date. I want to eat dinner with you while I look at your beautiful body."

Huh? Me? Beautiful body? Hello, I'm 42 and had a child. I have varicose veins, a permanent tummy bulge, and back fat (it's minimal but it's there.) To say that feelings of immense self-consciousness and vulnerability enveloped me is putting it mildly. Then again, only Preston could cause me to feel somewhat open and okay with the whole thing.

So, standing in my kitchen completely naked, sipping red wine and eating grape and avocado salsa and chips with a man I'd met no more than a week ago was a vastly sexy experience. What was funny, though, was that we actually had very normal conversations, as if we were having lunch at a restaurant, two ordinary people getting to know each other.

"This is awesome," said Preston about the salsa, "Where'd you get it?"

"I made it."

He seemed surprised. "Really?"

"Yeah," I said. Then I opened up the fridge, took out another container and took the lid off. "Try this."

Preston dipped a chip in the container and then put it in his mouth. "Wow, what is this? It's really good."

"Eggplant salsa," I said with pride. I realized right then that for the first time in what seemed like years, I felt proud of something I'd created, other than my daughter, of course. Feeling gratified simply by making salsa that I knew deep down really was good gave me a sense of self-confidence I'd been missing for a long time.

Cute naked guy had another bite. "This is like really amazing and I'm not just saying that," he said.

"Thanks. If you want to take some home, feel free. I've got plenty more in the fridge. I also have black bean salsa, and I think, fusion peach salsa."

"What's with the salsa obsession, Baby?" he asked.

"I have no clue," I replied, "I'm just into making salsa all the time. All different kinds. It's crazy!"

"Do you just make it, or do you eat it, too?"

"I definitely eat it. I joked, "Actually, I read somewhere that cilantro can act as an aphrodisiac. Maybe that explains my attraction to you."

"Give me a little more credit than that," he teased.

"Here's my theory," I said to my date, who looked oh so sweet right now, his cute little cheeks moving as he continued to chew, "I think for a long time, I've felt numb, unresponsive to anything or anyone besides my family."

Suddenly, my eyes filled with tears as I realized how much Preston Christiansen had actually done for me in this short time, not just with his hard abs, but with his unrestrained attitude and his soft-hearted demeanor. I literally had to take a deep breath so I wouldn't break down.

I continued, "The taste of the lime juice that I use in every salsa I make is so tart and so sour, and I like the sensation...the pain almost...of the acid on the insides of my cheeks." I felt a tear spill out of my eye. "Feeling that makes me realize that I can still feel. Does that make sense?"

Preston looked into my eyes and nodded slowly. Then he gave me a big bear hug, I think because he didn't really know what to say.

I let his strong arms temporarily protect and shelter me from my hideous past, and I realized right then just how much baggage I was carrying around. I still had so much to work out, so much to understand, so much to accept, so much to learn. And gardening and making salsa, although therapeutic diversions, couldn't even make a dent in my healing process. I was starting to think, however, that Preston Christiansen was the catalyst who was bringing me to the beginning of my road to recovery. And I adored him for that.

I pulled away from the hug, wiped a tear, looked at him and said, "We have a thing, you know."

"What do you mean?"

"You're seven years younger than me. And let's be honest, my body isn't half as good as most of the girls you're probably used to dating. It doesn't matter, though, does it?"

"First of all, that's not true about your body, but the age difference...no, that doesn't matter."

"We lead completely different lives. We spend our days and nights doing extremely different things. You have a social life, I have a child. You have a time-consuming job. I have salsa. We're polar opposites."

I wanted to ask him if our relationship was more than sex, but I didn't, because I knew he would say yes, whether it was or it wasn't.

"In some ways, yes, we're polar opposites," he smiled, "But you're right. We have a thing."

I realized right then, Preston had just answered my question. This was more than sex.

We put the salsa away and headed back upstairs. And we slept. And I rested in a peaceful way that I hadn't in so long. It was bizarre. I could actually feel my heart opening up. And from this point on, as we began to see each other regularly, the opening got wider and wider, and our relationship, although still highly physical, started to grow.

A few nights later we went to a movie, and then of course back to my place. When we walked in the door, Preston practically tripped over a ball that Isabelle had left in the middle of the kitchen floor.

"I'm sorry," I said.

"It's okay," said Preston, picking up the toy and examining it. "Hey, a *Magic Eight Ball!*" he exclaimed, "I used to have one of these!" He closed his eyes. "Should I go home?" he asked.

"What?"

His eyes remained closed. "I'm asking the ball," he said, gently shaking it.

I was smiling from ear to ear.

Preston opened his eyes and looked at the ball. "My sources say no," he read.

"Well, that's good," I joked.

"Should I take Emma upstairs?" he asked the ball, shaking it again. "Concentrate and ask again," he read.

"Should you take Emma upstairs?" I played along.

Preston shook the ball again and read the answer. "Without a doubt."

"Does it really say that?"

He showed me the ball and sure enough, the *Magic Eight Ball* was in support of our relationship.

"Are we going to have fun up there?" Preston asked it. He read the answer. "Most likely."

We both chuckled. Then, Preston began kissing me. "Will I ever get enough of Preston?" I whispered in between kisses.

He shook the ball and answered, "Don't count on it."

"Does it really say that?"

"No," he chuckled. Then he showed me the ball and to my dismay, the real answer was, "Yes, definitely."

"That's not good," I said.

Preston had to shake the ball three more times before we got the answer we both wanted. Then he threw the *Magic Eight Ball* across the room and began kissing me again.

Chapter 8

"Let me make this clear," said Luke, through his heavy breathing, "I was a Blackhawks fan long before they won the Stanley Cup. Not a lot of people can say that."

It was Saturday, and Luke and I were jogging on the path. I'd dropped off Izzie at my parent's house for an hour so I could work out, and let's be honest, so I could see Luke again. Yes, I was deeply involved with Preston now, but part of me was intrigued by Luke, and I wanted to get to know him better. And since he hadn't asked me out on a date, I wasn't cheating. Besides, even if I *was* on a date, it wasn't like Preston and I had discussed not dating other people. I had no idea what he was doing when he wasn't with me. Honestly, I didn't think he was seeing other women, but maybe I was being naïve. As for myself, Luke had asked me to go jogging. That was it. And there was no harm in that.

"So, you don't like the Cubs, you like the Bears and the Bulls, but when it comes to the Hawks, you're a true fan," I answered, my breathing the same if not worse than my running partner's.

"It's not that I don't like the Cubs. In fact, I love going to the games. They're fun. I just don't have a lot of interest in baseball. But I've always loved watching hockey. Can I tell you a secret?"

"Sure."

"I always wear my Duncan Keith jersey while I'm watching Blackhawks games." He chuckled, "Even if I'm not with my boys."

I giggled, "Really?"

"Yeah. It's good luck. Swear to God."

I couldn't stop smiling. "You're like a little boy."

"It's juvenile, I know. But it makes me happy."

We ran for a little while longer and then Luke asked, "So, how did your date go the other night?"

"Uh...good." I was so glad at this point that we were running, so Luke couldn't see how flustered and red in the face I suddenly got, thinking about the fact that if he only knew how good things were...

"Really?"

"Yeah. You seem surprised."

"Not surprised. A little jealous, actually."

I turned to him, but he wouldn't look at me. He just continued to jog. "If you're jealous, then why don't you do something about it?!" I wanted to shout at him. I couldn't, though. I was afraid to hear his answer. Plus, I wasn't sure I wanted Luke to do anything about it. I was in a relationship. It was way too early to define it, but Preston was more than I could handle right now. So the fact that Luke was keeping things platonic was a good, good thing.

"So, how about you? Are you dating anyone?"

"No."

"Why not?"

"It's complicated."

"Luke, we have twenty more minutes before we can stop running. Tell me."

"I will. Just not now. Is that okay?"

"If anyone understands just how okay it is, it's me. I get not wanting to talk, but I *am* interested."

Luke was finally able to look at me. He smiled, "I appreciate that."

After a few minutes of silence, Luke asked, "So, have you gone out with him again?"

"We've had two more dates, actually."

"Really?"

I giggled, "Yeah, you seem surprised again."

"So, you're in a relationship."

"Why are you acting territorial?"

"Protective is a better word."

I suddenly felt like Luke was my big brother, and I loved it. It felt so safe and secure, and it made me feel young and protected. Yet, there was a part of me who felt very sexy around Luke. The way he looked at me gave me certainty that he was attracted. And that made me feel like a woman. And feeling both those things at the same time was a very appealing combination. I loved it!

"Look, does the guy treat you well?" Luke asked.

Does he treat me well? Ha! The heart stopping details of my sex life were the first response that popped into my head, but since I knew Luke wasn't asking how Preston treated me in bed, I simply answered, "Yes, he does."

"Well then, that's good. Because after what you've been through, you don't need any more shit."

I laughed. "You're a great guy, you know that?"

"Tell that to my ex."

That's the exact moment I realized something. Luke Sullivan had major issues, and that probably had something to do with why he wasn't pursuing me or any other woman. But I liked him. I *really* liked him.

A couple nights later, I went out with Preston again. We went to dinner with Stacy and John McGowan, the couple through whom we'd met. And although it was a fun evening, all I could think about through the entire meal was how much I was looking forward to the intimate after-party I was throwing at my place. Izzie was at my parents once again, and I was starting to feel a bit guilty about the fact that she was spending so much time there these days, but I was a desperate woman who needed Preston much like a crack addict needs a hit.

As we drove back to my house, I was so happy, thinking about holding and hugging and kissing and touching and all the other good stuff that was going to happen tonight in my bedroom. It seemed that with each date, I was diving in more and more. I didn't have the slightest clue where our relationship was going but that wasn't important to me. With Preston, I was living for now, and that was all that mattered. Logic, reason, judgment, and perhaps reality were becoming skewed. I didn't care, though. I just cared about having it continue.

We were halfway back to my place when all of a sudden Preston made a turn onto a dirt road and continued driving.

"Where are you going?" I asked him.

He kept driving without answering.

"Preston, what are you doing?"

No answer.

"Preston..."

He stopped the car, turned off the ignition, got out and opened my door. "Come with me," he whispered, taking my hand.

My heart was pounding. A few moments later, I found myself up against a tree. "I can't wait, Baby," he said, "I need you right now." He then lifted up my dress and began to touch me.

Oh my God! Was I really going to do this? I looked around. It was dark, not a single person in sight. "Preston, are you sure about this?" I whispered, "We could get arrested."

He chuckled and said, "It's fine, I promise." When he kissed me, I surrendered unconditionally and made love to my new boyfriend under a tree in a remote forest preserve. Very classy, right? Actually it was amazing and thrilling, a new Preston Baby high in the area of sexual deviance. But it didn't seem sleazy at all. It was sweet, and quiet, and sensual.

When it was over, Preston held me very tight. In fact, it was almost unnaturally snug, making me feel like he was grasping onto me out of some kind of fear.

"I really like you, Baby," he said, "but I don't want a girlfriend and I don't want to fall in love."

Wow. I realized right then I wasn't the only one with baggage. Maybe Preston wasn't as untainted as I'd previously thought. For whatever reason, he was guarded, careful, and wanting to make sure he kept up his wall. But he wasn't fooling me. He'd just given me a glimpse of some severe vulnerability.

Instead of pursuing anything, however, I decided to make him feel safe and protected. So, I responded by stroking his hair and answering softly, "Of course you don't."

"So why can't I stop shaking?" he asked.

Chapter 9

That Sunday, with thunder as loud as I can ever remember and rain coming down in buckets, Laura moved the rest of her things into my house. My niece, Audrey, who was headed to Europe the next day for a pre-college summer excursion with four of her friends came over to spend time with us and help occupy Isabelle while Laura and I unpacked. After a couple hours, Izzie watched iCarly, while Laura, Audrey and I sat at the kitchen table eating cool cucumber salsa and chips.

"I hate her," said my eighteen year-old niece, referring to Alan's bride-to-be, "Her personality is even more fake than her boobs!"

I snuck a peek at Laura's reaction. I could tell my sister got satisfaction out of her daughter's disapproval of dad's new girlfriend.

"Don't hate her," I managed to tell Audrey, "And don't hate your father, either."

"She's right," Laura added, "I can't stand your dad right now, but I think my anger will fade over time. He's a good man. He's just a little messed up." And there it was, my completely selfless, thoughtful, caring sister holding it together for her daughter.

"Are you going to be okay Mom?" Audrey asked, tears in her eyes.

"Yes," Laura answered, "I have a lot to figure out, a lot to deal with. In time, though, I think I'll be fine."

"I love you," Audrey said.

"Me too," Laura smiled.

Audrey wiped her tears, looked at me and then blurted out, "I heard about your new boyfriend, by the way."

"Word spreads pretty fast, huh?" I said, looking at Laura.

"Way to go, Cougar!" Audrey laughed.

When she left to go meet some of her friends for dinner and a movie, I called my parents to come over and eat with us. "We'll order a pizza," I said to my mother.

"Okay," she replied.

"What does Dad want on it?"

"Actually," she said hesitantly, "he's not coming."

"Why?"

"He's tired. I'll be over soon. I want mushrooms and black olives."

I obliged, hung up the phone, and immediately stated to my sister that something very weird was going on with my dad. I was getting this awful feeling he was sick and that my parents were hiding it from us.

While we waited for the pizza and for my mother, we played Chutes and Ladders with Izzie. Halfway through the game, Laura's cell phone rang. I burst out laughing.

"What?" said Laura.

Diana Ross was gone, the ring tone replaced with Natalie Imbruglia's "Torn."

"Is this what you do with your spare time now? Shop for ringtones?"

"If it gives me pleasure in life to shop ringtones, I feel I have the right to do so." She answered her phone. "Hello? Hi Marc, how are you?"

I could tell Laura was talking to her divorce attorney. She sat there listening, and as the seconds ticked by, her facial expression was changing. The smile faded quickly, a combination of shock and worry taking its place. Whatever he was telling her was also causing her to turn white. It was brutal to see.

"Thanks for letting me know," she said, "We'll talk soon." Then, she hung up and shouted, "That fucker!"

"Aunt Laura!" said Izzie, "You're in trouble."

"I'm sorry, Izzie," she said. Then, she turned to us. "That was my lawyer. Alan filed!"

"No offense, but are you surprised? I mean, if you're engaged to someone else, it makes sense to get divorced first, right?"

"That's not helping," Laura snapped.

"That being said, he could have gone about it in a better way. He could have told you himself instead of gutlessly hiding behind the courts and the lawyers, and letting them break the news to you."

"Thank you," she replied.

"Good riddance!"

"I guess so, but I can't believe how quickly he wants to get rid of me after more than two decades."

Laura was right, and I now realized how sleazy and cowardly my soon-to-be ex-brother-in-law's true nature really was.

"Look at me," I said, "It's going to be okay."

"I don't think so."

"Yes, it is," I said.

I hugged her tight, and that's when the doorbell rang and the door opened, our mother bursting in at the same time as the pizza guy.

Upon the sight of my dear, sweet mother, I burst out laughing.

"What's so funny?" she asked.

"Your pants!" exclaimed Laura, who was laughing too.

"What about them?" Mom asked, looking down. My mom had on a white tee-shirt and these bright orange, cropped cotton pants.

"I love you, Mom," I said, "But you look like an inmate from the Cook County jail."

Laura added, "Actually, the shade of orange for the Cook County prisoners is a little bit better of a shade than your pants."

This got a big laugh out of the pizza guy.

"This color is very in right now," Mom defended, turning to him and asking, "Don't you think?"

"Um..."

"Depends on who's tipping," I said with a giggle.

The pizza guy didn't give his opinion. My mom paid him, along with a big tip. The second he was gone, Laura blurted out, "Alan filed."

"He's fast, huh? Do you have a good lawyer?"

"I think so."

"Good," said our mother. Then she kissed Laura on the cheek, "Better to just get it done." She put her head down sadly and walked into the kitchen with the pizza, making a huge fuss over Izzie's sparkly headband. As we followed her, we were still giggling and cracking jokes about the pants.

Surprisingly the meal went well. There was lots of laughter and one slightly awkward moment when Izzie began asking me what ingredients her father liked on his pizza. But no one cared. In fact, I think my mother and sister thought it was good for Isabelle to ask questions like this.

"He liked sausage," I said.

"And black olives?" Izzie asked, holding up a black olive from her slice of pizza.

"Oh yes!" exclaimed Helene, "Your dad loved black olives!"

"Just like me!" Izzie exclaimed.

I looked right into my daughter's eyes, the ones that were so much like her father's and I answered, "Yes, just like you." And it took everything in my power not to cry. My poor, sweet Izzie, trying desperately to hold on to a piece of her father. Anything she could. And me, having such a wonderful time with another man. I'm not sure I ever hated myself more than I did at this moment.

"So, tell us what's going on," I finally asked my mother, "Where is dad and what are you hiding?"

"Later," she said, shooting a look at Izzie, who was waiting with baited breath for an answer. After dinner, my mom offered to put her to bed while Laura and I cleaned up.

"Hey, how about a glass of wine?" I asked.

"Oh, I don't think so," she replied, "It's late."

I completely ignored her, opened up a bottle of Pinot and poured us each a glass.

Once the kitchen was clean and half the bottle was gone, I headed over to a nearby bookshelf, took down my computer, and brought it to the kitchen table. I'm not sure if it was the wine buzz, or if what I was doing had been pre-meditated, but I logged on to the dating website, Match dot com.

"What's going on?" Laura asked me.

"I'm searching for men for you."

"What?"

"You heard me. I want to see who's out there for a gorgeous, newly single 44 year-old doctor."

Shockingly, Laura didn't object. She was quite enthusiastic about the idea, holding my wine glass and leaning into the laptop. "I guess it can't hurt to browse," she said casually.

I clicked on "I am a woman searching for a man."

"I have a problem with the wording of this," I said, waiting for the next screen to appear, "Is every woman who goes on this site searching for a man? I'm certainly not, and neither are you. Can't they instead word it, 'I am a woman curious to see single men?' Because that's what we are. Curious. Nothing more."

"I agree!"

"What age bracket should I search?" I asked.

"I say 35 to 50. Anything over 50 seems old."

"I agree," I said, happily clicking away. The last thing I did was punch in my zip code. Then I hit search.

And then we waited. We waited in great anticipation for all the eligible faces in little boxes to appear.

"I don't know about this," said Laura, "It seems kind of desperate."

"Shut up," I joked, "Don't think about it and don't judge."

Approximately six seconds later, the pictures appeared. To our dismay, they were horrendous. Each guy was worse than the next. There was YourPrince68, who would cause me to pretty much want to kill myself if he was my prince. Then there was goodguy2know1203, and although he looked like a good guy, he also looked like he was about seventy years old. Johnclassof89 had potential, but I was finding his thick mustache a bit too cheesy.

"Lookingforcowgirl," Laura read, just before letting out a scream of terror, which I feared may wake up my innocent little daughter.

"Sounds like a twisted psycho who likes to tie girls up!" I said with a laugh.

"How about this guy," Laura asked, pointing to Takeme44, "I'd take him."

"You would?"

"I'd take him to get his haircut and a shave!"

"And to the gym!" I added.

We both burst out laughing. Two single women were having a great time bashing the gender Laura loathed at the present moment, the guys she had it in for, just because they were guys, and for no other reason except that they were of the same sex category as the person who had deeply hurt her.

"What's going on in here?" asked my mother, who had just walked in, her orange pants still getting a laugh out of us.

"Mom, please promise me you'll throw those in the garbage tonight when you get home," Laura said.

She ignored her. "What are you two doing?"

"Take a look at these guys," I said, turning the computer toward my mother's chair so she could get a glimpse, "I'm trying to find dates for Laura."

"Match dot com?" Mom asked.

"Yup," I answered, "It's an online dating website."

"J-date is better," said my mother, "That's what my friends tell me."

"Please," said Laura, "I can't look anymore. Log off."

"Oh well, it was worth a try." And then, just as I was about to close out of the site, I froze.

"What is it?" Laura asked.

I continued to stare at the screen.

"What is it, Em?" she asked again.

I looked up at her, my eyes glossy (not entirely from wine). "Look at this guy," I said, pointing to a photo with the name "Den0507" under it, "I have a really weird feeling about him. He looks nice. And normal. Laura, do you find him attractive?"

"Yeah," she said, "He's nice looking. He looks like a big teddy bear."

"He's cute," said my mother, leaning in, "He's definitely not Jewish, but look at those pretty eyes."

"Click on his profile page," said Laura.

The three of us silently read his profile. Den0507 was divorced with two kids and was a mortgage broker. He lived in our town, and was forty-three years old.

"Do you think his name is Dennis?" Laura asked, "That's kind of a bad name."

"Denny's a good name," I answered back, trying to sound hopeful.

We read on. Den0507 liked to work out, go to movies, go out for nice dinners, mountain climb, kayak and...

"Oh my God!" I practically shouted, "It says here his favorite food is chips and salsa!"

"And look at this," Laura exclaimed, pointing to the text, "His favorite movie is <u>The Hangover</u>!"

"What's <u>The Hangover</u>?" asked my mom.

"It's one of Emma's favorite movies. She's obsessed with Bradley Cooper."

Mom smiled, "Interesting. Maybe it's fate."

I looked at Laura. "No, he's for you."

"No way," she answered, "Salsa and <u>The Hangover?</u> He's yours."

"But what about Preston?"

"You mean, your little boy toy?"

I gasped as dramatically as I possibly could to make it clear to her that I was deeply offended.

"Oh, please, I'm just being honest."

"He's more to me than that."

"I know, but come on. He's not your soul mate."

"I'm sorry, am I looking for my soul mate?"

"He's serving a purpose in your life," said my mother.

"Look, I'm not trying to be a jerk," said Laura, "but honestly, you're in a relationship that's mostly physical, and the other man in your life is Luke, your new best friend."

"What's wrong with being friends with Luke?"

"You can't be friends with Luke."

"Why not?"

"It's a classic When Harry Met Sally scenario," she said.

"I loved that movie," said my mother.

"Well, you're wrong," I snapped, "We're actually going running again tomorrow morning. He hasn't asked me out. I'm telling you, it's platonic."

"He's either involved with someone or he's gay," she said.

"Luke Sullivan is not gay!"

At that moment, the weirdest thing happened. My mother, a normally strong, energetic, happy woman began to cry. Both Laura and I gasped, as we'd rarely seen her break down.

"Oh my God, Mom, what is it?" asked Laura.

"Is it the pants?" I asked, "We just want you to look good, I swear."

Mom looked up at us, her face looking so sad and distressing, it was frightening.

"Please, tell us," I urged.

She cleared her throat and said softly, "Your father's having an affair."

Chapter 10

*G*old *Medal Gymnastics* is the filthiest, most disgusting place imaginable.
I would have to bet that the thirty-some year old gymnastics studio
hasn't been cleaned since it opened. That being said, it just so happened to
be one of Isabelle's favorite places to go.

She had attended birthday parties there in the past, and after each one
would beg me to sign her up for classes. I never did, though, because we
always seemed to have too many other activities to fit in gymnastics. Plus,
would you send your child to classes at a pig sty?

"Mom," she had said to me a few weeks earlier, "My friend Katherine is
going to camp at Gold Medal Gymnastics."

I smiled at her hopeful tone and replied, "Oh, they have a camp there?"

Izzie had obviously done her homework, because she knew every detail
about the interim camp offered for the weeks between the end of summer
camp and the start of school. "Katherine is going Mondays, Tuesdays, and
Thursdays, from nine to noon."

"Interesting," I said.

"Can I go, Mom?"

"Hmmm…" I said playfully, pretending to be contemplating my decision and watching her hopeful little face, "I guess that might work." I figured even though the gym was beyond dirty and germ ridden, no one ever
died from going there, and if it would make my daughter happy, why not?

So I signed her up and here I was, dropping her off at the Petri-dish for influenza and every other illness on the planet. After I signed the release forms, I asked a member of the staff if the counselors were pretty diligent about having the kids wash their hands before snack.

"Oh yes, Mrs. Bloom," replied a little brunette girl, who was very apparently trying to model herself after Mary Lou Retten, and doing a great job, since she really did look like her. "We make sure of that," she added with a wink.

Mary Lou seemed extremely insincere, and I was sure she rolled her eyes the second I was out of sight. So just as another precaution, I said a silent prayer to God that Izzie wouldn't bite her nails over the next three hours.

The second I left the place, I called my parents house. After hearing the horrific news just twelve hours earlier that my seventy year old father was "banging Mrs. Feldman," a widowed seamstress who was doing a lot more than just hemming his pants, I couldn't focus on anything else but making sure my mother was okay.

Helene and Stan Bricker had been together for 45 years. Regardless of the bumps along the way in their path of life, the two had managed to stay together. They had survived both of their parents' deaths, my father's hip replacement, and their daughter's husband's death. They were a strong couple, and I wasn't going to let Mrs. Feldman with her needle and thread break up a long-term, not blissful, but certainly happy union.

When there was no answer, I tried my mother's cell. No answer. Then I tried my dad's cell, wondering what on earth I was going to say if he actually answered, which he did.

"Hi, Em." I knew immediately by the tone of his voice that he knew my mother had told me what was going on.

"Hi."

Silence.

"Em? Still there?" he asked.

"Yeah, Dad, I'm here."

"Look...I don't know what to say."

"How about 'I'm a jerk' and what I'm doing is horrible and I'm not going to do it anymore?"

"It's complicated, Em. I feel terrible about it, but I need to figure out what's going on."

"It's pretty clear what's going on, Dad. You're sleeping with another woman."

"Look, Emma, I already got an earful from your sister this morning. How about cutting me some slack?"

"Really? That's all you have to say? How's your wife? How's Helene?"

"Your mother and I have to work this out."

"No, *you* have to work this out. Dad, I love you, but why are you doing this to her? To *us*? *Our family?*"

"Please don't judge me, Emma. Please? You have no idea how I feel."

I didn't know how to respond, so I didn't.

"Look, I have to go. I'm at the dentist and I'm about to be called in."

"Okay, where's mom?"

"She went to get her hair done and then shopping, I think."

"Okay, bye."

"Emma, wait."

"What?"

"I love you. I'm really sorry, sweetie."

With tears in my eyes I responded, "I love you too, Stan. I'm mad at you, but I love you."

I hung up and fought back tears till I reached the grocery store parking lot. I would soothe my pain once again by buying mangos and then making the latest concoction in my head, minty mango salsa.

Once in the produce department, I gently weeded through the mangos, thinking about how conflicted I was about my dad, the cheater. How was he any different than Alan? Perhaps he was worse. I couldn't even imagine what Laura must have said to him. She was most likely ten times as angry as I was. Then again, he was my dad. How could I hate him for anything?

At his moment, I got a text from Preston. "Thinking of you..." it read.

I stood there, mango in hand, feeling like a spell had just been cast on me. 'How did he do it?' I wondered. What kind of magical power did he have on me? One little text and all thoughts, problems and issues vanished. Temporarily, of course. My heart was now pounding and thinking of only one thing: P.C.

I put a few mangos into my cart, smiling and feeling happy and giddy. The three words Preston texted had me in a frenzy, and I was bursting with joy and excitement. By the time I got to the check-out line, I realized what I desperately needed to do.

"Can you come over?" I texted back, my shaking fingers making it difficult to text.

I paid for my fruit and walked to my car.

"When?" he texted back.

"Now."

Two minutes later, now in my car, another text. "I'll be there in ten."

So there it was. Basically, Preston got my text and then made the decision to leave work and come to my house for one simple reason: sex.

Who had I turned into? Here are some names that came to mind: *Cougar, MILF, Horney housewife.* That being said, I was so frantic about seeing him, I felt as if I was losing control, and the only person who could calm me was the person who was causing my craziness. And while feeling this way scared me to death, I loved it, too, because I felt alive.

I pulled into my driveway. Seconds later, Mr. Gorgeous pulled in behind me. I got out of the car, took the grocery bag out of the back, and smiled at him. He gave me a wide grin back, but neither one of us spoke a word. Not even hello.

What happened next seemed like something out of a movie. Without either of us uttering a single word, Preston followed me into the house. Once inside, I turned to him, feeling almost as if I was at his mercy. He took me in his arms and began to kiss me. I dropped the bag, put my arms around his neck and kissed him back with passion I never knew existed within me. Clothes came off on the living room floor.

Keep in mind, this was a Monday morning. A thought popped into my head, which was that all over town, people were sitting in their offices, drinking their morning coffee, gossiping about the weekend with co-workers, sifting through e-mails, and basically beginning the work week. And here I was, half-naked on the stairs, my hands covering the tanned six-pack abs of a man I couldn't get enough of.

At this moment, I realized something important. I was really, really living. How many people could actually say they texted their boyfriend at work on a Monday morning and he came right over on demand? It made me feel sexy and young and special.

Eventually, we made our way to my bed. We made love for a long time, during which he whispered, his body on top of mine, "Look at me."

I did what he said, but a second later he repeated himself. "Look at me, Baby," he said with intensity, "look into my eyes."

"I sort of thought I was doing that," I wanted to say, but I complied and looked as directly at him as I possibly could.

It was scary to stare so intently into his dark brown eyes because they were almost haunting me now. I felt like in return, Preston was able to see right through me and into my soul. 'How much of my core could he see?' I wondered. Could he tell that I felt like the happiest woman on the planet? Did he surmise that at this moment in time, I felt like I had no past? It was as if there had never been a tragedy. I truly felt like every worry, every care, and every negative feeling I'd ever experienced (included my most recent worry, my dad's infidelity and my parents rocky marriage) was far, far away. Preston Christiansen was bringing hope and courage back into my body. Strength and will were returning to me.

I was experiencing the feelings of pure ecstasy and bliss that most people don't have during their entire lives, and for the first time, perhaps since Sam died, I felt like I was being given a gift. Yes, I was now a single mother, having to deal with loss and with the stress and pressure of handling life alone. But on the flipside, I had the kind of excitement and adventure reserved only for a woman in my situation, and in that regard I felt extremely lucky.

"If I ask you to do something for me," he whispered, "Would you do it?"

"Anything," I replied instantly, my voice filled with desperation to give to this man whatever he needed or wanted.

"Would you let me watch you with someone else?"

I froze. 'Anything but that,' was the first response that popped into my head.

Preston must have sensed how I felt, because he gave me a gentle smile and kissed my forehead. "Sorry, Baby, I didn't mean to freak you out."

"It's okay," I lied. Shocked and now somewhat dazed, I got up and put on a tee-shirt. "I better get going," I said with a nervous smile, "I have to get Izzie soon."

"Hey," he said with a chuckle, pulling me back to bed, "Please don't be upset about this. I would never want you to do anything you didn't want to do." Now he was kissing my collar bone, and I was returning to my desire for the man whom I'd adored unconditionally, pre-threesome suggestion.

He continued, "It's just that you're so beautiful. Everything about you. And I would be completely in heaven if I could watch someone else touch you, and then have you for myself."

I silently said to God, "I promise I will never actually go through with it, but just let me appease this person I'm mad about." Then I whispered to Preston, who had now begun kissing each of my ribs, "Let me think about it, okay?"

The rest of the morning in bed was still amazing, but I was having difficulty blocking out Preston's request. The line had been crossed, the boundaries had shifted, and I felt foolish for thinking that I knew Preston, when in reality, he was a stranger. And I was a little bit scared of him now. Not scared because I thought he would force me to do something I didn't believe in, or that he was a bad person for being into group sex, but afraid to admit the realization Laura had brought to my attention not too long ago.

Preston and I weren't soul mates. We were not going to get married and live happily ever after. Our relationship was physical and not much else. Not that that was such a bad thing, but I had to face the truth that our time together would be ending someday, and that in and of itself was very scary and sad.

I picked up Isabelle and spent the rest of the day at the pool with her, swimming and relaxing in the hot sun. At the snack bar, she saw a little girl sitting on her dad's lap and eating an ice-cream cone, and I could have sworn I saw tears in her eyes.

"Hey, Izzie?"

"Yeah?"

"Are you okay?"

"Yes," she answered, her lower lip quivering.

"Want to talk about something?"

"No, mommy," she said, "I just want to see my daddy."

"I know," I consoled her, lifting her onto my lap, "I know."

We sat there in silence for a few moments until I said, "Hey, Izzie, I'll make you a bet. I bet you can't jump off the high dive."

"Yes I can!"

"I bet you can't," I teased.

"You're on!" she laughed.

This led us over to the diving boards, and I spent the next hour watching Izzie, who was happy again, not thinking about how she didn't have a dad, but rather jumping off of the boards, alternating between the high dive and the low dive. As for me, Sam was on my mind the entire time. If he was alive, would we still be married? Who knew? But what I did know is that my daughter would be so much better off if she still had a father. Survivor's guilt. It was truly exhausting sometimes.

When we got back to our lawn chairs, I received a text. "I can still smell your perfume on me. I love that." As usual, my heart began to beat and my desire for Preston reignited instantly.

I texted back, "I'm wondering, will I ever get enough?"

"I hope not" he answered.

I smiled while reading the response, but I found myself in somewhat of a fog, finding it difficult to stop thinking about the weird proposal he'd put on the table. Would I ever have a threesome? And what was he talking about? A guy or a girl? And why did that matter? I would NEVER have a threesome! 'NEVER!' I told myself. 'Never say never,' myself answered back, startling me.

Relaxed on the chair, watching my daughter doing hand stands in the pool, I began to actually consider what Preston requested. Maybe I *could* be with two people at the same time. Maybe I was being what I always accused Laura of being: closed minded. I mean, I'd never dreamed of being in a relationship like I was with Preston, so anything was possible, right?

Confusion was setting in. On one hand, I didn't want to change who I was, and the bottom line was that I was a good girl. Threesomes were just not me. Then again, I was beginning to think I would do just about anything to keep the interest and heart of the man whose visits I was now dependent on as much as oxygen. In other words, I wanted Preston Christiansen to love me, and I couldn't deny that any longer.

Tears welled up in my eyes, but I quickly had to wipe them away when I heard my daughter shout to me from the pool.

"Mommy, mommy! Come swim with me!" she yelled, "I want to see you do a hand stand!"

I smiled at her and stood up. "Okay, here I come!"

Her face gleamed with excitement. How wonderful it was to have a little person love you like this.

I got into position to dive into the pool. Maybe a good plunge into some cold water would clear my head. If not, maybe a stellar hand stand would cause all my uncertainty and confusion to fall out of my head. Hopefully, it would stay at the bottom of the pool forever.

"Come on, mommy!" she shouted, "Dive!"

"Okay! Here I come!"

I lunged forward, and the second my hot skin made contact with the cool water I had the strangest thought. 'Did I miss my period?' I wondered.

When I came up for air and looked at Izzie, I must have had a really weird look on my face because she asked, "Mom, what's wrong?"

I think I knew right then that I was pregnant.

Chapter 11

That night, after Izzie was in bed, my two drinking buddies and I were once again at the kitchen table, sipping Pinot Noir. I was doing the responsible thing, taking small sips and trying not to have more than a half a glass since my intuition was telling me a little Emma was inside of me. Even though I couldn't begin to decide whether or not I was going to actually have a baby, I felt like drinking alcohol was probably a bad idea.

"How could I have gotten pregnant?" I'd asked myself over and over again. "We used condoms every time," I found myself repeating in my head. I had no proof I was pregnant, but in my heart I knew I was. Maybe a condom had broken one night? I didn't think so. Was there even one time when perhaps we'd gone without protection? It finally hit me. The forest preserve. That night, it had been spontaneous, and it was the one time Preston and I had unprotected sex.

"I'm going to move out for awhile," my mother announced.

"What?!" Laura and I shouted at the same time.

"Shh..." our mother scolded in a whisper, "Someone is sleeping!"

"Mom, are you crazy?" I asked.

"Yes Emma, she is," Laura replied.

"Look, I need a little space. I'm so angry with him. Plus, I'm not even sure he's going to stop seeing her!"

"Of course he is!" said Laura, "He has to."

"No he doesn't," said my mother, "He has to *want* to end it with Mrs. Feldman. I don't want him back out of guilt or obligation."

"He'll end it," said Laura, "I'm sure of it."

"I hope you're right," I said.

"I'm not so sure I care," said my mother.

Laura replied, "Of course you care."

My mother's eyes welled with tears when she looked at me. "Up for another roommate?"

My jaw was on the ground. "Uh...sure. But are you sure, mom?"

"For now, yes. I think your father and I need to be apart."

"You can sleep in the bed with me," Laura offered.

"Thank you," Mom said.

My mom then switched gears and looked at me. "Hey, what's wrong with you?" she asked, "You seem like you're hiding something."

"No," I lied, "Everything's fine."

"You do seem a little weird tonight. Is everything okay?"

"Fine," I lied again.

It was tough to keep my secret from my family, but I decided there was no reason to get everyone in an uproar until I went out and bought a test, which I was planning on doing the next day. Fortunately I was able to hold them off for the night, probably because we had lots of other issues on the table. Both my parents situation and my sister's divorce were pretty huge, not to mention what ended up being the highlight of the night: Laura's announcement.

"So," she said with hesitation, "I have a date tomorrow night."

"What?" I replied, "This is great! Who is it?"

"A doctor from the hospital. Someone told him I was separated and he asked me out. His name is Ari Bega. He's Israeli."

"Wow! I'm so happy for you!" I said.

"It's great, honey," said our mother.

"I bet he's gorgeous!" I exclaimed, "Since he's Israeli and everything."

"He's pretty cute," said Laura.

"How old?" asked Mom.

"Around my age, I think. He just got divorced and has two daughters."

"See?"

"See what?" she asked.

"It's already starting. And you thought no one would want to date you."

"Will you help me find an outfit?"

My sweet, sweet sister, so strong and sure of herself when it came to her job, yet so insecure, almost possessing a teen-age-like mentality when it came to her physical self-confidence, and I knew it was only going to get worse now that she was single again. "Sure," I said with a smile.

My mother looked pleased. I guessed she was happy her daughter had so quickly gotten up the courage to put herself out there. As for me, I was thrilled for Laura. I went to bed that night ecstatic for my sister but sick about *my* situation. So sick in fact, that I tossed and turned for what seemed like hours.

That night, in total, I think I got approximately twenty minutes of sleep. I spent it crying, thinking, trying different sleeping positions, and watching *Seinfeld* re-runs. During commercial breaks of *Seinfeld* and between the bouts of weeping, I tried to come up with the answer for how in the hell a forty-two year old woman using condoms every time except *one time* could possibly end up pregnant. One time!

From around 3:30 until 6:00 when Izzie woke up and crawled into my bed, I thought about the two options I had. One, have the baby. Yeah, right. I think I'll complicate my daughter's life even more by bringing a brother or sister into our home, whose father is a commitment-phobic sex addict. That thought only brought on more tears.

Option number two, have an abortion, which in the Jewish religion isn't really a huge deal. It's sort of not discussed, which I always believed meant that it was okay, just don't talk about it. The Jews, who are pretty much the chattiest group of people on earth, and who talk about everything under the sun in life, conveniently leave the topic of pro-life versus pro-choice out of their realm of conversation.

Browsing in the pregnancy test aisle at *Walgreen's* the next day, searching for the perfect brand to give me my official pregnancy test result, I wasn't sure which option I'd go with, but I realized the first thing I had to do was tell Preston. Not because I was realistically thinking of having his baby, but because something was telling me he'd want to know. After all, he'd just told me not to hide anything from him.

Plus, as immature as he seemed, Preston was also very intelligent, and he had good, decent morals (with the exception of thinking threesomes were okay), which made me believe that when it came to most issues he was an ethical person who would consider both options carefully. That's why I felt that going right for terminating the pregnancy without even letting him know was wrong.

"Eighteen sixty-five," said the cashier.

I pulled out my credit card and swiped it to pay for the pregnancy test. While the cashier was bagging my little item, I looked around the store to make sure no one was witnessing what I was buying. *Walgreen's* was pretty empty, so Miss Paranoia could relax. No neighbors had discovered my dirty little secret.

"Thank you," said the cashier, handing me the bag.

I headed for the exit door, thinking about how in less than ten minutes I would have confirmation that I was with child. Then, as I was walking out, I got a huge shock. Guess who was walking in? *Den0507!*

I recognized him right away because he looked exactly like his picture: adorable, nice, very big and bulky, and huggable. And those eyes... We glanced at each other and he gave me a polite smile. I think I smiled back, but I wasn't sure. My heart was beating out of my chest and by the time I got to my car, I considered going back into the store and pretending I forgot something so I could meet him. I didn't, though. How could I? I was a single mother who was carrying some young guy's child. This was not the time for *Den0507.* This was the time to figure out what I was going to do with playboy Preston Christiansen's baby. *Den0507* and his salsa loving personality were for down the road. Possibly. Right now, the focus had to be on me and my children (both of them), so I headed home.

Minutes later, standing at the bathroom counter, I gasped when I saw the plus sign on the test. I wasn't the least bit surprised, so why I was acting shocked was a mystery to me. Right then, I decided to call the father and drop the bomb before I lost my nerve.

I went downstairs and picked up the phone, and just as I was dialing Preston I got a text. Great... He was texting me, probably something sexy and seductive at the exact time I was calling him to give him the news that he was going to be a daddy.

I looked at the text. Surprisingly it was not from who I thought. It was from Luke. It read, "Hey Emma, want to run again tomorrow morning?"

"Could this day get any weirder?" I asked myself. I texted Luke back. "Kind of busy this week. Rain check?"

Luke texted, "Sure, just let me know. Hope all is well. Lucky's potty trained, by the way."

The irony... "I might be potty training someone in the near future," I could have texted back. Instead I went with, "Congratulations," and then I smiled, thinking about Luke and his cute effort at being funny.

Every time I heard from Luke, which was usually a text or a voice mail message, or a short conversation, it felt safe and nice. Upon hearing or reading one of his messages, I would always feel like things in my life were going to be okay. I don't really know why. It was just a warm, fuzzy feeling. Luke had a way, without even trying, of helping soothe and calm me in a protective, big brother type of way. Although, admittedly it was more than that. There was undoubtedly an underlying attraction. But for now, I was so wrapped up in my current, highly explosive relationship that I wouldn't let my mind go there and think of Luke in any kind of romantic way.

As I hit Preston's number on my phone, I considered the fact that maybe the timing of Luke's text was a sign. It was my friend telling me, "It's okay. Just call him. Everything's going to turn out fine."

"Hey, Baby," Preston answered.

When I heard the name "Baby," I had the sickest feeling I think I've ever experienced.

"Hey," I said, "Can you not call me that anymore?"

"Okay," he responded with a chuckle. Then a moment of silence followed before he asked, "Why not?"

I took a deep breath and then decided to go out to my courtyard and tend to my beautiful garden while I broke the news. I figured that watering my gorgeous rose bushes might calm me down and help me to get my words out easier. The neighbors to the left of my house had just moved out, so the place was vacant. The people to my right were in Martha's Vineyard for the month of August, so they weren't around either. That's why I felt free to speak outside, knowing no one would hear my scandalous secret.

"Um...just because." I said. "Because your baby is having a baby!" I wanted to shout. But I didn't. Instead I stood there in my garden without saying anything.

"So what's up, Emma?" he said, stressing the name "Emma."

Before I could even turn on the hose, I began to weep. I sat on the steps outside my door, and cried and cried.

"Oh my God! What is it?" asked Preston.

I composed myself, tears still streaming down my face and snot running down my nose. "The thing is," I managed to say. Then more crying.

"Take a deep breath," he said.

"The thing is, I'm pregnant."

What followed was complete and utter silence on the other end of the phone for what seemed like ten minutes. In reality, I think it was about four seconds.

"Hello?" I said.

"I'm here, Baby..." he stuttered, "I mean...sorry. I'm here *Emma*..."

"Can you believe it?"

"How?"

"The forest preserve."

Another estimated two seconds of silence and then, "I don't understand. I mean, you're like forty-one years old."

"Forty-two."

"Oh," was all he could say.

"What should I do?" I asked softly, "I guess I should have an abortion, but I don't know."

"Look," he said, "You just blew me away. I need to think. Is that okay?"

"Yes. We both need to think about what to do."

"Right."

"I'm really scared, Preston."

"I know Bab...sorry. I know. Let me call you later."

He hung up, and I just sat there in a daze, completely out of it and thinking, "That's it?" I'd just told my lover I was pregnant. He'd said he was "blown away" and that he'd call me later. End of conversation. I seriously was on the phone with Preston for less than two minutes. I wondered right then just how deep (or how shallow) our relationship really was.

Although very thoughtful and sweet, Preston, not knowing what else to say, had simply ended the call. Was I on my own with this one? Was I going to have to make the decision myself? It clearly was looking that way.

I managed to get through the rest of the day acting normal, reading to Izzie, making dinner with my mom, taking Izzie out for ice-cream, all the

old, familiar rituals to try to return to normalcy, as if following a normal rou-
tine and doing everything the way I always did would make the pregnancy
turn out not to be real. Maybe I'd wake up tomorrow and realize it was just
a dream. Yeah, right.

Just before 8:00, I dressed Laura and sent her on her date with Ari. I'm
not lying when I say it took sixteen outfits before Laura agreed to wear a black
halter top and the *True Religion* jeans I made her buy a few months earlier.
My sister had a bod that millions of women wished they had. Unfortunately,
in her own warped mind, she was unable to see how physically attractive she
was. She never could. And now, with what Alan had just sprung on her,
that he was basically dumping her and marrying a twenty-six year old, I
knew it wasn't going to help her self-image, physical and otherwise, one bit.
Nevertheless, my sister seemed pretty pleased with her appearance when she
walked out the door to go meet her date.

"Hey," I said to her as she walked to her car, "If you get into a situation..."

"Yeah?"

"Look in your purse, in the side zipper pocket." Then I burst out laughing.

Laura opened her car door, and before even getting in, she placed her
purse on the seat, unzipped the side pocket, and pulled out the two condoms
I'd stuck in there. "Very funny. What are you? Seventeen?"

"No, I'm middle-aged and responsible," I answered, when in reality I
wanted to throw up because I realized I should have made sure there were
condoms in *my* zipper side pocket.

With a wave and a nervous smile, my sister was gone. That's when I
went inside and called my mother, who told me she and my father were in
the middle of a discussion and that she would speak to me in the morning. I
put Isabelle to bed around 8:30 and decided to curl up into my bed and read
a book. Instantly, I fell asleep. At around 9:00, I heard my Blackberry ring.
I dragged myself out of bed and answered it.

"Hey," said Preston.

"Hi," I answered, my voice groggy, "Where are you?"

"I'm still at work. Can I come over? I want to see you."

"Sure," I smiled.

Within ten minutes, Preston was at my door. When I opened it, he took
me in his arms and hugged me for a long time. It felt strange. We weren't
attacking and groping each other, and kissing passionately like we usually

did. We were grasping one another, both feeling scared, and needing each other for emotional support.

"Isabelle asleep?" he asked softly.

I nodded, "Come in." Then I took his hand and led him to the couch. "Want something to drink?"

"I'm good," he said with a sad smile, "How are you?"

"Good," I lied.

"Emma," he began, "I've been sitting at my desk all day in a daze."

I gave him an empathetic nod.

Preston then took my hands and looked me in the eyes. His voice was shaking when he said, "I think you should have the baby." Then he took his hands and gently pulled up my tee-shirt halfway. "Hi Baby," he whispered to my belly.

I sat there frozen, trying to absorb this unbelievably surreal moment. The next thing he did was put his lips on my stomach and gently kiss it. And then, Preston Christiansen, the ultimate playboy bachelor, set his head down to rest on my belly and on his child. And then he began to weep.

Chapter 12

Henry Horowitz was my dentist. He was recently divorced, and when I say recently, I mean like four weeks recently. Henry's union had officially ended a month earlier, and in celebration of his newly single status, he decided to throw himself a big, huge, extravagant divorce party.

I had received the invitation a couple weeks earlier, and when I showed it to Laura we both cracked up. On the front of the card was a picture of a donkey. Below the animal it read, "The divorce was a pain in the ass…" The inside read, "…but it wasn't half as bad as the one I was living with!"

"This guy seems hilarious," Laura commented.

The invite continued, "Please come celebrate my status change on Thursday, August 20th at 7:30 p.m. – Claudia's Bistro." Henry had hand-written a note below that read, "No happily married people allowed. Also, everyone attending is required to bring a single friend, male or female."

"So will you go with me?" I had asked my sister.

At the time, I didn't know I would be extremely pre-occupied with the recent discovery that I was carrying Preston's child, so I wholeheartedly accepted, and actually thought going to the party would be a riot. Now, at this moment, walking into the shindig, I felt physically sick to my stomach. And no, I was not experiencing morning sickness.

I still hadn't told Laura about the baby and by no means was I telling her tonight. I mean, why ruin a good time? Honestly, I was dreading telling her, certain she'd be irate that I even got pregnant in the first place, not to mention furious if I told her I was considering having the baby. Laura would without a doubt try to talk me out of it. So, I was stalling.

We walked into Henry's bash, which was packed. I would have guessed there were about fifty people in attendance, mingling, nibbling on passed hors d'oeuvres and sipping wine.

"Which one is Henry?" Laura asked me.

I pointed to him. Then I looked at my sister and judging by her expression, I felt the need to say, "No, he's not gay."

"Really?" Laura asked, "Are you sure? Maybe that's why he got divorced." She added, "Not that that's a bad thing. I'm not judging."

I smiled as we watched my very effeminate dentist talk to some girl and admire her outfit. It was when I heard Henry demand that she spin around so he could have the full view of her new *Rock and Republic* jeans that I realized just how metro sexual Henry was. And possibly gay. Truly good-natured, though.

I went on to tell my sister that Henry didn't get divorced because of his female demeanor, but because his wife went to law school a few years earlier, fell in love with one of her professors, and was currently planning her second wedding.

"Ouch," was Laura's response to the story, "I can relate, I guess."

"No, you can't!" I scolded, "It's a completely different situation."

"How do I look?" she asked, "Does this top make my boobs look too saggy?"

My beautiful sister, once again blind to her outer beauty.

I felt sorry for her. That is, until her cell phone rang. This time it was Beyonce's "Irreplaceable" that was Laura's ring tone de jour.

I burst out laughing and Laura did too. But her laugh turned serious when she looked at caller-ID.

"What's wrong?" I asked.

"It's Ari again," she said with a frown, "This is the sixth time he's called me today."

"Stalker?"

"Yup. It's horrible. We had one date, and it was nice, but now he won't leave me alone. He calls every hour. And he texts too."

She proceeded to show me several texts from Ari, who now seemed more like a desperate psycho than a nice-looking Israeli doctor.

"Every single one of his messages starts out with 'Sweetie,' 'Honey,' or 'Baby!'" she exclaimed.

"Yuck!" I said, nausea creeping up again when she said the word baby.

"I just got separated! I don't want to be anyone's sweetie or honey or..."

"I know, I know..." I said, trying to avoid hearing the "B" word again.

"How do I get him to leave me alone?" she asked.

"Really want to know?"

"Yes! Help me!"

I grabbed the phone out of her hand and texted Ari. "Please don't call or text me again. I'm getting back together with my husband."

When I gave Laura back her phone and she looked at the text, she was exasperated. "Why did you do that?!"

"Now he'll leave you alone."

Laura gave me a big grin and replied, "Okay, then."

We headed to the bar. On our way, several people approached us and introduced themselves. I felt like we were thrown into a pack of wolves, divorced women eager to get a glimpse of the competition. As for the men, they seemed to be trying to decipher whether we were viable candidates for their love lives or not.

The first person we spent a decent amount of time talking to was a girl named Georgia McBride, who had been brought to the party by Henry's divorced cousin, who was her personal trainer. Georgia was one of those women who didn't have a particularly pretty face, but her body spoke volumes. It was possible Georgia's was the most perfect figure I'd ever seen, complete with big round flawless breasts (which I suspected were fake but who cared), a teeny tiny waist, and muscular (but not too big) thighs that were sculpted, yet not bulky looking.

"So how long have you been single?" I asked Georgia.

"Three months," she replied, "Well, the bastard moved out three months ago."

Bastard? So here it was. I guess when you go to a divorce party, you're bound to meet some cynical and bitter people. "I'm sorry," both Laura and I said.

"It's okay," she smiled, sourness in her voice. "I obviously wasn't good enough for him, so he had to go out and sleep with half of Illinois."

We listened wide-eyed for the next few minutes while Georgia explained to us how her husband had been having an affair with a woman he worked with. Apparently, the woman was really into swinging with other couples, and had somehow talked him into joining her in her trysts.

As Georgia went on about the dozens of women her husband had slept with while his girlfriend watched, all I could think about was how the father of my unborn child had wanted to do something similar with me. I suddenly felt sick to my stomach standing here with this poor woman, who had probably perfected her body so her husband would be attracted to her, when in fact he was a closet sexual deviant.

Was Preston the same? Did having group sex make someone a freak? What if you only did it one time? Was that different? I wasn't sure, and I was conflicted beyond belief. I took a deep breath and realized I needed a drink.

Wait a minute. I can't have a drink! I told myself.

"Are you okay?" Laura asked me.

"Actually, would you excuse me?"

Laura continued to talk to Georgia while I made a b-line for the bar, which was just a few feet away. When I got there I ordered a Diet Coke.

"I'll have the same," said a guy who appeared out of nowhere.

I looked over at him, startled because I hadn't seen him come up next to me.

"Hi," he simply said to me, "I'm Tony." Then he offered his hand.

"Emma..." I said during the hand shake. Tony was tall and somewhat attractive, with jet black hair and a fit physique. His eyes had this very kind, gentle look to them, almost as if he'd been through a lot, which I guessed was probably the case if he was at this party.

"How are you connected here?" he asked.

"Henry's my dentist. How about you?"

"Henry and I went to college together. I got divorced about two years ago. I brought this girl with me, who I met on E-harmony. We're just friends," he explained, as he handed me my drink and took his, "Anyhow, she just left because see that guy over there?" Tony pointed to a guy who was now talking to Laura.

"Yeah."

"That's her ex-husband. Dan, I think his name is. He coincidentally ended up here with some girl, and my friend refuses to be in the same room with the guy. And they've been divorced for like four years!"

"Wow."

"I know," Tony replied, "At some point, don't you think people should just let it go?"

"I guess," I said with a sad smile, "But we don't know the whole story."

"Are you divorced?" asked Tony.

I looked directly at him, and like I always did with people (except for Luke), I lied. "Yes. How about you?"

Tony's answer was shocking. "No. I'm not divorced. Actually, my wife died."

I'm pretty sure I gasped. "I'm so sorry."

"Thank you."

"If you don't mind me asking, how did she die?"

"Heart attack."

Another gasp. "Really?"

Tony nodded sadly and then said, "The thing that's so hard about it for me is, we didn't really have the best marriage. We fought all the time. And now, I feel guilty about her death."

"What a coincidence," I wanted to add. I didn't though.

"Why do you feel guilty?" I asked him, "You didn't want her to die, did you?" It was strange. I was asking the questions to Tony, but wasn't I sort of asking those same questions to myself?

Tony smiled sadly, "No, but let's be honest. We'd probably be divorced if she was alive."

It was weird. That was exactly how I would have answered. I suddenly felt as if Tony was placed here next to me to help me.

"How about you?" he asked, "What happened with *your* marriage?"

"Long story."

Tony gave me a really kind smile and said, "Sorry. Didn't mean to pry. Then again, we're at a divorce party. What else are we supposed to talk about?"

I couldn't help but laugh, and something at this moment made me feel like Tony and I were about to become friends.

Tony pulled out a business card. "Listen, if you ever want to talk," he said, handing it to me, "If you ever want to get together, I'd like that."

"I'd love that, actually," I smiled. And I meant it. Tony wasn't hitting on me. He wasn't even asking me out on a date. He was just a nice guy, probably a little bit lonely, and wanted a friend. And there was something so likeable about his demeanor that made it all very acceptable, refreshing, in fact.

We put each other's numbers into our cells, and then Tony said, "Somebody told me once that eventually everyone learns how to deal with their baggage. Do you think that's true?"

I gave him a wide grin, "I don't know. My baggage is pretty heavy."

"Then put it down!" he exclaimed.

All I could do was grin. He was right. I wanted to put my baggage down so badly. I'd told my late husband a million times how sorry I was. I'd told God a million times how sorry I was. My baggage was still so heavy, though, to the point where it was making my biceps sore. And until recently, I hadn't had even the slightest clue about how to let it go. But now, between Preston and Luke and my unborn child, and seeing my sister suffer, and seeing my mother suffer, and now, meeting Tony, a guy in my exact situation, I was starting to figure out how to forgive myself. And it was liberating beyond belief.

I think I'm going to leave," said Tony, "But hey, before I do, I saw you talking to that girl over there." He motioned to Georgia, "She's cute. What's her deal?"

I walked Tony over to Georgia, introduced them, and left them alone to get to know each other. As I walked away, Georgia gave me a wink and I knew instinctively that I had just made a love connection.

My next order of business was to check on Laura, who was still in deep conversation with Dan, Tony's date's ex-husband. It was nice to see my sister smiling from ear to ear and show some interest in a guy, even though the guy's character was in question, based on the bad reference I'd gotten indirectly from Tony's date.

Then came the shock. Just as I was about to go talk to Henry, who was standing by the door, something made me turn around and look back into the crowd. Standing there smiling and waving to me was none other than Luke. Why I was so surprised I wasn't sure. Luke was single. This was a party for single people in a small suburban fish tank. Wouldn't it make sense that he would be here?

He was dressed in jeans and a light blue pullover. Tonight was the first time I'd ever seen him in anything other than running attire, and I had to say, he looked utterly adorable. I waved back and saw him heading toward me. And then something even more shocking happened. A cute, little brunette took his hand and began walking with him. I panicked. Was Luke on a date? Is *she* the reason Luke was keeping our relationship platonic?

"Emma!" he said happily when he reached me, "How are you?"

"I'm fine," I responded, trying to look happy to see him and not jealous of the woman who seemed extremely territorial.

"Emma, this is Patty," said Luke, "Patty, this is Emma Bloom, my running partner."

Patty was really short, but really pretty.

"Hi," she said with a sugary smile.

"Hi, nice to meet you," I managed.

Patty then felt the need to declare ownership of her man, because she turned to Luke. "Hey Hun, I want you to meet Henry. Come with me." Then she looked at me, "So great meeting you, Emma!" she gushed. Then she turned and walked away, practically pulling Luke with her.

Luke turned around and gave me a dashing grin and a big wink, and at this moment, I wanted to run after them. I wanted to shout, "Hands off, Shorty!" But how could I? Luke and I weren't dating. We were acquaintances at best. He'd just introduced me as "his running partner!" The bottom line was, we'd gone for a few runs together on the path, and we'd had some nice talks. That was it. He wasn't mine.

Plus, hello! I was knocked up with someone else's baby. Someone who was giving me strong signals that he wanted to be a part of the child's life, and maybe mine, too. I was with Preston. Luke was obviously with Patty. And that's the way it was.

I realized right then, I didn't want to wait another second to tell Laura what was going on. I walked over to her and Dan, who were now in a seemingly cozy conversation. It was so strange to see Laura in a situation like this and witness her acting flirtatious. After all, I'd never really seen her with any man other than Alan, and that relationship had always seemed so domestic and non-romantic. For the first time, perhaps, I was seeing my sister in a whole new light. It was refreshing in a way.

"Hey sis," I said, "Are you almost ready?"

"You want to leave? Already?" The disappointed look on her face made me feel guilty, and made me realize how much she liked Dan. Still, I pressed her.

"Yeah, is that okay?"

"Sure," she said sadly. Then, switching gears and with all smiles, she declared, "Emma, this is Dan. Dan, this is my sister."

I shook Dan's hand. He was very handsome. I wondered what might be lurking behind his good looks and charm that made his ex-wife despise him so much that she had to leave the party. For now, though, I didn't care. He was cute and he was making my sister happy. That's all that mattered to me. How bad could the guy be? I was smart enough to realize there were two sides to every story, and Dan seemed okay to me. For the moment, he had my blessing.

We chit-chatted for a couple minutes and then I turned to my sister and said, "Ready?"

She gave Dan a fake pout and said, "Got to go."

"Can I call you?" he asked.

"Sure," said Laura in an enthusiastic voice I'd never heard before. Was this my serious, doesn't know how to have fun, Orthopedic surgeon sister? She was like an alien to me at this moment.

I watched Dan program Laura's cell number in his phone, and I almost made a crack about her ring tone, but decided to keep my mouth shut.

We said good-bye and Dan actually kissed Laura on the lips. As we exited the party, I took one last glance at Luke and Patty. They were both smiling and in a conversation with another couple, so neither one of them noticed Laura and I breeze past them and out the door. Patty, the shrimp, had her arm around her date's waist. No touching on Luke's part, though. That spoke volumes.

I wondered how they got together. Luke had made it very clear that he wasn't dating. What changed his mind? Could he not resist her? Who pursued who? How long had they known each other? Had they kissed?

Once outside, I turned to my sister. "I'm so sorry. I know you liked that guy and that you wanted to stay. I just couldn't."

"Are you okay?" Laura asked me.

"Luke was in there."

She gasped. "Why didn't you point him out?"

"I just had to get out of there. He was on a date."

"Oh. I'm sorry," she said sadly.

"I'm so bothered by it."

"Was the girl cute?"

"She was okay. It's not Patty who bothers me. It's the thought of Luke dating. I mean, what if it's serious?"

"Aren't *you* in a relationship?" she asked.

"Laura, I have to talk to you about something. Can we go to *Starbucks?*"

Chapter 13

"**A**re you crazy?!" This was my sister's reaction to finding out she was going to be an aunt again.

"Please calm down and let me explain," I pleaded, taking a sip of my grande skim decaf misto.

"There's nothing on earth you could tell me that would make having a baby seem like a good idea at this juncture in your life. It's bad for you, bad for your boy toy, and very very bad for your child!"

"There's the judgmental sister I know and love so well," I replied.

"Please, you know I'm right."

"Laura, Preston cried!"

"How touching."

"You're awful."

"And you're being really stupid."

At this point, I chose to grit my teeth and try to tolerate Laura's abhorrent behavior. "Please try to see this as a blessing. This is a gift, a miracle."

"And what about supporting the miracle?" she asked, "Did you guys talk about that?"

"Yes, of course. Preston said that he would be more than willing to take care of his baby financially. He makes a lot of money. But you're missing the most important point. He wants to raise our child too. He said that. I promise."

"Em, what about Izzie? Hasn't she been through enough already without adding a sibling into her life, whose father is an eternal playboy?"

"I've thought about Izzie, and I think she would learn to see this as I do, as a wonderful addition to our lives. This baby is part of our family, and although our family dynamic is a little different than the norm, we're still a family and that means something. And we will continue to be the same family, plus one." I hesitated and then finished, "Or maybe two, if Preston decides to become a part of it in any significant way."

"What do you see happening with him? I mean, are you two going to get married?"

"Any way you could tone down the sarcasm just a touch?"

"Answer the question."

"Neither one of us has the slightest clue. I think it's best to let things progress naturally and see where the future takes the two of us. Who knows? We may end up living happily ever after."

"Oh my God," Laura exclaimed.

"What?"

"I understand now," she said with a smirk.

"What?"

"You think that Mr. Single hottie player boy is going to marry you when you have his baby."

"No, I don't," I defended.

"Yes, you do. You think that Preston is going to take one look at his new baby, and then all of a sudden want monogamy, a family, and dinner with the kids every night at six."

Furious at this point, I stood up, "So you have it all figured out, I guess."

Now Laura stood up too, and was almost shouting. "Mr. City loving boy, who loves clubbing and Cubs games and boating on Lake Michigan with his buddies, is going to move out to the suburbs and live with you and Isabelle and your baby, and make all your problems go away!"

"Shut up, Laura!" I shouted, knowing full well that I sounded just like I did in seventh grade. I could feel the stares from all the coffee drinkers at neighboring tables, but I didn't care. "I can't believe how judgmental you're being!" I finished.

"You're confusing being judgmental with being honest," she shouted back.

I felt my eyes brim with tears. "Thanks for being so supportive," I said softly. Then, I turned and walked out.

"Emma!" my sister called out, but I didn't turn around. In fact, I started running, and I ran all the way home, which was okay, because it wasn't more than a quarter of a mile.

When I got to my house, my mother, the babysitter, was all over me. "What happened? Why are you out of breath? Where's Laura?"

"We...had a fight."

"Are you crying?" she asked, trying to get a closer look at me.

I put my head down and tried to hide the tears and smeared mascara that was running down my cheeks.

"I'm fine, mom. Everything will be okay." I kissed her cheek. "Thanks for watching Izzie. Was she okay?"

"She was great," she said, "I'm worried about you guys."

"I just need to go to bed," I said, "We'll talk tomorrow. Are you okay? Are you staying over I hope?"

Apparently, my parents were still in negotiations, discussing the fallout of my dad's affair with Mrs. Feldman, the slutty seamstress. The only info my mother had offered earlier was that they were trying to work things out.

"What's that supposed to mean?" Laura had asked angrily.

"Well, I'm not sure I want to," my mom had said.

"Of course you want to!" Laura snapped.

"Why?" I'd responded, "Her husband's the cheater, not her." Those words had left my sister speechless.

"Yes," said my mother, "I'm sleeping here." She seemed very sad about that. I hugged her tightly, and although I couldn't see her face, I knew she was crying. I was too afraid to turn and confirm her tears, though, because the thought of my mother this upset was overwhelmingly devastating, and for tonight, I couldn't take anything else.

"Good night, Mom," I said, "I love you. It will be okay. I promise."

I headed upstairs and that's when I heard the front door open. "Is Emma here?" I heard my sister ask my mom.

"Yes."

I heard them talking, but couldn't really hear what they were saying, and didn't care. I just wanted to go to bed. After checking on Izzie, I got into my PJ's and then went into the bathroom to wash off my makeup and brush my teeth.

I was standing at my bathroom sink, drying off my face when Laura appeared in the doorway.

"Hi," she said.

I didn't answer her. Instead, I grabbed a tiny bottle of Lancome overnight eye cream and began putting it around my eyes.

"Another free gift with purchase?" she asked with a smile, obviously hoping to lighten things up.

I turned to her. "You know, Laura, you held my hand while I buried my husband, and I can't even count the number of times I cried in your arms over the past year. And now, after knowing all you know about me and what I've been through, you can't even find it in your heart to support something I want so badly."

"I don't want to fight with you," she said, "But I can't support you on this."

"Why?" I urged, "I've always supported you. I never told you this, but when you were getting married at 23, I thought you were crazy. But I never said anything because it was *your* life, not mine. So, I kept it to myself and stood by you. You're a workaholic. You've never had any fun in your life. And that bothers me. But, I never said anything because it's not my place. And tonight, I wanted you to act the same for me. I wanted you to say, 'I don't agree with what you're doing, but I will stand behind you.' And you didn't. I can't believe it. You're my sister!"

"That's right. I'm your sister. That's why I won't stand here and watch you screw up your life!"

Now I was ready to explode. "Did you even hear one word I just said?!"

"Look, I'm tired. I'm going to bed," she responded, turning to leave.

"Why am I not surprised?" I answered bitterly as she walked out.

Chapter 14

I couldn't deny that Laura might be right. I mean, what was I thinking? Just because Preston told me to have the baby, that made it okay? Was I going to have a threesome for him too? What kind of power did this man have over my judgment? Life all of a sudden began to feel like it was spinning out of control. I was the driver, and I was traveling on dangerous roads, with a dangerous person, doing dangerous things.

I thought about the divorce party. I'd met all kinds of interesting people. There was Tony, the guy whose wife died, who was offering me his friendship. Then there was Georgia, the woman with the perfect body, whose husband felt the need to be a swinger. Where was the justice in the world for HER?

And Luke. On a date with Patty! Why did I care so much? Luke and I weren't together. We'd never even been on a date. Just like me, he had the right to go out with whomever he wanted. So why was I having such a hard time with it? Because at this moment, I decided to finally admit something to myself. I barely knew Luke Sullivan, but I had this weird feeling gnawing at my gut, telling me there was something special happening between us. And the way Luke had winked at me tonight, I knew he felt it, too.

I had this vision of Luke in my future in some significant way. Not necessarily marriage. I wasn't ready to think about walking down the aisle with anyone. But there was a connection, and a feeling of familiarity about Luke that was lodged in my core. So there it was. The guy who was a noteworthy part of my future was on a date, and I was pregnant with someone else's baby. Not good. Very unsettling.

I looked closely at my face in the mirror. Did I even recognize myself? I, Emma Bloom was having some random guy's baby. It was nuts. Had I lost my mind? I pulled up my shirt and looked down at my stomach for a long time. Inside of it was a very teeny tiny person, actually just a bunch of cells at this point, multiplying together as the seconds ticked by. Still, a growing human being was inside of me, its father a non-committal party boy who loved crazy sex with me (and probably a lot of other women).

I touched my tummy and whispered, "Hi, Baby," and as the words came out of my mouth the weirdest thing happened. I heard a text come through. I went over to the night stand where my Blackberry was and read it.

"How is my baby, Baby?" it read, "Say good-night to him or her for me. Can I see you tomorrow night?"

My heart suddenly soared. This was the first glimpse I had that Preston might actually step up to the plate and come through on this whole thing. Maybe he was capable of being a good father. Maybe things would work out. Maybe my old school, judgmental sister was wrong.

I fell asleep with my anger fading, happiness and excitement taking their place. I would make Laura understand. I would make everyone understand. It would take time, but they would all have to deal with it. Because having been through hell and back, this was my time to do what I wanted. I was having a baby! Creating a life! And yes, maybe the circumstances and the dad weren't ideal, but having watched the pain of my child missing her dead father, I was perfectly in tune with death and loss. I was not going to apologize or back down, or even make excuses for giving the joy of life.

Thankfully, the next morning, when Isabelle and I and my mom woke up, Laura was already gone. She had an early surgery at the hospital. Only my sister would go to a party and stay out late, knowing she had to get up at the crack of dawn to go to work. I felt beyond guilty thinking about this, because I knew Laura went to the party for me. And this morning, I was happy to have her out of the picture.

I was able to hold my mother off and not get into detail about my fight with Laura, but she did show me a note Laura left me that read, "Emmie, I'm sorry about last night. I just want you to have a good life and I'm worried about you. Everything I say, I say because I love you. L."

"What does she mean she wants you to have a good life?" asked my mother while pouring *Frosted Flakes* into Izzie's bowl.

Pouring the milk, I answered, "Mom, it's complicated. I'll tell you all about it." I motioned to my daughter, ever so grateful that I could use her as the excuse not to share my secret. I finished, "You know...after 9:00, when gymnastics starts." I looked at Izzie, who was watching *Big Time Rush* and not listening to us. My adorable little girl, who had no clue that her life was about to erupt (again). The guilt was killing me.

"Fine," said my mother, "I'll wait here."

I actually had no intention of telling my mother anything yet, but I figured I could drop Izzie off and then call her from my cell and tell her I'd talk to her later, that I had some errands to run. What a weasel I was. Nonetheless, I wasn't ready to face Helene with the news of her third grandchild.

Then, low and behold, as luck would have it, my dad called shortly after this conversation and asked her to go out for breakfast with him. So my mother left before us.

I dropped off Isabelle and headed home. There were so many things I could do to preoccupy myself till it was time to pick her up. I could work out or run errands. Or, I could make salsa, or work in my garden. But by the time I pulled into my driveway, I knew exactly how I wanted to spend my morning.

I quickly changed into my bathing suit, grabbed a towel, threw some sunscreen and a bottle of water into a beach bag, and got back into the car. And then I headed east. I lived twenty minutes away from the beach, and could honestly count on one hand the number of times I'd taken advantage of that in seven years. Today, with the morning to myself and so much on my mind, I had a strong urge to sit on the sand and look out over Lake Michigan for the next couple hours.

The second I reached the beach, I took off my flip-flops and walked onto the sand. It was the best feeling the in world. The weather couldn't have been more perfect. I looked at the glistening water and then I looked up at the sky. It was all blue, with one little puffy cloud off to the side. And it was at this moment, I realized how small I was, and how small my problems were. Looking at the big sky and the massive body of water put everything into perspective. I smiled, took a deep breath and a big exhale. And then, the weirdest thing happened. I looked down and noticed an iphone lying in the sand.

"Whoever just dropped their iphone is majorly cutting into my beach time," I said to myself as I walked up to the shelter where some lifeguards were sitting and chatting.

"Hi," I said, feeling like I was interrupting some teen-age chit chat.

"Hey, what's up?" said a friendly guy who reminded me of one of the Jonas Brothers.

I handed him the phone. "I just found this in the sand."

"Okay, thanks," he said.

I smiled, turned around, and literally bumped into someone, who turned out to be Luke.

"Emma!" he exclaimed, grinning from ear to ear.

I giggled, "Oh my God! Luke, hi!"

"What are you doing here?"

"I just decided to come here. You?"

He laughed. "Same thing! I swear to God. Are you here by yourself?"

"Yeah."

"Me too! I woke up this morning and it was a gorgeous day, so I decided to blow off work and go to the beach. I've seriously never done that before. The boys are on a field trip with camp, so here I am. I can't believe you're here!"

I was smiling so wide my cheeks were hurting. "I can't either!"

"Actually, I just lost my iphone," he said.

"Is this it?" asked Nick Jonas, holding up the phone.

Luke examined the phone. "Yeah! Thanks, man."

"She found it," said the lifeguard, motioning to me.

Luke gave me a huge smile. "Really?"

I nodded.

"Unreal! So, would you like to sit together?" he asked with a chuckle.

"Sure."

Luke then did something that stopped my heart. He took my hand. I could have sworn I heard one of the lifeguards say, "Aw..."

Luke and I walked about 30 feet to the spot where he had his towel, and the entire way, all I kept thinking about was how much I loved Luke's hand in mine.

"Is this okay?" he asked.

"Yeah." I put my bag down and spread out my towel next to his.

"I really can't believe this," he said, sitting down, "It's crazy, isn't it?"

"It is."

"Great, huh?"

I didn't answer Luke. Instead, I asked, "So...did you have fun last night?"

"Yeah, good party. You? Who were you with?"

"My sister. Who were *you* with?"

"Patty Rubenstein, a girl I went to high-school with. She just got divorced."

"Are you guys dating?"

"Um...not really."

"You either are or you're not."

"Now who's being territorial?" he flirted.

He was right. I was. But how could I not be? Here I sat, feeling that familiar feeling you get when you're on a date with someone you really like, yet in my belly I was carrying the child of another man. All I could do was smile bashfully and say, "Touché. If you like her, I'm happy for you."

"Look, I shouldn't have said not really. I should have said no. Patty and I are friends. We've known each other for thirty years. We reconnected through facebook, and only because we're both single. We're just friends, I promise."

"Patty thinks you're more."

Luke smiled, "Maybe she does, but trust me, we're not."

"Because you don't date."

"Right. Because I don't date."

"Still not ready to talk about it?"

Luke shook his head.

I smiled, "Boy, when it comes to bottling things up, you have me beat, which is pretty impressive."

"It's just...really complicated. Soon. I promise."

I smiled at him. "Okay."

"So, how about *you?* How's the young guy? Are you still seeing him?"

"Yes. I'm actually having his baby," was the honest answer, but I certainly wasn't going to say that. So, instead I answered with an awkward smile, "Good. Really good."

"You don't have to be embarrassed by it. I think it's great."

"You do?"

"Yeah. Is he still treating you nicely? I'm just making sure. I'm protecting you. *Not* being territorial."

"Well, thank you," I said politely, "Yes, he's treating me just fine."

"How does it feel being in a relationship? Do you like it?"

I turned my head to the side to look at Luke, who was doing the same to look at me. It was so odd. I could have been lying next to Laura and talking like this, and I would have felt no more comfortable with my sister than I did at this moment. "Yeah," I smiled, "I do like it. I don't really think I'm in a long-term relationship, but it's really okay." At that moment I was thinking, "Then why the *hell* are you having his baby?"

"I agree. I'd be worried about you if the first guy you got involved with after your husband was someone serious. What you're doing is good. It's healthy."

I was dying to add, with sarcasm, "Healthy's for sure. I've created a human being."

"So, is the guy totally hot? I mean, if I saw him, would I be intimidated?"

I was still looking at Luke when I answered, "He's pretty hot, but..."

"But what?"

I gave Luke a big grin. "He doesn't have your eyes."

Luke's instant wide grin confirmed that he was digging me hugely. And that made me happy.

We lounged with our faces in the sun and talked for the next hour and a half. Not nonstop, though. Much of the time was spent soaking up the sun and relaxing, to the point where I thought Luke had fallen asleep a couple times. It was comfortable, very natural, and I felt at ease.

We did go for a swim in Lake Michigan, and at one point, Luke found a football that didn't seem to belong to anyone, so we played catch in the water. I thought back to the last time I'd swam in a large body of water with a man. It was on my honeymoon in Jamaica, seven years earlier. And as I recalled the trip, I suddenly began to feel guiltier than O.J. because right now, here on Lake Michigan, with a man I barely knew, I was having more fun than I did all those years ago. Something about being here with Luke made me ask myself a question that caused me to hate my own guts. "Why couldn't I have been on my honeymoon with *this* guy?" I wondered. I answered myself, "Because then you wouldn't have Izzie, you unappreciative, horrible, and I might add PREGNANT person."

God, I hated myself for having these thoughts. But I couldn't deny the truth any longer. No, I didn't want Sam to die, but it was time to be honest and admit that the foundation for our marriage and our relationship in general wasn't very strong. There wasn't a lot of substance to it. If I could feel like this, so at ease and so natural with a man I barely knew, what feelings of significance had I ever really had with Sam? It was sad, but very realistic.

A couple hours later, when Luke and I parted ways in the parking lot, I felt like the natural thing to do would have been for him to kiss me. On the lips. He didn't, though, and I hoped that the look of disappointment I knew I had on my face wasn't too obvious. Then again, I wasn't allowed to kiss Luke. I had Preston. And his baby! I was living two separate lives now. Actually, three.

One life was that of a middle-aged sexpot, cougaring like nobody's business. The next, an infatuated groupie, trying to grasp a little bit of a relationship with a guy who was carrying some baggage, but who seemed otherwise normal, aside from the secret he was keeping that I wanted so much to know about. And my third life, the life of a mother with a sweet, innocent child, both of us still grieving my dead husband. Only now, in addition to that pain, I was beginning to acknowledge that the man I'd vowed to spend the rest of my life with probably would have ended up being my ex-husband had he survived his car crash.

I was three people. And I didn't care for any of them at this juncture. But I did care for Izzie. And I was completely obsessed with Preston. As for Luke, all I can say is, I was falling. Hard.

Chapter 15

"Mommy, can I water the garden?" Izzie asked me as we were pulling into the driveway.

"Sure, that would be a huge help," I smiled, "But jump right in the shower when you're done." Coming from Gold Medal, Izzie was surely in need of some hot water and soap.

"Ok, Mommy," she said, leaping out of the car and heading to the back patio.

I pulled into the garage and headed into the house, feeling relaxed and happy. I had just spent a wonderful morning on the lake with a very special man. My insides felt all warm and fuzzy, my thoughts of Luke and our new friendship (or whatever it was) unable to leave me.

Suddenly I heard Izzie cry, "Mommy! Mommy!"

"What is it?!" I shouted, racing to the back patio door to see what her urgency was.

"Look!" she exclaimed.

I opened the door and there stood my daughter, holding a dozen pink roses that were wrapped in cellophane.

"These were on the steps," she said, "Aren't they pretty?"

I was stunned. "Yes, they are."

"Are they for us?" she asked.

"Let me see." I took off the little white envelope that was taped to the cellophane and opened it. "For my babies. Love, Preston," it read. My heart pounded.

"What does it say?"

I looked at my daughter and flat out lied. "It says thank you," I smiled.

"Can I read it?" she asked, coming up to me, "I can read now, you know."

Instinctively, I folded the card, put it in my hand, and made a fist to hide it. "I know you can read, sweetheart," but it just says thank you. I helped a friend with something and she wanted to thank me so she dropped off flowers."

"What did you help her with?"

"Uh...I made some salsa for her."

"Why?"

"Why does it matter?" I asked with a nervous giggle.

"Mommy?"

"Yeah?"

"Are those from a boy?"

"Izzie!"

She was only six, but man, she was smart. "What?" she asked defensively.

"Are you watering the garden or what?"

"Fine. I'll butt out," she conceded, handing me the roses.

"Thank you," I said with a smile. Then I kissed both her cheeks and walked into the house, still unable to believe Preston dropped off flowers.

While Isabelle was in the shower, I called and thanked him.

"Can I come over tonight after you put Izzie to bed?"

My first thought was Laura. A, we were in a fight, and B, this was the worst time for her to meet the father of her future niece or nephew. Then I thought of C, which was myself. "Sure," I smiled, "Come around 9:00."

Laura got home from work around 6:00 and tried to apologize to me. I was in the kitchen making Isabelle a hot dog, and making apple salsa.

"Are those walnuts you're putting in that salsa?" my sister asked.

My assistant, who was sitting on the kitchen counter mixing the ingredients, answered, "Yeah, and there's cinnamon in it too."

"Yum!" said Laura, "Can I try?"

"Sure," answered her niece.

Laura put a spoon into the bowl and then tasted the salsa. "Em, I swear to God, you should go into business! This is yummy."

I completely ignored her.

"Hey, Izzie, will you go upstairs and get me a hair band?" Laura asked. It was obvious that her motive of sending my child away was to be alone with me.

"Sure," said Isabelle, jumping off the counter and running off.

"Em, please talk to me."

"Nothing to say," I answered coldly.

"You can't see things clearly!" she exclaimed, "You're not thinking. I'm trying to help you!"

I turned to her. "Laura, you're the one who can't see things clearly. Stay out of this. If you're not going to stand by me, then butt out."

"Stand by you? And watch you ruin your life? And your daughter's life?"

I couldn't take it anymore, so I shouted, "Watch me ruin my life? What a joke! I watched you ruin yours twenty-three years ago! I knew marrying Alan was a mistake, but I stood by and let you live your life! And I never judged you! All I want is your support. I think what I'm doing is the right thing. You don't know how I feel!"

"No, I guess I don't," she answered sadly.

"Here, Aunt Laura," said Izzie, back with the hair band.

"Thanks, cutie," she said, giving her niece a kiss on the cheek. Then she said to me, "I'm going upstairs to change, and then I'm going out. Please think about what I said."

I didn't answer back. Instead I watched my daughter chase after her aunt and ask where she was going. I heard Laura tell her she was going out to dinner with a friend. I knew right away it was a date. I also knew it was with Dan from the night before.

When my sister left my house, I never even looked at her. Major guilt crept in because I knew she'd probably struggled with her outfit and that she was wishing she had my opinion. Still I stayed away, acting cold and bitter and angry.

Later that night, I put Izzie to bed, and she asked me why I was angry at Aunt Laura.

"We just disagree about a lot of things," I told my daughter.

"What's disagree?"

"We have different opinions about things."

"I don't understand."

"Someday you will, when you're older."

"Do you still love Aunt Laura?"

"Oh yes," I said with a smile, and right then I began to soften about my sister, "You can disagree but still love someone."

"Are you guys best friends?"

I laughed, "Yeah, I guess we are."

"I knew it."

"Well, you and I are best friends, too, aren't we?"

"You and me?" she asked.

"Yeah! You and me!" Then I hugged my daughter as hard as I could.

"Hey mommy?"

"Yeah?"

"Were you and daddy best friends?"

"Yes, sweetie, we were."

"Did you and Dad ever disagree?"

"Man, you're smart!" I declared, "Go to sleep!"

I must have kissed her good-night 25 times before I left the room, perhaps trying to make up for what she had just confirmed: her knowing that her mom and dad used to argue.

I shut her door, and then went downstairs and into the kitchen. I took out the apple salsa, some chips and apple slices, and put them on the table for my date. Preston arrived promptly at 9:00, and the way he kissed me was heavenly. I wasn't sure if it was my imagination, but there was meaning in it, as if our relationship had suddenly transformed from lust into something deeper.

We ended up sitting at my kitchen table, eating the chips and salsa and talking about the baby.

"What do you think it is?" he asked me.

"Boy."

"Really?"

"Yeah, I just have a gut feeling."

"Can we name it after me?" he asked.

"No way," I said with a laugh.

"Why not?"

"I'm having a hard enough time figuring out how I'm going to tell my mother I'm having a baby whose legal last name is going to be Christiansen!

If I tell her his first name's going to be Preston, I think she may go into shock."

Preston laughed. Then he did something endearing and unforgettable. "Come here," he whispered, taking me onto his lap. He lifted up my t-shirt and kissed my stomach. "Are you going to get really big?" he asked.

"Yup," I said with a laugh.

He kissed it again. Then he gently kissed my lips. Then he kissed me harder. And harder. And we kissed for a long time.

It was interesting because ordinarily, clothes would have been flying off of us, but now, everything seemed to be different all of a sudden, like our relationship had just changed. Granted, my daugh/ter was upstairs sleeping, and I wasn't going to risk having sex in my house while she was there. But still, neither of the two people who previously felt it impossible to keep our hands off of each other were interested in doing anything besides kissing. And it seemed like both a good and a bad thing.

After we were done smooching, we plopped on the couch and watched TV. Ironically, the movie He's Just Not That Into You was on, starring my boyfriend, Bradley Cooper. Preston had his arms around me, and that's when I started to think about Luke. Sitting here with Preston didn't really feel natural. Lying on the sand with Luke did. Preston was the fun, wild, spontaneous guy in my life. He wasn't supposed to be the person watching Bradley Cooper and cuddling with me. Luke was. Or maybe someone else. But not the man with whom I ate salsa naked, or the person who I had sex with in a forest preserve. This is not the man to watch TV and snuggle with, and let's be honest, have a baby with. I mean, Preston had never even met my daughter, other than for five minutes at the McGowan's house. Nevertheless, life in my belly always seemed to win the argument against reason. So, I continued to accept fate and go with it.

When he left, Preston kissed me good-bye and gave me a smile I knew was genuine.

"I still can't believe we're doing this," I said softly to him.

"Me neither," he said, "But for once in my life, I'm taking responsibility and it feels good. It feels really good."

I wished right then I could say the same, but I didn't feel that way. Preston was supposed to be my boy toy. Now he was turning out to be the father of my child who would be in my life forever. And regardless of my feelings for Luke, it really didn't seem right.

Then again, the events that had taken place in the past had shaped who I was now. Sam's death had led me to isolation and misery like none I'd ever experienced, followed by a crazy physical attraction that had led to a life. And that made logic go right out the window. Following protocol seemed so unnecessary. There were no rules anymore. Just life and death.

Preston and I were having a baby. That didn't mean we had to get married and live happily ever after. I felt okay with accepting the fact that God gave me a fetus. It was a miracle, and that was good enough for me. And my sister didn't understand this. Probably never would with her closed-minded attitude and her pragmatic approach to life. But I did.

This was life on my terms, no one else's. The accident that now lived in my belly was mine and Preston's. He or she was also my daughter's sibling, who we would all love. And regardless of my gut instinct telling me I was nuts for going through with this, once again, I felt like the miracle of life was taking precedence over normalcy.

And then, just as I was feeling peaceful and happy and somewhat serene for the first time all night, that's when I went to the bathroom and saw blood gushing out of me.

Chapter 16

Dozens of emotions were running wild inside of me. Panic, shock, confusion, devastation, sadness. The worst one of all, though, was relief. I sat there thinking, 'I'm off the hook,' these words ironically making me even more upset because I felt guilty for being partially thankful that I was losing this baby. Then again, I was losing this baby! The child who was inside me, even if just for a short time, was never going to be.

I began to cry, the tears flowing as fast as they did in the dark days of the previous year, the year of Sam's death. I sobbed for a long time. Then I took a shower, wondering the entire time while hot water streamed down on me, how I was going to tell the father.

Do I call him? Do I tell him in person? I asked myself, as beads of sweat began to form on my forehead, caused both by hot steam and the anxiety of thinking about how hard Preston might take the news. I got out of the shower, put on some sweats, and fell asleep in literally less than a minute. I was wiped out.

Very late in the night, I was awakened by the noise of someone coming up the stairs. I knew right away that it was my sister. I looked at the clock. 3:22! Laura, Miss Conservative was getting home from a date in the early morning hours! I found myself very happy for her. Perhaps for the first time in her life, she was allowing herself to have fun. In my eyes, my sister was finally living.

I wanted so much to go talk to her, but I couldn't bring myself to get up for two reasons. First, I was still extremely angry with her, my idiotic stubborn side stopping me from giving in, and secondly, I was drained and weak and exhausted, not to mention in pain due to severe cramping. When my thoughts shifted from Laura and Dan's date back to my now empty womb and my baby who would never be, I began to weep again. I cried quietly until I eventually fell back asleep.

Awake again at 6:30, still in a little bit of pain, I was tossing and turning, trying to fall back to sleep. A few minutes later, I made the decision to give up and go downstairs. And once I found myself standing in my kitchen with nothing to do, I did what I always did. I made salsa. It was the one task always guaranteed to cause a diversion, and right now I sure needed one.

I opened the fridge and took out two large green peppers, a bunch of cilantro, two jalapenos and a large watermelon. Then I began furiously seeding and cutting and mixing, anything to take me away from the realization that I had to deal with loss. Again.

"Watermelon salsa?" I heard Laura say, "Now I've seen it all."

I turned to my sister, who was standing there in a t-shirt and socks, looking exhausted, but happy.

"Hi," I said flatly.

"Hi?" she laughed, "You actually said something to me?"

I couldn't help but giggle.

"Listen," she began, "I have to tell you something."

"Laura…"

"No, let me say something. I want to apologize. You were

right. If you want to have a baby, I shouldn't be talking you out of it. I've always been too much of a conformist, too old-fashioned. I'm sorry, Emmie." She hugged me, and that's when I lost it, and I mean *really* lost it. I began to sob uncontrollably.

"Shhh," said my sister, who was like a means of life-support to me at this moment, "It's okay. I'm here with you and I will help you, and we'll make everyone understand. And I'll love your baby just like I love Izzie."

I pulled away from her embrace and managed to say through tears, "No, you don't understand. I lost the baby."

Laura gasped. "What? When?"

"Last night before I went to bed," I said, breaking down again. My big sister immediately pulled me to her and held me tight.

She whispered, "It's okay." She put her soothing hand over my hair and said, "I'm so sorry."

I pulled away and looked right at her. "Thank you," I said softly, "Thank you for accepting me for the person I am. I appreciate it."

Laura took a big piece of my hair and put it behind my ear. Then she looked into my eyes and said softly, "Things happen. How we deal with them is how we find out what we're made of."

"You're right."

"You should probably call your doctor today and tell her."

"Okay, I will."

"And drink lots of water and Gatorade and stay in bed and just rest today."

"Yes, Doctor," I said with a smile, "I will."

Laura hugged me again and I cried for what seemed like a long time. "Thanks for taking care of me. You're a good doctor."

Laura laughed.

"And a good sister."

"So are you, my sweet Emmie."

"Please don't call me that."

Still embraced, we both cracked up.

After a few minutes, Laura declared that she needed coffee badly. As for me, I continued making the salsa.

"So...how was last night?" I asked with a giggle.

"Great," she smiled.

I started clapping and shouted, "Yay!!"

Laura laughed.

The morning continued to improve when Isabelle woke up. Seeing her face brought everything back to reality. How thankful I was for her! After breakfast, I dropped her off at the gymnastics place. Then I decided it was time to call Preston. Laura had gone back to sleep, so I figured I'd get it over with. I stepped outside and sat on my back porch, looking at my beautiful garden, ironically the same place I'd chosen to tell Preston he was going to be a father, and I called.

"Hi," I said when he answered.

"Hi, Baby!"

There was no need for small talk. I didn't try to cushion it and I didn't try to tell him lightly, I guess because there was no nice or easy way to say it. So I just simply said it.

"I lost the baby."

"What do you mean?" he asked.

"I had a miscarriage," I said flatly.

The silence that followed was torturous. Waiting for his reaction was painful. Finally, after what seemed like ten minutes, he spoke. "Are you okay?" he asked softly, "I mean, are you in pain?"

God, he was sweet. Preston's gut reaction made me realize what a genuinely good-hearted person he was.

"Not really. A little bit maybe," I answered.

"I'm really sorry." Now he appeared to be in somewhat of a daze, and I got the feeling he was having a hard time grasping the news.

"I am too." My eyes welled up with tears. "I really mean it. I would have loved to have had your baby, Preston." Was I lying? I wasn't sure.

There was more awkward silence. A strange feeling suddenly crept up on me. It seemed as if the two of us had just lost the road map that had shown us how to connect. I now felt like I was on the phone with a stranger. "Say something," I finally said.

"I seriously have no idea what to say."

"Well then, I guess we should hang up."

"Let me call you later," he said, "Is that okay?"

His words were unconvincing and as I said good-bye, I wondered if I was ever going to talk to him again. I realized right then how little I knew this man, whose baby I had actually committed to having. What was even worse was the fact that if I never heard from him again, I wasn't so sure I cared.

Everything had suddenly become so confusing. How could I have craved him and wanted to have his baby one minute, and felt so disconnected the next? I was beyond mixed up and messed up and screwed up. I was a basket case who needed one thing at this moment: more sleep. I went upstairs and plopped down on my bed, my eyes closing seconds later. And then I slept. And interestingly enough, I dreamed about Luke.

His arms were wrapped around me and I was kissing him, not only with my lips but with all of me, my core, my bones, my veins and my blood, as if

I needed him to know that although we were technically platonic friends, he was already buried deep in my heart.

We kissed and kissed, and Luke made me feel secure and protected and out of danger. I felt a sense of calmness, as if being in his arms would make everything okay. Ironically, though, the intensity of my feelings were making Luke dangerous to me. As long as his soft lips were on mine, covering them and keeping them warm and cozy, I was anything but calm. I was panicky, actually, unable to deal with the intense feelings and vulnerability taking over my soul.

All of a sudden, Luke stopped kissing me. He put his hand on my belly and asked, "What do we have here?"

I looked down and suddenly I had this big round pregnant stomach. I was eight months pregnant. "I don't know what you're talking about, Luke," I said, "It's gone. There's nothing here."

Luke looked down again. "Are you sure?"

That's when I woke up. My heart was pounding. I sat up, realizing I was dreaming. I felt unbelievably relieved, but it was a bit strange that I had just had such an intense kissing dream about Luke. Then again, spending time at the beach with him had been incredible, and even with everything going on, he was lodged in my head. Or let's be honest, maybe in my heart, too.

Chapter 17

Ironically, just like the day Laura moved in with me, it was pouring down rain with thundering and lightning the day Helene packed up and left her husband of more than four decades to move in.

When she called my cell phone to tell me she was five minutes away, I told her to wait in the car, and that I'd pull my car out of the garage so she could pull hers in. That way, we'd be able to unpack the car without being outside.

The minute Mom got out of her car, though, no one unpacked anything. Instead, Helene started to cry. Right there in my garage, I held my mother in my arms while she sobbed for what seemed like a long time.

"Where's Izzie?" she finally asked.

"She's inside reading a book with Laura."

"I don't want her to see me crying," said Helene.

"Okay," I said, wiping my mom's tears with the sleeve of my shirt.

"I just can't forgive him," she said, "And I'm not so sure he's sorry for what he did." She was no longer crying, but the look of sorrow on her face was almost worse.

"I'm so sorry, Mom," I said, putting my hand on her arm, which seemed so little to me now, so fragile. The rock solid, strong mother I had known all my life now seemed weak and wounded all of a sudden.

"Go inside and relax," I said, "I'll bring the stuff in."

Laura told me later that the second Mom walked in, Isabelle asked, "Grandma, are you crying?"

"Oh no," Helene lied, "I have awful allergies."

"I think my dad had allergies, right Aunt Laura?" she asked.

"Yes, I remember that," my sister answered.

That night, the four of us had dinner together and my mother explained to Izzie that she was going to be staying with us for a little while.

"I know. I saw the suitcases."

"Oh."

"Why?" asked Izzie, "Did you have a fight with Grandpa?"

"They're just taking a little time apart from each other," I explained gently.

"Are you getting a divorce?" she asked.

"No!" I interjected.

My mother looked at her, "Maybe, sweetie."

Izzie looked really scared.

"But please don't worry about it," my mother continued, "Grandma's very strong. Whatever happens, I'll be okay. And I'll always love you. And so will Grandpa."

Izzie got tears in her eyes and then so did I. 'How much more could she take?' I wondered. First, her dad dies, then her aunt gets separated and moves in with us. Now, her grandparents were splitting up, with her grandmother becoming another houseguest. If I was still pregnant and had to tell her she was also going to have another sibling, I wasn't so sure she could have handled that piece of news. I found myself thinking that there really was truth to the statement, "Things happen for a reason."

After three games of *Operation*, seven hands of *Uno*, and four books, I put Izzie to bed.

"Is Grandma going to be okay?" she asked.

"Of course."

"Will I ever see Grandpa again?"

"Yes! He's my dad. Why wouldn't you see him?"

"At least he's not going to die."

"What?"

"Well, divorce is better than dying."

"Yes, I suppose it is, smart girl."

"I am smart, just like my dad, right?"

I leaned over and kissed her on each cheek. "Yes, you are very smart just like your dad."

When I came downstairs, two women were seated at the kitchen table eating salsa. That's when I decided to tell my mother about the pregnancy and the miscarriage. Laura actually held my hand while I spoke.

My mother listened the whole time, never interrupting with comments or questions. A look of shock was on her face throughout my entire story.

"So, are you completely disgusted?" I asked.

"Disgusted?" my mother responded, her eyes welling up with tears, "No, I'm not disgusted. I'm very sorry that happened to you."

"Thanks for being such a cool mom," I said. She really was. Here was a woman in her late sixties, who had slept with one man in her life. Now she had two single daughters. "Cougar" and "boy toy" weren't in her vocabulary until I became one and got one. My good-hearted mother, who was naïve until the day her husband chose to cheat on her was not passing judgment on me for anything. Not for having casual sex, not for becoming pregnant, and not for deciding to have a baby with a young womanizer.

I went on, "I hope you know that I realize how careless I was."

"That's good," she said.

"But," I said with a tearful smile, "I have to admit, I'll miss him. I enjoyed every minute of that relationship."

"How do you know it's over?" asked Laura.

"I just think it is."

"Well, you enjoyed him. Isn't that what life's all about?" said my mom, "And isn't it better than sitting around feeling guilty over a dead man you didn't kill?"

Now I cried on my mother's shoulder, literally. I felt like I was five years old again, and it felt safe and comfortable and wonderful. I needed my family beyond belief at this moment, and they were here for me. They had always been here for me and for that, I felt very lucky.

My dad called a few minutes later. Laura picked up the phone.

"Hi," I heard her say in a cold, unemotional voice. He must have asked her what she was doing because she then said, "Just sitting around with YOUR family, kind of wondering why YOU'RE not here." After a few moments of what I suspected was dad apologizing, Laura said, "Look, I don't really have anything to say to you right now. My husband just left me for another woman. You're pretty much just like him."

I glanced over at my mom, who had her head down. Then I heard Laura say, "Hold on." She handed me the phone.

"Hi, Dad."

"Do you feel the same as your sister?" said Dad.

"No, of course not. But, I am wondering what you're thinking."

"Can we get together and talk, Em? I haven't seen you in awhile."

"Sure."

"Sure, what?" said my mother.

"I can hear your mother. Is she sitting right there?" he asked.

"Yes."

"Okay, can we have coffee tomorrow?" he asked.

"Let me have a little more time. Is that okay?"

"Sure."

There was silence, and both Laura and my mother were just staring at me.

"I love you, Em," said Dad.

Right then, I caved. "I love you too, Stan."

Laura shook her head in disapproval and I couldn't even look at my mother, because I felt like I was being disloyal. But he was my dad!

I added, "I'm really mad at you right now, but I still love you."

"Thank you, Em." It was at this moment, I could have sworn my dad was crying.

"Talk to you later. Tell your mother and sister I love them."

"Okay, bye, Dad."

I hung up. "He said he loves you guys," I said softly. Both of them just sat there.

The next couple of weeks at my house included lots of wine drinking, salsa eating, talking, crying, laughing, and bonding. Three heartbroken women and one adorable, innocent child were living together, sharing each other's lives, and it all seemed to make sense, as if God had put us all together to learn from each other and help one another. And I have to say, I found it unexpectedly enjoyable, under the circumstances of course.

There were nights the three of us would sit up and talk for hours, my mother mostly listening, and seemingly reflecting on things, and my sister exploding with her newfound sexuality. Yes, Miss Prim and Proper was now sleeping with Dan, and finding out what it was like to actually have great sex.

"He is so hot!" she told us, "I never thought sex could be like this."

"It's pretty fun to sleep with a guy who's actually attractive, huh?" I joked.

Laura and my mother burst out laughing.

"I'm really happy for you," I said, "I mean that."

"Thanks," she said with a smile. Then she looked at our mother, "Do you think I'm a slut, Mom?"

My mother answered to both of us. "You girls don't think I know anything, do you?"

"What do you mean?" I asked.

"Just because I was a virgin when I married your father, it doesn't mean I don't appreciate good sex!"

"Please don't go here," said Laura.

At that moment Laura's phone rang. *"Fly me to the moon, let me play among the stars...let me see what spring is like on Jupiter and Mars...in other words, hold my hand..."*

"Thank God!" I shouted, "Interrupted at the perfect moment!"

"Is that Frank Sinatra?" asked my mother.

"Yes," exclaimed Laura as she went to answer it, "Dan and I both love Frank Sinatra.

When my sister answered, we could hear Alan yelling at her in the background. "What the fuck?" I heard him say. Strangely enough, Laura was not fazed by it. In fact, she was smiling.

"It was a joke, Alan," she said calmly. Then I heard more shouting on his end, and Laura continued to smile, almost holding back laughter at this point. "Don't be mad," she said, "I apologize." More yelling. "I have to go now," she said, "It's late. Good-bye Alan."

She ended the call and then burst out laughing.

"What was that all about?" we asked her.

"I was over at the house today and Alan was upstairs...and his cell phone was sitting on the kitchen counter..." She began laughing again. "...and I changed his ring tone!"

"To what?" I asked.

Laura started singing the Dean Martin classic, *"You're nobody till somebody loves you...you're nobody till somebody cares..."*

Giggling and singing, I joined in, *"You may be king, you may possess the world and its gold..."*

Suddenly Helene joined in, and now the three of us were blaring out, *"but gold won't bring you happiness when you're growing old. The world still is the same, you'll never change it. As sure as the stars shine above...you're nobody till somebody loves you. So find yourself somebody to love."*

The image in my mind of the three of us singing and laughing together will be etched in my brain forever. Two sisters whose philosophies in life were at opposite extremes, and their mother, who was somewhere in the middle, were now connected by the thread of heartbreak. And we were making the best out of the cards we'd been dealt. In retrospect, we were actually flourishing.

The loss of my baby was still raw, the sadness gnawing at my gut twenty-four seven. But during these days of living with two additional roommates, I also found great solace in spending time with my daughter. There were only a handful of days left until school started, so I took advantage of Isabelle's time off and did all kinds of fun kid things.

I found it easy to temporarily forget the heartbreak of not hearing from Preston while sitting close to my daughter, holding her tight, going twenty-five miles an hour down a mini-roller coaster at *Great America.* Examining giraffes at the *Lincoln Park Zoo,* holding her hand while she stuffed popcorn in her little mouth was a quick fix and a means to not think about my parents' and my sister's splits. And thoughts about what might have been, my second child, were somewhat easily put on the back burner while we walked through the *Harry Potter* exhibit at the *Museum of Science and Industry.*

Perhaps the best form of therapy for my delicate mental state were my daughter's kisses and hugs and giggles, and the funny little comments that came out of her mouth. "Mom?" she said to me one day while she happened to catch me coming out of the shower and toweling off, "Why are your boobs so ugly?" I burst out laughing.

One night, she came over to me, put her hands on my hair and kissed my cheek.

"What's that for?" I asked.

She looked at me with her big blue eyes and long eyelashes and answered, "You're a good soul, Emma."

With a child like mine, I was sure I could survive anything. I had to. She was my number one responsibility in life. Actually, she *was* my life. And she was the reason I was able to accept the loss of my baby and begin to move on. That being said, healing was certainly a process.

The Saturday before school started, Laura took her into the city for tea at *The American Girl Place*. As for Helene, she said she had some errands to run, and then she was going to the *Lexus* dealership to look at cars. Apparently, her lease was up in a couple weeks and she was deciding what car to get next. So here I was, home alone for the first time in a long, long time.

"Do something fun for yourself," Laura told me before they left, "Go get a massage, or workout, or go shopping!" Although very appealing options, none of those things were how I chose to spend my afternoon. No more than ten minutes after all of them were gone, I made a phone call. I called the person who had been on my mind since that lovely day at the beach. I called Luke.

Chapter 18

"Is this the hottest girl in Willow Ridge?" is how Luke answered his phone.

As I giggled, all I could think was, "if you think I'm hot, why aren't we dating?"

"Are you up for a run?" I asked him.

"Right now?"

"Yeah."

Luke hesitated for a moment and then said, "Sure, why not? Can I bring Lucky?"

"Of course."

"Although," he said with hesitation, "Is it going to rain?"

"Don't be a wimp."

"Fine."

Not more than twenty minutes later I was on the neighborhood running path with Luke and his dog, jogging at a pretty good pace and loving the feeling of the very light misty rain that had just begun to come down. I felt as if my entire body was getting a facial, cleansing away all the dirt from my recent and not so recent past. Add to that, I was with Luke, who in the handful of times I'd been with, never failed to make me feel great. I felt contented, calm and safe, yet full of enthusiasm, almost bubbly.

"So, tell me something good," Luke said.

What was good? Hmmm… Do I tell him my parents were on the outs and that my mom was living with me now? Do I share the fact that the same applied to my sister? Or, how about telling him that I've been avoiding my dad for weeks? Then there was the miscarriage. Do I tell him about that, and that the father is M.I.A? Would Luke enjoy hearing that? Tell me something good, he had said. What was good? I wondered. Then, it hit me.

"Isabelle," I answered, *"She's* good."

This began a long conversation about children, both Luke and I sharing stories, bragging and joking about our kids, and offering each other advice about similar kid problems and issues.

It was fun to compare stories. As much as I enjoyed the conversations I had had with Preston, we never really talked about my child, and it took being with another single parent to make me realize how much of a void that left in the relationship. Being in the same shoes gave Luke and me a commonality, a bond that Preston and I would never share. That didn't make Luke the right guy for me, or Preston the wrong guy for me by any means, it was just another connection I felt with Luke. He would understand me in a way Preston never could. And it made the pull to him even stronger.

A few minutes later, Luke's phone rang. He pulled it out of his pocket, looked at caller-ID, and then ignored the call and put it back.

"Nothing important?" I asked, sensing almost with certainty it was a girl. And again, I seethed with jealousy.

Luke chuckled nervously. "Patty."

"Oh."

"You were right. She *does* think we're more than friends."

"But you're really not?"

Luke looked at me. "No, we're not. I swear! Friends. That's it."

"Friends."

"Yes!"

"Like us?"

Luke abruptly stopped jogging. Lucky stopped too, and then so did I. Little raindrops began to take the place of the mist. He turned to me and said, "No, not like us. Emma, I really like you. Do you know that?"

I nodded slowly, but I really didn't understand.

"You and I have a connection and I haven't really been able to figure out exactly what it is." He gave me a smile that stopped my heart and finished, "But it's something."

I was standing there speechless, rain now coming down in buckets.

"Do you agree, or is this all me?" he asked.

More silence on my part.

"Say something!" he exclaimed.

Suddenly I burst into tears. To my surprise, hearing Luke tell me he had feelings for me was overwhelming. Maybe I was crying because I was relieved that my attraction to him wasn't one-sided, or maybe I was just happy. Whatever the reason, my feelings for Luke had just been validated, and that gave me a sense of pure relief. Add raging hormones, separated parents, a separated sister and a womanizer who'd just disappeared and it made sense that Luke's tender admission was the final ingredient needed in the recipe for a major meltdown. Standing in the now pouring rain with Luke and his dog in the middle of a semi-remote jogging path, I was now sobbing, probably harder than I had in over a year.

"What is it?" Luke asked.

Lucky was trying to comfort me by licking my leg.

I kept on hysterically crying, unable to speak. Standing here with a man I didn't know very well, who understood me and captivated me at the same time was almost too much to take. Being with Luke suddenly made sense, as if this was how things were supposed to happen, as if he was rescuing me. I suddenly realized that part of me had thought of Luke in this way since the first time I saw him standing over me and my bleeding knees.

"Let's get out of here," he said, putting his arm around me, "I'm taking you to my house. Is that okay?"

I nodded and we walked to Luke's. He had his arm around me the whole way there, but neither of us said a word the entire walk home.

When we got to his huge stone mansion I thought about the last time I'd been here. It was the day of my first date with Preston, and I didn't stay very long that day, since I had to rush home to get ready for the man who I didn't know at the time would impregnate me and then vanish into thin air when I lost his child.

Last time I'd been in Luke's castle the world looked bright. I had no clue that I would soon be facing loss once again, this time the death of an unborn child. I also didn't know my mother would be living with me. Now, being back at Luke's again, I realized how quickly life can spiral out of control.

"Put these on," he said, handing me a t-shirt and a pair of sweatpants with a drawstring. He also gave me a towel. We were both soaked, and while I changed in the bathroom I could hear Luke talking to Lucky and toweling her off.

A couple minutes later I came out, sat cross-legged on the living room couch and waited for the main man who I assumed was upstairs changing his own clothes. I had calmed down significantly and was now just feeling exhausted from my meltdown, plus a little bit stupid for losing it like that in front of someone I had seen half a dozen times max in my life. Luke had just seen me unravel, and I wondered what he would think about the authentic Emma.

A minute later he appeared in the doorway and gave me a sympathy smile. He looked really cute, his hair wet, his University of Wisconsin sweatshirt old and torn, and his red nylon basketball shorts showing off his muscular thighs. This guy was the definition of adorable.

"Feel better?" he asked gently.

I nodded and said, "Thanks, Luke. Sorry for the meltdown. I have a lot going on."

"Feel like telling me about it?" he said, sitting down next to me on the couch.

"I don't even know where to begin."

Chapter 19

"Just say it," said Luke, his eyes looking right into mine.

My heart was pounding, my vulnerability so intense I wasn't sure if I could handle it. But I wanted to. For the first time in so long, I wanted to really open up to someone. And in my heart, I felt this person was safe.

I never took my eyes off of Luke. My voice was soft, the words coming out slowly. "I had sex in a forest preserve and I got pregnant. And then I had a miscarriage." I held my breath and waited for a response.

The look on Luke's face was one of complete and utter shock. It was easy to see I had really flabbergasted him.

"Please don't judge me," I went on, "I'm not sure if I can handle that."

"Who am I to judge anyone?" Luke said with a half smile, "I judge myself every time I look in the mirror."

"Why?"

"Because look at my life. My wife dumped me... I'm a single dad... I'm sorry, aren't we talking about *you?*"

"What's wrong with being a single dad?"

"Well, the thing is, the more time that goes by, I realize maybe I wasn't such a good husband."

"Why do you think that?"

"I just think I could have acted better, maybe handled certain situations differently, been a little more thoughtful."

"I think anyone could look back and see mistakes they made in a marriage. Don't you?"

"I guess."

"But you can't change what you did or how you acted in the past. You just have to learn from it and try to be a better person moving forward."

Luke smiled gently, and I realized right then that I should heed my own words.

"So, the young guy you're dating. Was he the father?"

"Yes."

"And what's with the forest preserve?"

"It was spontaneous. I'd never done anything like that before."

"Not judging," he said, "just curious." I suddenly felt like I was talking to my best friend. He continued, "And then you found out you were pregnant."

"Yes."

"And then you lost it."

"Yes."

"Were you relieved?"

"I have mixed emotions," I said, "I thought I wanted to have the baby. You know, the miracle of life."

"I could see that," he said.

I took a deep breath. "Can I tell you something?"

"Sure."

"The night my husband died..." I stopped. The words wouldn't come out. It was like if I said them, that would make it real, which it was, but still, I couldn't speak them.

"Just say it," Luke said softly, "Whatever it is, it's okay."

Tears now dropping down my cheeks, I replied, "No, it's not okay. It will never be okay. The night my husband died, he and I had had a huge argument. I was shouting at him and I told him I hated his guts. And then...he left. He got into his car and he left. And then he crashed. And died."

Luke hugged me really tight. How strange it was to have someone I barely knew, a guy I wasn't even dating, comforting me with his strong arms after I just chose to confide in him, a random neighbor who'd come into my life because of a bizarre fall. It was almost poetic, fairytale like.

At this moment, with my arms firmly around him and the side of my face nuzzled under his neck, I thought about pulling a *When Harry Met Sally,* by planting a passionate kiss on him and officially turning our friendship into a love affair. I didn't, though, for two reasons. One, sex was the last thing on earth I wanted. In fact, I didn't care if I ever slept with another man for the rest of my life. And two, what if Luke rejected me? He hadn't asked me out, yet I knew he had feelings for me. But if he wasn't dating me, then chances were maybe he didn't want to sleep with me. So, I held back. I will never know to this day, whether he would have responded had I made a move.

"I'm so tired, Luke," I whispered, "So tired of feeling guilty."

"Can I ask you something?"

"Yeah."

"What was the fight about?"

I pulled away from him, took a deep breath and began telling Luke the story. "There was this girl...Jill Sadler...she worked in Sam's office. They worked for a financial consulting firm. Jill was really cute, a lot younger. I met her at the company Christmas party that year. So anyhow, I was suspicious that something was going on. Sam started becoming cocky, and making comments like, 'You better appreciate me. Other people do,' and 'If you ever left me, it wouldn't take me long to find someone else.' And I asked him, 'Where's this coming from?'"

As I was telling Luke the story, it was funny to watch his expression. He was wide-eyed, intently listening, waiting for the climax of the whole thing. Trust me, he wasn't disappointed.

"He told me that Jill had been asking him to get together, but that he wasn't cheating on me. A couple nights later, we were arguing about money or something, and Sam had had a few drinks during dinner. I said to him, 'If you think I spend too much, maybe you're with the wrong person. Maybe you should be with Jill.' And Sam responded, 'Maybe I am.'"

Luke actually gasped, to the point where it made me crack a little smile.

"Luckily, my daughter was in bed so she didn't hear the ranting and raving and screaming and shouting and name calling that went on. Years of pent up hostility on both our parts was being released, and while it was well needed, it was almost surreal because I realized right then how unhappy both of us were in our marriage."

"Wow," said Luke.

"So then I asked, 'Sam, are you having an affair?' He responded, 'We've kissed a few times.' And that's when I went nuts. I told him to get out."

I put my head down and said almost in a whisper, "And I told him I hated his guts."

I looked up at Luke and finished, "And then he left. He got in his car after about four beers mind you, and he left. And I never saw him again."

Luke nodded and said with sincere sadness in his voice, "I'm really sorry."

"Now do you understand?" I asked, "I told my husband to leave. I told him to get in the car and leave after he'd been drinking."

My voice began to rise, "I told him to drink and drive because I wanted him out of my sight." I shouted, "I killed my husband!"

"Oh my God, no, you didn't!" Luke responded, "This isn't your fault!"

"Yes it is! It is!"

"No! He killed himself, Emma. Or fate killed him. Not you!"

"If I didn't kick him out, he'd be alive today."

"You're not God. You had no control over what happened." Luke took my shoulders in his hands. "Emma, I don't know you that well, but I know one thing. You'll never have a good life until you forgive yourself for something you absolutely did not do."

"I don't know how," I said through tears.

"Let me ask you something," he said, "Let's say *you* were the one who was cheating and let's say Sam had asked *you* to leave that night. And let's say you got into your car and got into an accident and died."

"Okay..." I said with the kind of chuckle one makes when you think something's creepy.

"Let me finish," said Luke, "Let's say you're up in heaven looking down at Sam...God forbid, of course..."

"Yes, God forbid."

"Would you blame Sam? Would you think it was his fault that you died?"

"No, not at all. I'd blame myself for cheating and then I'd blame bad luck."

"So why the hell are you blaming yourself? Do you really think Sam is up there in heaven blaming you for his death?"

I looked up at the ceiling and suddenly I had a smile on my face. I looked back down at Luke. "No, I don't think Sam blames me."

"Then stop blaming yourself. Look, time's going by and years are being wasted for no good reason. You're a good person. I'm sure of that. And you deserve to be happy. Sounds like your husband had some major issues. I'm not glad he died, but he did it to himself. You had nothing to do with his death. You did what any other woman in the world would have done. Do you understand that? Tell me you do."

I nodded slowly, and suddenly it was like the light bulb just went on. Had Luke, my new friend, gotten through to me by saying pretty much the same thing my mother and sister had been telling me for a year? I suspected so, and I didn't understand why hearing this from Luke was different than hearing it from my family, but it didn't matter. Something had stuck. The message was beginning to resonate.

I must have looked really tired because Luke then told me to lie down on the couch. I did as I was told, and he grabbed a blanket off a nearby chair and covered me with it. Then he picked up a small couch pillow and put it under my head. "Take a nap," he said, "Just rest. Relax and rest."

"Thank you," I whispered, closing my eyes.

Luke sat on the edge of the couch, put his hand on my hair and gently rubbed my head. "Guilt is exhausting," he said softly, "No more. Promise me."

"Okay," I answered, barely audible at this point because I was already dozing off. And thank God for that because if I had any energy at all, I would have blurted out, "I love you, Luke Sullivan!" Instead I fell asleep in about five seconds.

The next thing I knew, I was waking up. It seemed like a lot of time had gone by. The first thing I did was sit up, feeling somewhat panicky. I ran over to where my wet clothes were lying in a pile and retrieved my Blackberry to make sure no one called me, and to see what time it was. 5:00! Had I really been asleep for three hours? Luke's flat screen was on, the sound barely audible but the picture as clear as crystal. It was ironic. The movie, Limitless was on, my hottie, Bradley Cooper looking as cute as ever.

Suddenly I heard a loud snore. I looked over at the big recliner chair and there was Luke, fast asleep. He was holding the remote and his head was tilted back. He was out, big time. I smiled as I thought about how my dramatic life had exhausted this poor guy, who was just your basic ordinary single dad trying to move on with his life.

"You're the best," I whispered to him, now on my knees in front of his chair, watching him snooze and thinking about how much he'd been here for me today. I was getting to know him. He was becoming my friend. Plus, I was attracted to him. All of him. Not the out-of-control, crazy, physical attraction I had for my now ex boy toy. This was very different. I had the desire to kiss Luke and touch him and hold him, but it was more stable, more mature, more solid, deeper.

"Wake up Luke," I whispered, softly touching and moving his arm.

He jerked his head up quickly. "Did I fall asleep? What time is it?"

"5:00," I whispered.

"Wow," he said, still trying to wake up.

I stood up and then he did. "How are you?" he asked.

"Good."

"Feel better?"

I nodded, "I do."

"Hungry?"

I thought about it for a second and realized I couldn't remember the last time I ate. "Actually, yes."

"Let's order some food."

"Sure."

I called Laura to make sure she and Izzie were home, and to see how their day was.

"Where are you?" my sister asked.

"I'm at a friend's house," I answered, "I'll be home in a couple hours. Is that okay?"

"What friend's house?"

"Just a friend."

"Preston?"

"No."

"Emma, tell me!"

"I'm at Luke's." I looked at my friend, who was perusing a few take-out menus. He looked up at me and smiled. I smiled back.

"Luke's?" my sister practically shouted.

With a giggle, I said, "Thanks, Laura. I'll see you soon. Tell Izzie I love her."

Luke opened up a bottle of wine and we had a glass while waiting for our pizza to arrive. We talked and laughed and gossiped about people in our neighborhood, both wanting light, fun conversation versus the serious topic we'd covered earlier in the day. Spending time with Luke was relaxing, and the ease of hanging out with each other came especially natural. It was like no other relationship I'd ever experienced, sadly enough, not even my marriage.

"So, I know you're Jewish," Luke said, "But what were you telling me the other day? You're not really Jewish? You're..."

"*Sephardic.*"

"What's that?"

"It means that my family descends from the Middle East, not Europe, like most other Jewish people."

"So, do you speak Arabic?"

"I know a few words."

"I want to hear! Talk to me in Arabic."

"Why?"

"Because it's hot."

I said a few words in Arabic and Luke looked like he was thoroughly entertained.

"How do you say butt?" he asked.

"Butt?"

"Yeah. Butt. Behind, rear end, derriere, Ass."

I laughed. "Teso."

"Teso?" he chuckled.

"Yeah."

"How do you say pretty?"

"Fatin."

"Emma," he joked, "You have a really nice teso."

I laughed and Luke said, "And when you smile, you're fatin."

"You're flirting with me in Arabic."

"Yeah," he grinned, "I know."

"You know what?"

"What?"

"I'm not sure anyone has ever made me smile the way you can."

Luke gave me a wider grin that literally melted me.

"I'm so glad I know you," I said.

"Me too," he smiled.

And then he leaned over and kissed me on the lips, and I wish I could define what kind of kiss it was. First of all, there was no tongue, therefore it was hardly a romantic kiss. Yet it was soft and slow, and much longer than a kiss of pure platonic friendship. It was something in between, just like our relationship was.

The two of us were smack in the middle of the spectrum of nonphysical, nonsexual on the left, and passionate romance and true love on the right. Who knew what we were? The only thing I was sure of was a connection with so much power and so much energy that it didn't even matter what our official status was. Friends, lovers, soul mates...did it really make a difference at this particular moment? I knew for certain that at some point the dust would settle, and Luke and I would eventually figure out what we were.

For today, though, just spending time with him was enough. Being here was filling some void I'd had perhaps for a long, long time, maybe even forever. And that to me was worlds more important than having a clear cut definition of our relationship. I didn't need to know what we were. I just needed him.

Chapter 20

"You're glowing," Laura said to me with a big grin when I walked in the door.

"What's glowing mean?" Izzie asked.

"It means your mommy's happy," Laura answered.

I smiled at them and said, "Yeah, I'm happy."

"Hey, mommy, Grandpa called again," said Izzie.

"He did?"

"Yeah, I talked to him for awhile. He said he misses us."

I looked at Laura. "Did you talk to him?"

"Briefly," she said with sarcasm.

"He said you should call him," said Izzie.

"I will, I will," I said, not happy with myself for continually putting my dad off these days. "Hey, where's Mom?" I asked.

"She's not home yet," said Izzie.

I looked at Laura. "Really?"

"Yeah. I talked to her about an hour ago and she said she was going to dinner with a friend."

"Who?" I asked.

"I don't know."

"Mommy, where were you?" asked Izzie, her big blue eyes looking up at me.

"I spent the day with a good friend of mine," I answered, picking her up and placing her on my lap, "Is that okay? How was the American Girl Place?"

"Great! Who was the friend?"

"Uh..."

"Our friend, Luke," Laura responded for me, "He's an old friend of the family. We've known him for years. Nice guy..."

"Is he married?" asked Izzie.

"No, but he has two kids," I answered, "Twin boys. They're nine."

"Is he divorced?" she asked.

"How on earth is a six year old this smart?" I asked.

Isabelle answered, "I know lots of divorced people. My friend Gabriella's mommy and daddy... Paul's mommy and daddy... Aunt Laura... Grandma and Grandpa..."

"Maybe not Grandma and Grandpa, sweetie," I told her, realizing how Izzie's environment had sadly forced the little girl to grow up quicker than she would have otherwise.

A little while later, I put Izzie to bed, and then I went downstairs to find Laura snacking on some chips and salsa.

"What a surprise," I joked.

"So, tell me..." she said.

I told Laura all about my jog with Luke, my breakdown, our dinner and our kiss.

"He sounds nice," Laura said, "Although, I'm a little suspicious."

"I know. Something's going on with him. I think he might have a girl-friend. Maybe she's married or something."

"That's terrible!"

"Please don't judge. I don't know that for sure, I'm just guessing. The thing is, there's something about Luke that I trust. I don't think he's a snake or a liar. I think he's genuine. Just a little confused. You know, he's got baggage."

"Everyone who's divorced has baggage," said Laura, "I just came to that realization."

"Dan?"

"Of course," she said with a smile, "but he's hot, and fun and..."

I then saw my older sister's face turn a dark shade of red.

"Are you blushing?!"

She put her hands over her cheeks. "No!"

"Laura, you're 44 years old and you're blushing at the thought of great sex! Jesus!" At this very moment, I realized how new casual sex and lust was to my very sheltered, sexually repressed sister.

"The things I do with Dan...I've never done those things before. It's really embarrassing to talk about, and I'm ashamed to say it, but I like it. I like it a lot."

I gave Laura a sad smile, sad because it had taken her this long to let herself be human and enjoy good sex. But I was happy that at least she was experiencing it now. "There's nothing wrong with what you're doing, Laura. It's natural and it's fun and you're not hurting anybody. You're finally living."

Laura gave me a big grin and said, "You know, I kept saying to myself, 'Why did God do this to me? Why did God make Alan leave me?' And now, I feel like maybe it was because of this. I'm not saying I'm going to live happily ever after with Dan, I'm just saying that I feel lucky that I get to have this much fun. I realize now how bad and how wrong my marriage was. For two people to live together for 20 years and have sex once a year at most just isn't right. There was no spark. Nothing. Ever. And now, now I like being sexy. I like my body. I like that a really good-looking man wants to touch me." Laura had tears in her eyes when she finished, "I feel so pretty."

"I'm so happy right now!" I practically shouted, "You ARE pretty! And now you realize that!"

We continued to talk and talk and talk and it was wonderful to see "the new Laura," self-confident in her newfound sexuality, and so happy.

When it got to be around 9:00, and my mother still was not home, I called her cell. Voice mail. 9:30, voice mail again. 10:00, voice mail again.

At 10:05, Laura left her a message. "Mom, it's us. If you don't call me back in the next ten minutes, I'm calling the police."

I shouted in the background, "And then we're calling dad! We really don't have a choice! We're worried about you!"

Then we waited. Both my sister and I were on pins and needles. Where on earth was our sixty-seven year old mom? At 10:08 we got our answer. Our mother sent her very first text (of her life). "I'm fine. With friend. Don't worry and don't call anyone! And don't wait up!" At the end of her text was a smiley face.

"The woman's never sent a text, and she's already inserting smiley faces?" Laura practically shouted, "What if someone forced her to text that?"

"I don't think so," I laughed.

"Is Mom on a date?" Laura asked.

"Sure sounds like it."

We decided to go to bed, hoping Helene knew what she was doing, that she was safe, and that she would be back soon.

All night I tossed and turned, realizing that if I could just fall asleep, my mother would be home when I woke up, everything would be fine, and there would be a perfectly logical explanation for her going on the lamb. I just couldn't sleep, though. My mother wasn't here, I had no idea where the woman was, and I was troubled.

At 6:15 the next morning, I got up and looked in the guest room. Laura was asleep. Alone. And that's when troubled turn to panic. I woke Laura up, and the two of us were complete wrecks for the next few hours. We called my mother but it went right to voice mail. We texted, but no return texts.

Laura called her office and told them she couldn't come in until later, and then paced in front of the TV while watching the *Today* show. As for myself, I did the one thing I knew could somewhat calm me down. I made salsa. With Izzie sitting on the kitchen counter helping, I created my latest invention, artichoke salsa. At exactly 9:15, my mother waltzed into the house.

"Where have you been?" Laura scolded.

When I took one look at my mother, the mother I'd known for forty-two years, I knew. The woman looked contented and relaxed and giddy, all at the same time. She reminded me of a young girl with her sparkling eyes, her wide grin and her rosy cheeks.

"Go upstairs and get dressed," I said to Isabelle, "I'll be up there in a minute."

The second she was out of sight, I looked at Laura. "Mom had sex."

My mom started giggling, while Laura responded, "That's really funny, Emma." Then she looked at my mother. "Mom, we were so worried! Where were you?"

"Your sister's right," Mom said.

"Wow...how do you feel?" I exclaimed.

Mom smiled, "Good."

"Why was your phone off? And why didn't you answer our texts? We were so worried!" said Laura.

"So, who's the guy?" I asked.

Laura's mouth was hanging wide open, as if she was appalled.

"What?" I asked.

"Are you condoning this?"

"What are you talking about?" I asked.

Laura began chewing me out, as if my mother wasn't even there. "You think it's okay that our mother spent the night out with a man?"

"Not only do I think it's okay, I think it's great if she's happy. Are you?"

"Yes," she smiled.

"So, who is it?" I asked, "Do we know him?"

"No. He works at the Lexus dealership," she answered.

"You picked up the guy trying to sell you a new car?" I asked.

"Yup."

"What's his name?" I asked.

"Harry Rakowski."

"Not Jewish," I joked.

"No, not Jewish," Mom said with a smile.

"How old is he?" I asked.

"He just turned sixty."

"You cougar!" I shouted.

My mom laughed.

"That's really nice," Laura interjected, "Calling our mother a cougar. Great..."

"Lighten up, Laura," I said.

"I'd think you'd be happy for me," Mom said to her, "My husband cheated on me. We're separated. What am I supposed to do? Sit around by myself?"

Laura looked at her sadly and said, "No, Mom, I don't expect you to sit around. But spending the night out...don't you think that's kind of..."

"Kind of what?" asked my mother, "What about Dan? Haven't you been spending the night out with him? Have I said one thing?"

"It's different," Laura answered.

"How so?" I asked.

"It just is!"

"Look, Laura, you better get used to it," I said, "Our mother's single. So is Dad. Both of them are allowed to do anything they choose. Don't you want them to be happy?"

"Oh, look who turned into Miss Optimistic all of a sudden. You've been in a coma for like a year. All you do is make God damn salsa, and now you think you're an expert on happiness?"

"That's unfair!" said my mother.

"And rude," I added.

"Look, I'm not going to sit here and listen to the details of my mother spending the night out with some random guy," Laura said, "It's disgusting!"

"The way you're acting...your attitude...that's what's disgusting!" I shouted.

"Are you guys fighting?" we heard. I looked over at the doorway and there stood Izzie.

"No honey, we're not," I lied.

At the same time, my mother said, "Of course not."

"Then why are you shouting?"

"We're not," I said, "Want to go to the zoo today?"

"Yes!"

"Okay, then go make your bed, brush your teeth and put some socks on."

Izzie started cheering and ran back upstairs.

"I guess we'll never see eye to eye on these kinds of things," Laura said sadly.

"Why are you only thinking of yourself?" I asked, "Can't you understand how she's feeling? She just had sex with the second person in her life. Can't you focus on *her* instead of how *you're* feeling about it?"

Laura ignored me and turned to my mother. "Look, I love you, but I can't handle this right now." She kissed Mom's cheek. "I have to go to work."

After Laura left the room, my mother took my hand. "Thank you for understanding," she said.

Chapter 21

During my freshman year in college, in Psychology 101, I remember learning about how a person deals with grief, and the seven stages of healing, the third stage being anger. My costly education was now coming back to me, as I realized I was approaching stage three.

The anger I felt for my judgmental sister opened the floodgates to many things I was angry about, including what my dad did to my mom. He cheated. My dad was a cheater. And I currently found myself furious at him. Yes, I was happy that my mother seemed happy, but maybe in a sense I was like my sister, feeling like the only man my mother should be with was my father.

Then there was the loss of my unborn child. It was beginning to infuriate me all of a sudden. Where was the justice? Hadn't I been through enough having a husband die? Why was God making me suffer more? It seemed so unfair. I found myself enraged.

Over the next few days, all I wanted to do was hit someone. Jogging was a good outlet. Everyday I'd go for a run in hopes that physical activity would help me blow off some steam. I ran and ran and ran and ran, (without Luke, which I'll get to in a minute) and it would help, but only for about an hour. After that, the fury would return within me.

Why was I so angry? There was more. I was furious with Preston, who I hadn't heard from in weeks. What a complete jerk! I thought to myself. After all the intimate moments we shared, all those times in bed, all the kind sentiments. How he could just stop calling was mind boggling. Didn't he care enough to follow up with me? Didn't he want to see how I was feeling? The playboy was now showing me who he truly was, and it was brutally painful.

Did I think I was the exception? Did I think Preston, the man who told me he didn't want to fall in love, loved me? Sure, maybe for a fleeting moment he thought he could change. But ultimately, he knew who he was. He knew he was a player. And I knew that too. I had always known it. I just didn't want to see it, because I had some sick fantasy that he would become someone else for me. And now I realized how naïve I was. Reality was infuriating.

And then there was Laura. We hadn't spoken for a few days, living like strangers, just as we had when we had our fight about my pregnancy. Only this time, Laura wasn't trying to make up with me. She was still angry, too. But I'd have put money on the fact that I harbored more resentment than she did, simply because bitterness seemed to define me these days.

And last, but definitely not least, there was someone with whom I was so completely irate, I couldn't even think about him without gritting my teeth. Luke. The man who was supposed to be my friend, the guy in whose arms I cried, the guy I trusted and confided in, on whose couch I'd slept, and whose pizza I ate. He had disappeared off the radar screen. I hadn't heard from him in almost a week. No phone call, no text, not one ounce of concern or compassion or follow-up.

He was actually worse than Preston, because although we had never been together physically, I felt more exposed to Luke than I ever had with my young boy toy. I trusted Luke. I opened my heart and soul and let him come in. I spoke Arabic to him for God's sake! And he was there for me. And now he wasn't. And I burned with anger when I thought about him.

Late one night, I headed up to bed. I was alone in the house with Izzie, my mother and sister presumably with their new boyfriends. When I checked on her, she woke up.

"Mommy," she whispered, "Will you sleep in my bed with me?"

"No honey. I can't."

"Why not?" she asked.

"Everyone sleeps in their own beds because we all get better sleep that way."

146

"Please, mommy?"

I sat on the edge of her bed and stroked her hair. "What is it Isabelle? Are you afraid of something?"

"I'm afraid you're going to die."

"What?!"

"Like Daddy."

"Oh my! Isabelle, I promise you, I'm not going to die. I not going anywhere."

"Promise?"

"I promise," I said with purpose.

"I miss my Daddy."

"I know you do."

"Hey momma?" she asked.

"Yeah?"

"Why does everyone have to sleep alone?"

My daughter's question stopped me in my tracks. I realized right then that she had just made an incredible argument. Why *did* everyone have to sleep by themselves? Who made up that rule? Did only people with marriage licenses get to snuggle? Was this the penalty for being single? I wanted to climb into bed next to my little girl and sleep there every night for the rest of our lives, but I didn't. Instead I leaned over, gave her a huge hug and whispered, "Cause that's the way it works. Tell you what. Want to sleep in my bed just for tonight?"

"Sure!"

Izzie and I got into my bed and she was back asleep literally in two minutes. I watched my beautiful daughter snore softly and wondered how I could be so angry at everyone when I had this breathtakingly gorgeous gift. Izzie was mine. How lucky was I? The sick part was, because I was so inexplicably angry about so many things, the conversation I'd just had with Izzie made me angry at Sam. How could I be angry with a dead man?! I fell asleep with tears in my eyes, wishing my all my hate and anger would be gone when I awoke.

Sometime later, I heard a knock at the bedroom door. I sat up in bed. "Come in," I said, still half asleep.

The door opened. Standing there with the saddest look and mascara running down her cheeks was my sister.

"Oh my God, what is it?" I asked

Laura began to cry and I jumped out of bed and went to her. "What? Please tell me!"

"Dan dumped me," she said, before practically falling into my arms and breaking down.

I must have stood there holding my older sister and letting her sob for ten minutes before either one of us spoke another word. I looked over at Izzie, still fast asleep.

Slightly composing herself, Laura suggested we go into the guest room. We sat on the bed and she explained that she had been out to dinner at *Casa De Michael* with a woman she worked with, and Dan was there with a very young girl.

"He introduced me to her, and I actually asked her if she was his niece!"

"Oh my God!" I responded.

"That's when he said, 'We need to talk.' And then he told Amber...that's her name, Amber...that he would be right back. He led me to the bar area and explained that even with the huge age difference, he's never felt this way before. He's madly in love with Amber and he's decided to only date her. I didn't even know he was dating anyone else!"

"Fucker!" came out of my mouth so naturally it was scary.

This made Laura laugh, but then she went right back into bawling, and continued crying in my arms for a little while longer. "You know, maybe I *am* just a self-righteous bitch. Maybe God's punishing me. Maybe I deserve all this because I'm so quick to pass judgment on other people."

"No Laura," I said, "God isn't punishing you. You're a good person. You are who you are, and you strive for perfection. And maybe that's not always the best thing, but I can't think of anyone I respect and admire more than you. Professionally and personally."

"Thank you," she said through tears.

"You're learning. So am I. So is Mom. None of us asked for this single life. But we got it. And we have to figure out how to live with it and be happy. For now, I think we're doing the best we can. It's brutal, but we're strong women. All of us." I realized right then, that if I actually listened to the way I had just spoken to Laura, I'd probably be a lot better off in life. I had impressed myself with my words. But I was a hypocrite because I wasn't living by them. I was too busy being pissed off.

"I love you, Emmie," she said. Then she lay down on the bed, still fully clothed. "I'm so tired."

"Then sleep," I said softly.

I played with my sister's hair until she fell asleep. Then I took off her shoes and kissed her cheek. And then I did the strangest thing. I went back to my room, quickly put on a little bit of make-up, grabbed a pair of *True Religions*, slipped a cute top over my head, and put on some heels. I scribbled a quick note and left it on the guest room nightstand. It read, "I'll be back in half an hour." The odds that anyone was going to wake up in the next thirty minutes were slim to none, but I didn't want them to worry, if in fact they did, and I wasn't there. With two sprays of perfume I was out the door, and headed to none other than *Casa de Michael* to let Dan know how Laura's sister felt about him.

During the three minute drive over there, all I could think about was how much I was looking forward to going off on this asshole who caused my sister pain. Under normal circumstances, I would never, ever do anything like this. But I wasn't normal these days. I was an angry, bitter person who thrived on this kind of thing. I now liked confrontation. I was at war. Looking back, I was fighting myself. But at the time, all I wanted to do was get into battle with anyone who would play, all because I was so totally unhappy. And tonight, Dan was the enemy.

When I walked into the Mexican bar and restaurant, I saw him right away, the guy who I thought was so charming at the divorce party, but who now just looked like a slimy jerk. He was giddy and his hands were all over his new young girlfriend. He didn't seem the least bit fazed by the episode that had occurred half an hour earlier. It now made sense that Tony's date had to leave the party the second she laid eyes on her ex-husband. God only knew what he had done to *her*.

It was time to rumble. I rolled my shoulders back, took a deep breath and approached the opponent.

"Hi," I said.

Dan looked right at me, his wide grin fading a bit. "Do I know you?" he asked. I guess I didn't make an impression on him at the party.

"I'm Emma…Laura's sister."

"Oh," he said curtly.

Now came the silence. It was actually a staring contest. I stood there and waited for him to say something else. After a few moments he caved. "So what do you want?"

"What do I want?" I asked, my voice rising steadily, "What do I want?"

Dan stood up. Amber just sat there with a worried look on her face. "Look, I feel really bad about that whole thing."

"How dare you!" I shouted. I could feel my face turning red and my body shaking. "My sister is a human being! She has feelings! And she's going through a really hard time right now. And she liked you! And depended on you! And this is how you treat her?"

"Hey, I'm sorry!" he pleaded.

"No you're not. After tonight you'll never even think about her again. You'll move on and focus on your current victim." I looked at Amber and finished, "Until you've had enough of her too. Then you'll do the same thing to her!"

"Shut up, bitch!" Amber said to me.

I had to give the girl credit. I liked the offensive. I had respect for it, probably because I looked up to anyone who got angry. Plus, it wasn't really her fault. So I ignored her, looked back at the perpetrator and said in a low, calm voice, "You sicken me. Don't ever bother my sister again. You're a disgusting pig. And I can only hope she didn't catch anything from you." Then I turned around and headed for the door.

I heard Dan shout, "That's really nice!"

Then Amber shouted, "Screw you!"

Their comments actually made me laugh, and I felt pretty good about what I'd just accomplished. I was so glad I'd come here and defended my sister. She deserved it. But I couldn't lie to myself. Part of me had done this for *me*. I couldn't deny that I had gotten great satisfaction from going off on Dan.

Then, just as I was walking out of the bar, my next enemy, a Mr. Luke Sullivan, happened to be walking in. The sight of him simultaneously disgusted and excited me. Half of me hated him. Half of me adored him so much it was frightening. I was about as indecisive as Izzie gets at Baskin Robbins, trying to choose between mint chocolate chip and bubble gum ice-cream.

"Hi, Emma!" Luke exclaimed. Then he put his arms around me and gave me a bear hug. Another guy walked in right behind him. Luke pulled away and introduced me. "This is my buddy, Rick Solomon. Rick and I work together. Rick, this is Emma Bloom." I shook hands with Rick and tried to smile while focusing on the fact that Luke had introduced me as "Emma Bloom," not "my friend Emma Bloom" or "my good friend Emma Bloom," or "Emma Bloom, the girl who recently came to my house and lost it, and now I have no clue what she is to me." Luke had to introduce me as only "Emma Bloom" because he really didn't know what I was to him. And that's when I made the decision to call him on it.

"Luke, can I talk to you?"

"Sure," he said. Then he looked at his friend and said, "I'll meet you at the bar."

Rick nodded. "Nice meeting you, Emma," he smiled.

"You too," I responded with a sugary smile, as I watched him walk away. Rick was kind of cute. Maybe for Laura, I thought. I did a quick left hand check and saw the gold band, however, and quickly dismissed the idea.

"You look hot!" Luke flirted, "If I was Bradley Cooper, I'd be all over you tonight!"

I stood there, unable to speak.

"So, what's up cutie?"

Cutie? How could he be so nonchalant? A week earlier, I'd been at his house, pouring my guts out, divulging private information, and basically letting him into my soul. Since that night, I'd heard nothing from the man. Nothing! And now, upon randomly running into him at a bar, he was acting like we were old friends. It was infuriating!

I took a deep breath and asked him the question to which I needed an answer, the question that was literally driving me insane. "Luke, what are we?" I asked.

He seemed confused. "What?"

"What are we?" I repeated, my body beginning to shiver and my teeth now clenched.

"What do you mean?" he said with a nervous chuckle.

My voice began to rise. "I mean, what are we? Are we friends? Are we more?" Now I was almost shouting. "I need to know." I paused for dramatic effect and then said very slowly and loud, "What…are…we?"

Luke stood there in frozen, as if he was digesting the question I'd just asked him four times. "What is it, Emma? What's the matter?"

I looked right into his eyes and said, "Luke, I need an answer from you. What are we? What am I to you?"

"You're my friend," he said with a smile, "My good friend."

I gasped, my mouth wide open, as if I just heard something extremely offensive. As for Luke, he had this look on his face like he felt he just said something wrong.

"*Friend?*" I asked sarcastically, "I'm your *friend?*"

"Well, maybe that's not entirely true."

"You know what, Luke? This is what I think of you. Either you have a girlfriend, or you just don't like me, or…you're gay. I haven't figured it out yet."

Luke chuckled, "Well, I'm not gay, so you can rule that one out."

"That's hilarious," I snapped.

"And I don't have a girlfriend, and I *do* like you."

"Then why are you so hot and cold? Why are you there and then not there?"

"It's complicated."

"How so?"

"It just is."

"That's it?" I shouted, "That's all you're going to say?"

"For now," he said softly.

"You know what?" I shouted, "I don't want to be friends with you. You're a shitty friend! Don't call me anymore. And don't text me either. You're never there for me when I really need you, so get out of my life!" I opened the door to leave, but turned around first to say, "And by the way, that kiss the other night…it wasn't that great!"

Luke was just standing there with a confused look on his face, and I could feel the stares from Rick and Dan and a couple other people in the bar as I angrily walked out. I didn't care, though. I was done with Luke Sullivan. In fact, I was done with men period. I hated them all. Luke, Preston, Dan, Sam, and even my own father. Men were the enemy. That was the bottom line. I decided right then, at that moment, I would never let another man hurt me ever again.

I had no idea that at this moment, a beautiful woman who was sitting at the bar listening to me rant and rave, had gotten up and followed me out.

Chapter 22

I hit the unlock button on my car remote, and was about to open the car door when I heard a voice. "Excuse me..."

I turned around. Standing before me was an absolutely gorgeous woman who looked about my age. She appeared very pure, with goodness radiating off her light, milky skin. I wondered for a second if she was real, or if I was hallucinating.

"Yes?" I responded.

"I just overheard that fight you had with your boyfriend," she said with her big, beautiful, very red lips.

Why I was focused on a woman's lips, I couldn't say. But I was. I was mesmerized by all of her, in fact. I was strangely attracted. Did I have a girl crush?

Her body was fit, but curvy and feminine too. And her long, black, wavy hair complimented her light skin and big blue eyes. She took her tiny, sparkling headband off and slowly shook her head, her hair swaying back and forth.

"That guy isn't my boyfriend," I answered, "trust me."

She gave me a sympathy smile and said softly, "Well whoever he is, he upset you. And I was wondering if you wanted to go across the street and have a drink." She motioned to *Stella's*, a tiny wine bar that stood a few feet away.

I was completely confused, wondering why a woman was asking me out for a drink. The look on my face must have been obvious because she added, "It's just a drink. Come. It'll be fun."

What was happening was almost surreal. It was as if this woman had just appeared here to help me. I didn't understand it, but for some odd reason, it didn't matter. Accepting her invitation seemed natural, like it was what I was supposed to do. "Okay, sure," I said.

She extended her hand and smiled, "I'm Alice." Her light blue eyes smiled too, and I found them so pretty, I was embarrassed and had to look away.

"I'm Emma," I managed, shaking her hand.

No more than five minutes later, Alice and I were sitting at *Stella's* sipping Pinot Noir out of big, wide wine glasses. "So tell me," said Alice, "What did that guy do to you?"

"He didn't do anything," I answered, "that's the problem."

"I don't understand."

"Well, my life basically stinks."

Alice didn't pity me, nor did she judge me. She just asked matter-of-factly, "Why?"

"I just had a miscarriage, and the father has basically forgotten my number, my sister's going through a divorce and just got screwed by one of those assholes in *Casa de Michael,* my parents just split up, my mother is living with me, and I'm not really speaking to my dad."

"That's a lot," replied Alice.

"One more thing. I can't figure out how to become Bradley Cooper's girlfriend."

"That actually sounds like the biggest problem of all of them," she joked.

I smiled sadly. "Told you my life stinks."

"Look, I don't know you at all, so please take this for what it's worth, an outsider's perspective, completely unbiased."

"Sure."

"First of all, I'm so sorry about your baby. I know what that feels like. I had a miscarriage also."

"Oh, I'm sorry."

"Thank you," she said with a sad smile, "It was a long time ago." Then she continued, "Here's what I think. There are a lot of things that are out of your control-- your parents, your sister, your baby… But do you realize how much you can fix?"

I was listening so intently that nothing in the world, including a fire, earthquake or major tornado could have taken my attention away from beautiful Alice.

"Do you?" she asked.

"How?" I asked, "How do I fix it?"

"With a new perspective, a new attitude about things," she began. And as I sat there listening, I was also gazing at her. She truly was a lovely person. I could never in my life remember being infatuated with a female like I was with Alice. She had a way of explaining things without being judgmental. Her message was harsh, but the delivery gentle. She was smart, but not a know-it-all. And she was empathetic, but not pitying.

"May I ask you a question?" she said.

"Sure."

"What do you do professionally?"

"Well, I have a daughter. She's six. I stay at home with her. Alice, I'm a widow. My husband had a pretty good insurance policy." I put my head down.

"You seem ashamed of that," said Alice, "Don't be. Being a mother is very important."

"Thanks," I smiled.

Alice was smiling at me, and so were her pretty blue eyes. "Emma, when you're not with your daughter, what do you like to do? I mean, for yourself? What are your interests?"

"Nothing."

"Come on," she urged, "There's got to be something. What did you do before you got married?"

"I was a pharmaceutical rep, but I never really loved that job."

"What *do* you like to do?"

"I can't tell you. It's silly."

"Just say it."

"Salsa," I said, "I like making salsa. *Lots* of salsa. I can't stop." I explained to Alice how I had at least twenty-five salsa recipes, and that I made so much of it so often, that I had now begun putting it in large jars and giving them to my neighbors.

"That's so cool," she exclaimed, "Have you ever thought about going into business?"

"Actually, my sister tells me I should all the time."

"Well, it sounds like you have the time, and you don't need money right now. Plus, there's not much upfront money involved. You really should think about it."

"What do *you* do, Alice?" I asked.

She explained that she worked for a huge publishing company and was an advertising sales executive for three of their largest magazines. I wasn't surprised that she was in such a lucrative career and in a prestigious position. Alice seemed like she made a good living, and it was so obvious she was a hard worker, determined and driven. She was everything I wanted to be in this regard.

"Think about the salsa business," she said to me, "I have a good feeling about it."

"Okay, thanks," I smiled, so appreciative of the free professional advice and motivational speech.

"So, tell me about the baby. Was that guy in the bar the father?"

I let out a laugh. "No!" Then I proceeded to tell Alice all about Preston, and I mean *all* about Preston. For some reason, it was easy to spill out the stories I'd kept to myself for so long. There was only so much I could share with Laura, only so far I could go, given my sister's conservative personality. But with Alice, I felt safe telling her in much more detail, the things that went on between Preston and me.

Interestingly enough, I found that as I poured out the steamy details of our relationship, I was gleaming, almost as if I was reliving it.

"Listen to the way you talk about this man," said Alice, "It sounds as if he was wonderful for you."

"Yeah, but it's over."

"So what? At least you had it. Most women can only dream of experiencing the kind of passion you've experienced. You had sex that took your breath away, a connection that found its way into your core. What a wonderful gift!"

This was the moment everything changed. "Oh my God!" I exclaimed, "You're right!"

Alice smiled, "Just enjoy the past and enjoy now. Don't worry so much about the future."

Alice was right. Even though my relationship with Preston ended the way it did, the relationship itself was special and important and lovely. How could I be angry at him when he gave me such wonderful memories?

"As I've gotten older," she said, "I've come to appreciate relationships and people for what they are. I don't see things in black and white anymore. It's not all or nothing for me now. It's okay if people turn out to be something in between. And I've been lucky enough to have been involved with some truly delightful people."

I started laughing a little bit. "It's so weird. I'm not angry with Preston anymore. He helped me through a very difficult period in my life."

"See?" she replied.

"Same thing with Luke!"

"Who's Luke?"

"Never mind!" I said with a laugh. Alice was amazing. So smart. Everything she said made sense. I thought about Luke. Why was I mad at him? He hadn't done anything wrong. Luke was there for me that day I needed him. He was a friend, maybe more, but for whatever reason, he was choosing to keep things with us platonic. And I could either be angry about it, or accept him for who he was, and take what he could give.

Even Dan. Why be upset with him? Laura would get over him quickly. That I knew for sure. And yes, maybe he handled things poorly. But Dan helped Laura too. Why not look at Dan as Laura's rebound guy, the guy who made her feel sexy and young and beautiful, perhaps for the first time in her life?

"Alice, I do have one question. How do you forgive your own father for cheating on your mother?"

"Hmm...that's a tough one."

"Well, I do owe it to him to hear his side. Do you know I haven't even seen him since my mother moved in with me? I'm talking weeks ago."

"Wow, that's hard."

"What a horrible person I am. I mean, he's my dad, no matter what he did."

"Text him," said Alice.

"What, like right now?"

"Sure."

"Good idea!" I got out my phone and texted my dad. "Would love to get together and talk. How about tomorrow?"

"Wow! I feel better already!" I exclaimed.

Alice just sat there smiling. "I'm glad."

"So, what's *your* story?" I asked her, "Any guys you want to tell *me* about?"

"No. No guys," she said with a giggle.

"Okay, that's cool."

Now there was a moment of really awkward silence and I couldn't figure out why.

"No guys," Alice said again, this time with a slightly devious smile.

"I don't understand."

"There are no guys I really want to talk about, know what I mean?"

"I'm confused."

"Maybe I could talk about some girls, get it?"

I just sat there, still confused, Alice still smiling. Then, it hit me.

"Alice, are you gay?"

She let out a little laugh and nodded. Out of nervousness, I responded with a giggle. Then she began to laugh again, and before I knew it we were both laughing heartily. I became borderline hysterical at one point, partly because of the wine, but mostly because all of a sudden I began to wonder if this woman I was absolutely smitten with was trying to get me into bed.

"I'm not hitting on you, if that's what you're thinking," she said, "I think you're beautiful and I'd say if you *were* gay, maybe I'd be interested. I know you're not, though, so please don't be uncomfortable. I'm having fun. That's all."

I looked into Alice's blue eyes and didn't know exactly what was going on, but one thing was for sure. I felt like I was someone else for the night. Here was me, Emma Bloom, having a drink with a beautiful woman who liked girls, and I was fascinated by the whole experience. I looked at Alice's full red lips and wondered if I could ever see myself kissing them. Surprisingly, the thought didn't disgust me. In fact, it was semi-appealing.

"I'm having fun too," I said.

At this moment, I got a text back from my dad. "I'd love to have coffee with you tomorrow. Thank you Em."

"I love you Stan," I texted back.

"Love you too," he texted.

"Thank you, Alice. I mean it. I'm having coffee with my dad tomorrow."

"That's great, Emma," she smiled with those big, beautiful red lips.

I asked Alice a million questions about when, how and why she changed her sexual status. I assumed since she'd had a miscarriage that she had once been a fan of males.

Alice explained that she in fact had been with men all her life until recently. She was married very young and had a child by the time she was twenty-three. Her husband was a much older man who liked younger women. He eventually left Alice and moved on to an even younger woman. She chuckled when she told me her ex-husband was presently engaged to his fourth wife, age twenty-five.

"How old is he now?" I asked.

"Sixty three I think," she grinned, "He's still cute, and he's a good father to our daughter. Charlie isn't a bad person. He's just trying to live forever."

"I love talking to you," I told her, "You see the good in everything and everyone."

"The thing is, I was really angry that Charlie dumped me. I was upset about it for a long time. And I really think that's normal and should be expected."

"Right..."

Alice then told me something that would perhaps change the way I looked at things forever. "The thing is," she said, "Some people, like me, get over it eventually, and some people never do. Some people learn to accept things that happen to them and move on. Others decide to stay bitter and never let it go. In my eyes, it's the most important choice a person can make. But there are those who never see it that way."

She went on, "I think that the people who cling to the resentment and try to place blame on other people end up being unhappy for the rest of their lives. And the smart ones, the ones who focus on themselves and how to make their lives better and richer, and learn to forgive and forget things they had no control over, are the people who end up living happy, productive lives. They are fulfilled." She added with a smile, "As I am today."

I was now officially in love with Alice, last name unknown. Her words were amazing! I felt like she should be a life coach. It was at this moment I realized how much I needed to fix my life. Yes, I was a good mother, and yes, I was starting to come to terms with Sam's death and forgive myself, but now it was time to concentrate on the future, or more specifically, the professional aspect of my future. I decided right then, I was going to look into the salsa business.

I stood up, leaned over Alice's stool and gave her a huge hug. "Thank you."

She simply smiled and said, "No problem." Then she added, "My advice to you is, stop thinking and start *doing*. Do things that make you happy. Work out, make salsa, do fun things with your daughter, date whomever you want. And if you just live your life and be happy, something amazing will happen."

"What?" I asked.

"Look at this," Alice said, dropping her head slightly down and gently closing her eyes, revealing her eye lids. They were covered with gold sparkling eye shadow.

"What am I looking at?" I asked, "Your eye shadow?" I wasn't getting the connection.

She lifted her head. "It was a free gift with purchase from *Estee Lauder*." I giggled, "It's nice."

"My point is, if you buy into what I'm saying, about letting go of the past and just living for today and being happy, and doing good things for yourself and for others, you get a free gift with purchase. The gift isn't eye shadow, though. The gift is much better. What you get is a vibe, a really good vibe."

"I still don't really understand."

"By being a good, upbeat, wonderful person, you're basically sending out a vibe that starts coming through with every move you make. People in your life start to see it, and good vibes come back to you. People you touch get the vibe, and amazing things start happening. If you're decent and nice and respectful to others, your behavior brings good things to you. It actually shows itself in other ways. Maybe not even with the people who are in your life today, but with exciting, new people and new things." She exclaimed, "I swear by this theory!"

This was an amazing moment. Not only had Alice just told me about the free gift with purchase, I suddenly felt as if she had just handed it to me. I couldn't ever remember feeling hope like I did at this very moment.

I was calm now, the anger in me rapidly flowing out of my body, and rays of sunshine making their way into my heart. I felt like I was beginning to feel at peace with everything. Sam's accident, the miscarriage...Preston...

Luke...my parents...my sister... All of these things were out of my control. What I *did* have a say in was my little girl and my professional life. What was I waiting for?!

I suddenly felt as if someone had just unlocked the chains keeping me captive in my self-loathing prison. Laura and my mother had tried hundreds of times to get this message through to me, but they hadn't been successful, probably because I wasn't ready to hear them. Luke had helped get me over the guilt and self-blame for Sam, but he hadn't caused me to get off my butt and pursue something professionally. It took an absolutely dynamic, vibrant, gorgeous stranger to give me the memo that it was time for me to get a life.

I looked at beautiful Alice, sitting there with her red lips smiling at me and the *Estee Lauder* free gift with purchase on her beautiful eyes. She was the angel who appeared in my time of serious need. She was, at this moment, the person who had given me treasures beyond belief, all without judgment and criticism.

"What are you thinking?" she asked excitedly.

I didn't answer Alice with words. I responded by standing up, pulling her toward me, and planting a passionate kiss on her big, beautiful red lips.

Chapter 23

Kissing Alice was bizarre, yet shockingly appealing. The first touch of her lips felt so dramatically different than any guy I'd ever kissed, so foreign to anything I'd ever felt. They were soft and delicate, and I felt like a guy and a girl at the same time. I felt sexy and beautiful and desired, but I also felt Alice's femininity too.

She was a good kisser, even though I had no one to compare her to. I truly was enjoying myself. However, after a few moments I had to pull away because thoughts of being seen making out with another woman in a neighborhood bar began to crowd my head, and I had no interest in acquiring the reputation of being the lesbian mom who tongues it in public with other girls.

"We really shouldn't be doing this in here," I said softly.

"Then let's go," Alice said with a smile. She put some money down on the bar, told me not to worry about paying, and out we walked.

"I'm parked right over here," I said, pointing to my car, not really sure where this was going at this point, and suddenly feeling a bit panicky. "I'm not gay!" I wanted to shout.

Alice must have sensed my apprehension because she said, "Would you maybe want to sit in your car and talk for a minute?"

"Okay," I said, feeling immensely relieved.

I wasn't grossed out by what I'd just done. I was glad I kissed Alice, actually. But now, I didn't want to do it anymore. Ever.

Once in my car, I looked at Alice, her pretty face so close to mine and said softly, "Just so you know, I'm really attracted to you. I think you're stunningly beautiful, and I think you're an amazing person. But the thing is, I have no interest in taking your clothes off, and I'm a hundred percent sure I'll never want to do that. It's just not me. I like men. I love men, actually. Yes, I hate them sometimes, but I love them, too. I love their hard bodies with no curves. I love their not so soft lips. I adore their deep voices and their complete inability to multi-task. I love love love their scruffy unshaven faces, and I love their strong arms around me."

"I understand," she said with a smile, "I really do."

"Do you think we could be friends? Platonic friends?"

"Absolutely," she answered. Then she leaned over, took my face in her hands and gently kissed my cheek. "You're lovely."

I drove Alice to her car, and just before she got out, we programmed each other's numbers in our phones. "I had a great time," she said, "Call me, okay?"

"I will," I said with a huge grin.

Alice opened up the door and got out. Then she leaned back in and said, "And if you feel too weird to call, that's okay too."

"Are you crazy?" I said to her, "I had a wonderful night with you. I'd love to see you again."

"Thanks," she said with a big grin. Then beautiful, sexy, delightful Alice slammed the door shut, and proceeded to do something I will remember for the rest of my life. She put her lips on the passenger side window of my car and gave it a big huge smooch, emphasizing her bright red lips as much as she could. Watching her mouth pressed hard against the now fogged up window made me laugh. Then she pulled back and waved good-bye.

I waved back and then watched Alice dig through her purse for her keys. I waited until she found them, opened her car door and got in. Then I drove away. And the second I pulled into my driveway, I texted her.

"You're like no one I've ever met before" I texted.

"Thanks, had a great time!" she texted back instantly.

I got home and checked on the three people who now resided with me. All were safe and sound. My mother and Laura were asleep in the guest room bed, and sweet Izzie was still sleeping peacefully in my bed. I sat on the edge of her bed for a long time just watching her breathe quietly, her cute little body snug under the covers. Then I began to talk to God.

I thanked him for giving her to me. And then I thanked him for tonight. I thanked him for sending Alice to me. I had walked out of my house two hours earlier, an angry, bitter woman who could only see the past and the mistakes and the darkness. I had come home an energetic, motivated person, wearing acceptance and grace on my sleeve. I was at peace. And the future seemed bright. It was time to make plans, all kinds of plans.

The next morning, I woke up at the crack of dawn, before anybody else in the house. Adrenaline was pumping through my veins, given that I now felt like I had a million things to do since today was day one of my new and improved life.

I went downstairs and made coffee, and while I waited for it, I happened to notice Laura's cell phone lying on the kitchen counter. Giggling the entire time, I changed her ring tone to Gloria Gaynor's seventies hit, *I Will Survive*.

Next I turned on my computer, and while drinking almost an entire pot of coffee, I surfed the net, researching the salsa industry. If I was going into business, I needed information.

An hour and a half later, I heard Izzie. "Hi, Mommy," she said, her voice like music to me. I turned around and when I saw her, I literally melted. I reached out to her and hugged her tight.

"Why are you squeezing me so hard?" she asked with a giggle.

"Because I love you," I said.

It was strange. I was seeing my daughter in a new light. Not that I didn't feel lucky to have her before, but I now saw Isabelle as a gift that keeps giving, every second of every day. And with the way I was planning to start living my life, with my new business and my new outlook on relationships and people in general, I felt so much more worthy and proud of being her mother. And that didn't mean I loved her more than I always had, but it made me significantly more appreciative.

Laura was next to make her way downstairs. "Morning," she said.

"Good morning!" I exclaimed, hugging her tight.

"What's wrong with you?"

"Nothing, Laura!" I said with a laugh, "Nothing!"

"I saw the note. Did you go out last night?"

"Yes! Yes, I did!"

My sister gave me a weird look. Then she gave Isabelle a look and both of them shrugged their shoulders. Laura then went to get herself a cup of coffee, while I whispered to Izzie to go upstairs and call her Aunt's cell phone.

Sure enough, a minute later, we all heard, *"Go on now, go...walk out the door...just turn around now...cause you're not welcome anymore..."*

Laura stood there confused and I said with a grin, "I think that's your phone."

She burst out laughing. Then she asked, "What's gotten into you? Something's different."

"Yes, Laura, *everything* is different. Tell me, are you okay?"

"Yes, thanks," she said with a sad smile.

When I looked into her eyes, I knew she was going to be just fine. She appeared very drained and depressed, the effects of the previous night. But I knew with a little time, just like Gloria Gaynor, and every other woman whose man dumped her, Laura would survive.

After Isabelle got on the bus for school, I told my mom (who was now up) and sister all about my night, starting with when I told off Dan.

"I can't believe you did that for me," said Laura, "Thank you."

"Well, it felt pretty good, I have to admit. But it really wasn't the right thing to do."

"I'm glad you see that," said my mother.

I then told my family about the rest of my night. I shared details about my conversation with Luke, and then I told them about the highlight of my night: Alice.

"You kissed her?" Laura asked, "Like on the lips?"

"Yes," I said with a laugh, "Like on the lips, like for a long time!"

Both Laura and my mother had these weird looks on their faces.

"Look, I'm not a lesbian. It was a one-time thing. I told Alice we're just going to be friends and she's fine with that. I really want you two to meet her. She's an amazing person."

"Sure," Laura answered. Not surprisingly, there was much skepticism in her voice, and I knew it was pointless to try to sell Alice to my sister right now. But I also knew that if Laura met beautiful Alice for three minutes, she'd fall in love with her just as I had.

"So, I have an announcement," I said.

"What?" they asked in unison.

I took a deep breath. "Starting today, I'm officially in the salsa business."

"That's great!" exclaimed Laura.

"Yes, it's wonderful!" my mother added.

"What's with the sudden surge of ambition?" asked Laura, "I mean, why now?"

I looked my sister in the eyes and said softly, "Alice."

She stared at me like I was nuts.

"Whatever the reason," said my mother, "It's a good thing."

Neither of them understood how I felt, and how much the previous night had changed me. It didn't matter, though. The bottom line was, thanks to my free gift with purchase, I was different now.

"Mom, if it's okay with you, I'm meeting Dad today for coffee," I said.

"Yes, it's okay," my mother replied with a sad smile.

"I'm still on your side, Mom. I hope you know that."

"You shouldn't have to take sides," she replied.

"I'm not ready to see him yet," said Laura.

"That's fine," said Mom.

At this moment, all I could think of was how badly Laura was in need of Alice.

An hour later, my sister left for work. I sent her out the door with a big hug and kiss, told her not to spend her day thinking about Dan, and that we'd have chips and salsa and a good girl chat when she got home. As for my mother, she left to get her hair done, and then to have lunch with her new guy. 'Weird,' I thought, 'but good!'

And I, Emma Bloom, spent the day researching my new business, formulating a business plan, and creating my new little company and its products. I took only one break during the day, and that was for my coffee date with Stan Bricker.

Chapter 24

George's Place, a Greek family-owned diner, happens to be right across the street from *Donatella's*, the tiny Italian restaurant in whose women's bathroom I almost had sex. I couldn't help but smile when I got out of my car and glanced over there. It made me miss Preston and my heart actually ached a little bit. In a good way, though. Thinking of him made me happy, not bitter.

I walked into *George's Place* where my dad was standing in the doorway. He looked nervous and I felt sorry for him because I couldn't even imagine how he must have been feeling. I now felt horrible for staying away for such a long time, and I was overwhelmed with the desire to put my arms around him. So, that's exactly what I did.

"Hi," he said with a chuckle, "Good to see you too, Em!"

I pulled away and smiled. "Hi Dad."

We got a booth in the back and ordered coffee right away. The second the waitress was gone I looked at him and said, "I'm so sorry."

"For what?"

"For not doing this sooner."

My dad smiled. He seemed a little sad, but generally he looked pretty good. "Well, I can't blame you for being mad at me. I did a terrible thing."

"Yeah, you did," I said sadly, "But I should have reached out to you sooner and heard your side of the story. What *is* your side of the story, by the way?"

Dad took a deep breath. "I never, ever cheated on your mother all these years. And then, I met a woman I was attracted to. She noticed me. She paid attention to me. She made me feel young and attractive. And I acted on it. I couldn't believe I was doing it, but I did. I felt so guilty, believe me, but that didn't stop me."

Just then the coffee arrived. As he put sugar and cream in his, he asked the waitress for some milk.

I smiled, touched by the gesture. "I can't believe you know how I drink my coffee," I said.

My dad just smiled at me and I felt like a little girl at that moment. "So," he said softly, "Your sister hates me. Do you?"

"Are you crazy?" I replied, "I could never hate you. Neither could Laura."

"She told me I'm no different than Alan."

"You're not."

"Maybe I'm worse," he said.

"No way!" I said with a laugh.

"Em, I don't know what happened. I love your mother so much, and I hate myself that I did this to her. If I could take it back, I would in a second."

"What are you trying to say?"

"Emma, I want to get back together with your mother."

"Oh my God!" I exclaimed, "Really?"

"Yeah, but doesn't she have a boyfriend now?"

"She told you?"

"Actually, Edna and I saw them a few days ago at the mall. They didn't see us, though."

"Mrs. Feldman's first name is Edna?" I asked, holding back laughter.

"Yeah, why? Is that funny?"

"Forget it."

"So, your mother...is it serious?"

"What? Mom and Henry?"

"That's his name? Henry?"

I nodded. "What about Edna?" I emphasized the name Edna.

"It's over. I swear to God. I'll never see her again. I promise. I want your mother back. I want my wife back."

"Because you saw her with another man?"

"No," he said, "Your mother had every right to start dating. This isn't about jealously, although the thought of Helene with another man is killing me. But the thing is, I don't love Edna. I loved one woman in my life. Helene. That's who I love and that's who I want. Em, how am I going to get her back?"

"Dad, I can't even believe how great this is!" I put my hand over his across the table and said with a grin, "I'll help you. Laura will help you too."

He looked up at me. "Thanks, Em. Boy, I'm a real dickhead."

"Um...people can hear you."

"Is it true or not?"

I smiled, "No. It's not true. You just got confused and you made a bad call. A really bad call. But I get it. I've made a couple of those myself."

"You're doing just fine, my sweet Emma."

"I love you, Stan," I smiled. A tear ran down my cheek.

The second I left the restaurant, I texted Laura. "Call me! It's important."

Less than a minute later my phone rang, and I got a huge surprise that cracked me up.

"*I kissed a girl and I liked it...the taste of her cherry Chapstick...*" sang Katy Perry on my phone. Laura had secretly changed my ring tone after I told her about Alice.

"Very funny," I said when I answered.

"What?"

"My ringtone."

"Well, now that you're a lesbian, I thought it would suit you. What's so important?"

"Guess who wants to get back together with Mom?"

Laura screamed really loud, and I told her she was being dramatic.

"Maybe you're rubbing off on me," she giggled.

We decided we had to come up with some kind of plan to sit our mother down and sell her on the idea of giving her husband a second chance.

"Tonight, after Isabelle goes to bed." I said.

"Wine and salsa?"

"Perfect."

"Hey, Laura?"

"Yeah?"

"Please call him."

"I was planning on doing that right now."

I hung up with my sister and suddenly felt inspired. My salsa business was becoming a reality, I had had a great talk with my father, and my parents were headed toward reconciliation. What a great day! And I realized, I had *made* it that way. And I had the power to make *every* day like this, just by doing things I liked, and doing the right things. I had so much more control over my happiness then I ever thought was possible.

Chapter 25

Early the next morning, 6:03 to be exact, I was sitting in my car watching Luke from a distance. He was at the start of the jogging path, stretching and waiting for me. I had texted him the night before, and told him I wanted to talk to him. His response was that I should meet him for a jog at 6:00. It seemed more like a command rather than a suggestion, and since I was the one who was hanging my head, I followed orders.

Even with his bed head and middle-aged tummy, Luke looked adorable to me. I thought about what it would be like to sleep with him, to be naked and to have his arms wrapped around me. It made me happy, but then it made me feel a little foolish because I was here to make amends with Luke. I wasn't here on a date with him. I had *never* dated him. Not even once. So, the fact that I'd acted possessive and psychotic two nights earlier was ridiculous and childish.

At the time, I was too closed-minded to respect his reasons for keeping things between us platonic. I didn't want to accept him the way he was. Now, with my new attitude, I embraced Luke as a lovely person, someone I adored, and a friend I wanted in my life, on the condition of what he was willing to give. No more than that. I now accepted him with no expectations, just an appreciation for his enriching my life in a way. And now, it was time to tell him this, with a major apology included.

"Hurry up, girl!" Luke joked as I walked toward him. He looked at his watch. "It's 6:04!"

I stood there speechless.

"What?" he asked with a big grin. His smile made me feel like a child. Flashes of Izzie's cute face popped into my head because I knew the look I had on my face at this moment was the exact same expression my daughter used when she was trying to say sorry for something.

Luke said with a kind smile, "Forget about the other night."

I took a deep breath and exhaled. "Luke, I'm so sorry. I was completely out of line. I didn't mean those things I said."

"What things?"

"I don't want to be friends with you...You're a shitty friend..."

"There's some truth to that."

"No, Luke," I said sternly, "You're a good friend. A really good friend." I took another deep breath and continued, "The thing is, I really like you. The other night, instead of yelling at you I should have told you that. I really like you and I don't understand why you don't want to see me more. I'm not asking to be your girlfriend. I'm talking about being friends. Just friends. Want to be friends with me?"

Luke seemed a bit taken aback.

"Do you?"

"Let me ask you something," he said, "How many licks does it take to get to the center of a Tootsie Pop?"

"What?"

He repeated, "How many licks does it take to get to the center of a Tootsie Pop?"

"I'm sorry, I don't understand. What are you trying to say?"

"Think about it, Emma. Do I want to be friends with you? Yes, I do. But how many times do you think we could go out and have coffee, or see a movie, or have dinner, or drinks? How many times do you think we could do that and stay platonic friends?"

"Who cares? Why does that matter?"

"Because it does," he exclaimed, "Look, I don't want to be platonic friends with you because I can't."

"Why not?"

"Because." Luke put his head down.

"Please, just tell me," I said gently.

He looked up at me. "My wife wants to try to work things out."

Talk about a shocker! "Really?"

"Yes. I didn't want to say anything because I don't know what's going to happen. But for my boys' sake, I feel like I have to try. And if I'm going to make it work, I can't have any other relationships with women." He put his head down again and said, "Especially you."

We stood there in silence for what seemed like a really long time, Luke unable to look up at me, and me unable to actually speak, due to severe shock.

"Do you hate me?" he finally asked.

"Oh my God, no!" I exclaimed, "Actually, I feel relieved because not knowing why you didn't want to date me was worse than this. I think…"

"Look, truthfully, it's not going very well with my wife and I. It's forced and we're both walking on eggshells and trying to push something that I think we both know isn't there. But to get someone else involved, and have a third party being part of the reason we fail for good isn't fair to anyone. And that's why I've stayed away. Or at least stayed away as much as I could."

I leaned over and kissed Luke's cheek. "You're a really good person, Luke. Whatever happens, I'm glad I fell on my face in front of you."

Luke smiled, "Me too. You looked pretty damn fatin with your knees scraped up."

I giggled, "Your Arabic's getting pretty good. Come on, let's run."

While we ran, I told Luke all about my salsa business and he gave me some much needed advice and ideas about advertising, marketing, and cost efficiency. I listened carefully and asked questions, feeling like I was getting a free seminar from a smart, successful businessman.

"How do you know so much?" I asked him, while we stood by our cars stretching.

"Trial and error, I guess."

"Your ideas are really helpful."

"I'm impressed. Starting a business takes guts."

"Thanks," I smiled.

"I'm here during the week, every morning at six. Join me again sometime?"

"Wouldn't we be using a lollipop lick if I did that?"

"Exercise doesn't count."

With a big grin, I opened my car door, and just as I was about to get in, Luke called out my name.

I looked up.

"Did you mean it when you said I wasn't that great of a kisser? I mean, am I really bad?"

"No, Luke, I promise. You're not bad. I'm so sorry about that." What I really wanted to do was shout, "If you only knew how I felt about kissing you!!"

"How do you say sorry in Arabic?" he asked.

"Assif. Why?"

"You're sexy when you speak Arabic."

"Hey, you're not allowed to flirt with me."

"I know," he said with a sad smile, and with that, I got in my car and shut the door.

I waved and drove away, and suddenly I felt a surge of relief. Things made perfect sense. Luke liked me, but he was doing what he thought was best for his family. And I couldn't blame him for that. In fact, I had respect for it.

Not being able to be with Luke stung like crazy, but I knew I'd be okay. So, now, both Preston and Luke were out of the picture, and that was good. The two had paved the way for me to focus solely on other things. I didn't need or want a relationship with a man right now. What I needed and wanted at this juncture was a relationship with my salsa business!

Chapter 26

O ver the next few weeks, the weather began to turn much cooler, and there was something in the air that made it feel like the season for productivity.

The day after I met with my dad, I dropped a few hints to Helene to see how she felt about the idea of a getting back together with her husband. She wasn't too keen on the idea, one because a major amount of trust was now missing from the rock solid marriage she once thought she had. But also, there was Henry. Mom liked him. I could tell. They'd been spending a lot of time together. She had even mentioned that she'd like us to meet him.

My dad began calling my cell phone every night to talk about her. Upon my advice, he called my mother and asked her to get together. Not surprisingly, she declined. So, he called her again. Again she shot him down. After she said no a third time, my dad was a wreck.

"I have an idea," I said to him over the phone one night, whispering because Helene was just a room away, "I can't guarantee anything, but it's worth a try."

The next day, Laura and I checked into a room at the brand new *Sheraton* hotel in our area. We brought along a big basket of snacks and fruit, and a bottle of wine. We booked a couple's massage for 6:00 that night. Then we took one of key cards over to our dad's house. The other key card, we gave to Helene.

Dad was gung ho about the plan. Helene needed to be sold. "I don't know if this is such a good idea," she said.

"I can understand that, but you owe it to yourself to at least talk to him," Laura urged.

I added, "Spending the night there doesn't mean you have to get back together, but at least see how you feel."

Our mother was skeptical, but I think in her heart, she knew her marriage deserved a fighting chance, so she agreed. "The only reason I'm considering this," she barked as we were practically pushing her out the door with her suitcase, "is because I know everything is already paid for."

"Whatever, Mom," said Laura.

My parents ended up staying at the *Sheraton* for three additional nights after the first one, and by the end of their stay, it was safe to say they were back together.

As for my salsa business, it was taking shape at a rapid pace. I was spending every free moment working on my products and getting them ready to sell. Coming up with the packaging and general appearance of the salsa took a lot of time, and I had to experiment with many different kinds of ribbons and labels and colors.

I chose to put the salsa in 12 ounce glass jars I'd found at the dollar store. They were very plain and needed to be decorated to catch the eye of the buyer.

The final products ended up looking amazing. Each jar had two ribbons tied around it, just below its lid. One was yellow, one was red. The labels were bright florescent green and were shaped like jalapeño peppers. *Solo Chicka's Salsa* is how they read. That was the name of my new company. Laura, myself and our newly back together parents had decided upon it late one night over wine and Kiwi salsa. Solo Chicka is "single chick" in Spanish. And that's what I was, a single chick. The name was catchy and cutesy, and I felt like it would sell.

I decided to start out with four kinds of salsa. I chose my personal favorites, black bean, Fusion peach, Grape and Avocado, and a basic hot salsa I called *Hotter Than Bradley Cooper.*

Yes, I thought Bradley was hot hot hot, but I also thought it would be a good conversation starter with store owners. Not to mention, Bradley Cooper fans were a good market for salsa consumption.

Alice helped me a lot with marketing strategies, pricing, and ways to find lists of grocery stores, gourmet stores, specialty shops, and fancy boutiques. We met for coffee a few times and I felt lucky to have this woman as a mentor and a friend. Each time I saw her, I found her strikingly beautiful, but I never had any desire to kiss her again. We were platonic. We were girlfriends. And that was perfect. And I could tell Alice felt the same.

When I was finally ready to hit the street and start selling, I was a bit nervous. But in an instant, sales came right back to me. In and out of stores I walked, prototypes in hand, asking business owners if they were interested in carrying *Solo Chicka's Salsa* in their stores.

I got lots of no's at first. "The economy's bad," "I just don't think people would buy it," "It's too expensive," and "It's nothing special," were some of the things I heard from people.

"What does being single have to do with making salsa?" a snooty store manager asked me one day.

"Uh…maybe when you're single, you have more time to make salsa?" I answered in the form of a question, realizing that was a really stupid way to respond.

My favorite rejection came when I gave a guy a sample. When he began chewing, he said, "I have to be honest with you. This tastes horrible."

My heart sank. Was my salsa horrible?

"That guy's an idiot!" Laura said when I told her the story.

"What a creep!" said my mother.

In her true nature, Alice chose not to make a derogatory remark about the guy's reaction. "It's just one opinion," she said with a gentle smile. This woman could motivate me to no end.

Into more stores I walked, rejection after rejection after rejection. I was dismissed and refused and denied and snubbed and rebuffed, to the point where I could almost no longer stand it.

Then one day, I took the jars into *Gifted*, a little gift boutique that carried fine china, crystal, stemware, kitchen accessories, and some gourmet food items. The owners were two older women, and when I say they freaked, I mean it. To say they were enthusiastic about *Solo Chicka's Salsa* is putting it mildly, no pun intended.

"Wow!" said one of the women, after tasting the grape and avocado salsa, "Fabulous!"

"And what a cute name!" the other one said.

"Who's Bradley Cooper?" said the first woman, as she perused the four samples I had set down on the counter.

"Oh, you know who he is," her partner explained to her, "He was in that movie...Valentine's Day."

"And The Hangover," I added.

"Oh, yes!" the first woman exclaimed. She turned to me and added, "How cute that you like him."

I stood there smiling and adoring these ladies.

"So, how much?" one of them asked me.

I gave them the price. Then I held my breath while the two women looked at each other for a moment. They just stood there, each one waiting for the other to say something.

I was just about to tell them I'd give them a twenty percent discount, (I figured anything to sell something) when at the very same time, both women exclaimed, "Give us two of each to start."

It was only eight jars of salsa, and I was only netting three dollars a jar. So I basically had just made twenty-four dollars, and that was before income taxes. Yet, still, I was so excited I wanted to scream at the top of my lungs. I had made a sale! It wasn't the money, it was the fact that someone wanted to buy something I made! This was a moment of self-worth I don't think I'll ever forget. I was now Emma Bloom, salsa business owner, who had earned her first dollar in seven years. I was overjoyed.

The two God-sent ladies who ended my losing streak happened to be the facilitators for the turning point of *Solo Chicka's Salsa*. From this point on, I began to sell with such confidence, such enthusiasm and such energy, that I became a sales machine on an endless roll. I almost never left a store from this point on without selling something. I suddenly knew how to handle every rejection I heard. If a store owner was lukewarm, I'd somehow find the perfect thing to say to get them interested.

I had a unique selling style. It made sense to not just sell the salsa, but to sell myself, the sole owner of a small business, a single mother, a once heartbroken, down-in-the-dumps, depressed and lonely women, and now, a happy, productive, inspired business owner.

I talked about my love and passion for making salsa, and how it was therapy for me. I told them about the fresh ingredients I used, and how there were no preservatives. I let them sample the salsa, so they could taste for themselves how good it actually was. But I also played up my personal life. I talked about being a single mother, and about dating, and about Bradley Cooper. And people listened. And they liked me. So they bought from me.

Even if an owner initially said no, I'd convince and charm them to buy just one jar, and then I would leave my business card, because I felt it in my bones that the jar would sell, and that they'd soon be calling me for more. And it was working!

I set up a website and began getting email messages for orders. It was completely insane, overwhelmingly unmanageable almost, but I was thrilled by it. Isabelle started helping me after school, and I found myself not only happy to be spending time with her this way, but also very proud to be teaching her about business and hard work and accomplishment. I realized I was being an amazing role model in this regard. I was showing my daughter ambition and achievement.

And late at night, while she slept, instead of spending my nights drinking wine and eating salsa with my sister, I was now standing at the kitchen counter making salsa half the night, while my sister sat at the kitchen table keeping me company.

"I'm so proud of you, Emma," Laura said one night.

I looked at the successful doctor, whose professional life had always come so easily and who'd known she was meant to be a doctor from such a young age. "Thanks. That means a lot to me."

"It's true. You're doing so well. You turned out to be such a great business woman, such a hard worker, so motivated."

"You know what? I'm really happy, and for the first time in my entire life, there's no man responsible for that."

"It's wonderful," she smiled.

Chapter 27

My business continued to thrive. I was completely self-sufficient. It felt like the time in my life to work, set goals, and achieve professionally. But, I did start to feel very alone and although that was okay, it was a little sad.

Preston was completely out of the picture. I hadn't heard from him in weeks. As for Luke, a couple of random texts between us had been the extent of our communication since the day he told me he was trying to work things out with his wife, the same day he compared our relationship to a tootsie pop.

I decided that since my professional life was now in place, maybe it was time for me to try a real relationship with a man. Not a sexual relationship like I had with Preston, and not a fantasy relationship with an unavailable man like Luke, but something that had the potential for more.

One night after Izzie was asleep, I went to Match.com in search of *Den0507,* the guy whose picture and profile had captivated me, the same guy I spotted while walking out of *Walgreens,* and the same guy whose favorite food was chips and salsa.

I pulled up the 35-50 year olds in my zip code. It was no surprise that the same match dot com-ers who popped up months earlier were still there. "Yourprince65," "Goodguy2know1203," "takeme44" and let's not forget "lookingforcowgirl," all remained ready and available to meet me.

Finally I spotted *Den0507* and found myself immensely relieved that his cute picture remained on the site. After all, wasn't it possible that Den could have met his soul mate in the past few months and taken his profile off? Fortunately for me, he was still searching for love.

I printed out the picture, cut it to size and put it in my wallet. Then, the search began. Over the next few days, I carried around Den's photo and showed it to people, asking them if they knew this mystery man. After all, not only didn't I know his last name, I didn't even know his first name. All I knew was that I was on a mission.

I pulled Den's picture out everywhere I went. At my bank, I handed it to the teller who waited on me. "Sorry, Mrs. Bloom, I've never seen that person." I showed it to a couple of my neighbors. "No, Emma. Never seen him. He's cute, though." In one week alone, I showed the picture to at least twenty-five people. Friends, my post man, a local florist, the guy who owned the gas station by my house, my hair stylist, Izzie's teacher, and pretty much every store owner I called on that week. Now I had two jobs, salsa saleswoman and private investigator.

"How can no one know this guy?" I practically shouted to Laura in *Starbucks*, after just having shown the picture to the woman who made my tall skim misto with no foam, "He lives in our town and he's single!"

My sister and I were spending Sunday afternoon together, taking advantage of an unusually long stretch of free time. My parents had taken Izzie to lunch and a movie, so the two of us decided to do what girls do best: drink coffee and talk. I invited Alice to join us, but she declined, as she was leaving the next morning for a two-week business trip to London and had lots of packing and last minute errands to run.

"Calm down," said my soothing sister, "You'll find him."

"I'm obsessed!"

Laura asked, "So what do you say to these people when you show them the picture? I mean, do you explain why you're looking for him?"

"No. I don't give any explanation and no one really seems to care," I answered, shrugging my shoulders, "It's pretty hilarious. Not one person to whom I've shown the picture seems even the slightest bit fazed."

"Maybe there's a little piece of everyone who understands the concept of desperation," Laura joked. "You know, you could always join match dot com," she suggested, "Have you ever thought of that? Then you could contact him right away."

"Are you crazy? I'd never put my picture on that site. What if Luke saw me?"

"First of all, I guarantee Luke's not on there. He's back together with his wife, right?"

"Thanks for reminding me."

"And secondly, if he did happen to go on there and see you, well, then he would be looking on there too, so what's the big deal?"

"I'd rather die."

"There's the drama I never get enough of," my sister joked.

We continued sipping our coffees, and then my sister proceeded to tell me about a new guy in her life. Actually, he wasn't really new, he was Tim McMillon, a guy we'd gone to high school with, who now lived in Texas. Tim apparently found Laura on *Facebook* and contacted her.

"Do you remember him?" she asked me.

"Vaguely. I think he was a nice guy."

Laura told me Tim was divorced with two kids, he was a financial advisor for Merrill Lynch, and the best part, he was coming here to visit her.

"I'm so happy for you!" I exclaimed. I really was. My sister had been so down about Dan.

"I'm not so sure there are that many good guys out there," she had said to me a few days earlier.

I had asked, "What about Luke?"

Laura's response was to make some snide comment about Tootsie Pops. I left it alone because I knew how she felt, and there was nothing I could say to change her mind. Some great guy had to come into her life to change her attitude about the availability of quality men in the world. And maybe that guy was Tim. I hoped.

Don't even ask how I had such a positive attitude about the opposite sex. My recent dating history painted a bleak picture, especially when it came to Luke, the man who I sometimes felt like I was in an imaginary relationship with. The amount of time I spent dreaming of him and lamenting over him and wondering how his marriage was going was unnatural, given the actual amount of time I'd spent with him in reality. I mean, how well did I really know him? Not well. Still, something kept me clinging to hope that Luke and I might someday be something.

"So, where's Tim staying?" I asked Laura.

"The Sheraton."

"Well, that's a good sign," I joked, "Should I book you a couple's massage?"

Laura laughed and then the two of us literally planned her outfits for the entire weekend. We chose her clothes and accessories and shoes in our heads, knowing full well she was going to have to model everything before any decisions were final.

Just as we were about to leave, I heard a cell phone ring, and I was confused for a second, until I realized it was my phone, and that once again, my sister had secretly changed the ring tone. I let out a huge laugh. She had changed it to some salsa tune, and I felt like I was in a Mexican restaurant.

"It's so appropriate for your business," she joked.

I looked at the number and didn't recognize it. "Hello?" I answered.

"Hi, is this Emma?" said some guy on the other end of the phone.

"Yes, it is."

"Hi, it's Tony Strong. I met you at Henry Horowitz's party."

"Oh, hi!" I remembered Tony immediately. He was the widower who had really made an impression on me. He had seemed smart, honest, practical, and rational. I wondered why on earth he was calling me after all this time.

"How are you?" he asked.

"I'm fine. How are things with you?"

"Great," he began, "Thanks for introducing me to Georgia. We're still dating."

"Really?" I asked. I looked at Laura. She was mouthing, "Who is it?"

I didn't want to tell her it was Tony, the guy whose date was Dan's ex-wife, who had to leave the party because she couldn't stand the sight of Dan. So instead, I held up my index finger and said, "Tony, can I call you back? I can't really talk right now."

"Actually, do you have just a minute? I'm calling because I have this friend. His name's Matt. I think you two may hit it off. Can I give him your number?"

"You want to set me up on a blind date?"

"Yes! Yes!" Laura whispered, "Do it!"

"Um, can you tell me about him?"

"I think you should just go out with him," Tony said, "Trust me."

For some odd reason, with absolutely no knowledge about Matt, I agreed to let Tony give him my number. The guy texted me the next day, and two days after that we went out. His last name was Bricker also, and we spent the first thirty minutes of our dinner date trying to figure out if we were related because if we didn't have that to talk about, we would have been majorly struggling for conversation. Boy, Tony was a great guy, but his matchmaking skills left something to be desired. He couldn't have been more off in setting the two of us up. At the end of the night, both Matt Bricker and I were very sure there was no connection.

I even pulled out Den0507's picture and asked him if he recognized the guy because I knew he wouldn't be offended. I wasn't into Matt Bricker and he wasn't into me. Ironically, he was the first person to actually ask me why I was looking for Den. I told him it was for a friend. Matt smiled and I knew he knew I was lying. I also knew he didn't care.

We said our good-byes and went our separate ways, and I was sure I would never hear from him again. I didn't leave with a bad feeling, however. Even though my date and I didn't have a connection, I had met a guy who seemed nice and decent. More importantly, though, I was officially becoming open minded when it came to dating. It was both good and sad. I was happy to be moving on, but a big part of me was still struggling with that old familiar widow's guilt that seemed to tug at my heart every time I was with someone of the opposite sex or having the least bit of fun. It was much less pronounced now, though.

A couple days later, I received a surprising voice mail. "Hi, Emma, this is Matt Bricker from the other night. Look, I'm going to be perfectly honest with you. I didn't really feel like we hit it off."

"Really?" I said to myself with sarcasm, as I prepared my third batch of *Hotter than Bradley Cooper* salsa of the day.

"So anyhow, I know this sounds really weird," he went on, "but I'd like to set you up with my friend. His name is also Matt. Call me back or send me a text and let me know if you'd be willing to meet him. He's really a great guy. I think you two would like each other." Matt Bricker left his number and said good-bye.

"There's no way, right?" I asked my sister, who was standing in the kitchen in slinky black top number five, one of the options she was modeling for her upcoming weekend with Tim McMillon.

"That's the one, by the way," I exclaimed, motioning to her halter top.

"Are you sure?" she asked, "I feel like my boobs look too saggy."

My poor sis, so critical of her physical appearance, when in reality, she should have been beaming with pride at how beautiful she was. I gazed at her without speaking.

"What?" she asked, "Saggy, right?"

I took her shoulders, pulled her toward me, and looked right into her eyes. "Listen to me, Laura. You are beautiful. You're not just smart, and a good doctor, and a good mother. You have a beautiful body and a beautiful face. Do you understand that?"

Her eyes quickly filling with tears, she said, "Alan obviously doesn't think so. Neither does Dan."

"Fuck Alan and fuck Dan!" I shouted.

"Mommy said a swear word," Izzie sang.

I whipped my head around and saw my daughter standing in the doorway. "Sorry, honey. I was just trying to make Aunt Laura feel better," I said.

"Someday you'll understand," Laura said, kissing Isabelle's cheek.

"That's a really nice shirt, Aunt Laura."

"See?" I said.

Chapter 28

The next night, I went out with Matt number two, who turned out to be perhaps the biggest jerk I'd met in all my life, almost to the point where it was humorous. Matt was 42, divorced with a ten year-old, a six year-old and a baby. We never actually got into why he got divorced, which I was sure was a nightmare in and of itself, but when I asked him if he had dated much since, his response was, "Actually, I'm dating two women right now."

"Really?" I asked.

"Yeah, do you have a problem with that?"

"Um...no... I guess I'm just surprised."

"Why?"

"Well, why are you getting fixed up on blind dates if you have two girlfriends?"

He answered, "One of the women I'm seeing is still married, so I don't think she's ready for anything serious. As far as the other one, well..." He began to chuckle in this very creepy kind of way and then continued, "...she's just friend with benefits."

"What?"

"You know, just sex."

I must have had a really weird look on my face, because he added, "What's wrong? You seem surprised."

"Actually, I'm just surprised you would share that with me."

"Are you judging me? Are you telling me you've never had a friend with benefits?"

"Is that the point?" I asked. I stood up and finished, "Honestly, I think I might go."

"You *might* go or you *are going?*"

"I *am going*," I said very loud and clear. Then I walked off, thanking God that I had taken my own car.

On my way out the door I pulled out Den's photo and asked the hostess if she recognized him. "Sorry, honey," she answered, "If that hottie had come in here, I'd have remembered him."

"Thanks," I smiled. Then I began to giggle and I laughed the whole way home. I wasn't angry. I wasn't even angry at Matt or the other Matt. Being upset wasn't worth my energy. I would look back on this as part of the whole dating experience that I was now going through as a middle-aged woman. And I found it very entertaining.

The very next day, I was at Trader Joe's and ran into a guy who I'd met years earlier, the very good-looking younger brother of a girl I went to college with. He told me he just moved to the area and confessed that since he was new in town and recently divorced, he didn't have many friends to go out with. So, when he asked me out, I said yes, even though I remembered him as being extremely arrogant, to the point where he came across like he thought he was God's gift. Guess what his name was, by the way. Matt.

Matt was a personal trainer in his late-thirties, and even though he truly was very much in love with himself, I didn't care. I was on a roll, so why stop now? I figured if I kept going on dates, eventually one of them would cause me to forget about Preston and Luke and Den0507, if in fact I never found him.

Matt and I ended up having a pretty fun date at a Spanish Tapas restaurant in the area. We drank lots of sangria, and although Matt surpassed his reputation (that came from all the women I knew who knew him) as being one of the most self-loving men in America, he had lots of redeeming qualities, such as a well developed (borderline fanatical) knowledge of body conditioning. It was interesting to hear his stories about some of the clients he trained.

I found being with him so entertaining that after dinner I suggested we go back to my place for a glass of wine. Matt happily accepted.

With Isabelle and Laura fast asleep upstairs, I spent the next half hour on my couch kissing my date. Matt was a pretty good kisser. The problem was I had to keep moving his strong trainer hands off of my buttons and zippers. Matt wasn't really getting the point that kissing was all I wanted to do.

Finally he whispered, "Don't you want me, Emma?"

"Um…"

Matt pulled away and looked at me in disbelief. "You're not sure?"

"Well, I'm just not ready for the whole physical thing, especially with my sister and daughter upstairs. I'm sure you can understand that, right?"

"They're heavy sleepers, aren't they?" he asked with a chuckle.

"I don't think I want to risk it," I answered, really wanting to say, "How would you know since you don't have kids?" and "You're hot, but I'm not dying to sleep with you right this second."

"Wow," he replied, "I'm shocked by your will power."

This comment left me speechless.

"This sucks," he continued, "I mean, I thought for sure we'd be having sex tonight."

I think at this moment I gasped.

"Don't act so shocked. I can tell you want it."

"Want what?"

"This," he said, putting his hand on his "package."

At this moment, I let out a nervous laugh and then had to put my hand over my mouth. I stood up, walked to the back door and opened it.

"What are you doing?" he asked.

"I'm showing you out. I'm not in the mood to be date raped right now. Can you please leave?"

Matt walked out, wine glass in hand and scowl on his face. When I shut the door and locked it, I found myself shaking. The date rape comment was semi-valid, and I realized I had put myself in a very defenseless, precarious position, where it could have happened. I was thankful that Matt didn't assault me, and I realized no matter how old a person got, the realities of dating stayed the same, and that I had to be careful.

At this moment, I wanted to call Luke and ask him to come over and rescue me from all the creeps named Matt I'd gone out with lately. Luke would never hurt me, in fact he would protect me and take care of me. He made me feel safer than anyone I'd ever known. He was my rock, my go-to guy, my big brother and my friend. But he was also the guy who was probably going to be a monogamous married man again. At this moment, I wondered if I'd be going out with Matts until I was 80.

I headed upstairs, still a bit freaked out by Matt, but thankful the situation ended the way it did. I checked on Izzie. God, I loved her. I was so lucky. Why was I so focused on men? Wasn't my daughter enough? Couldn't I spend the rest of my life raising and cherishing and enjoying her instead of dating Matts who were going from bad to worse?

By the time I got into bed, I convinced myself that family love was worlds better than romantic love. My child, my sister, my parents...they were my life, and they were all I needed. I felt like men only seemed to offer chaos, aggravation, disappointment, frustration and tragedy. I decided at that moment, I could easily bid farewell to all the Matts of the world and focus only on my career and my blood relatives.

But the second I hit the lights and found myself lying all alone in the dark, I realized I was kidding myself. I hugged my pillow and whispered to it softly, "Let me love you, Luke. Let me love you."

Unbelievably, the next morning, I got a call from one of the moms in Izzie's class, asking me if she could give my phone number to a "really nice, cute, single guy."

"What's his name?" I asked her, "Maybe I know him."

Her answer was comically astonishing. "Matt...Matt Hart."

I sat there unable to speak. Another Matt? I didn't know if I could take it.

"Hello, Emma? Are you still there?" the woman asked, "Do you know him?"

"Um...no, I don't."

"So should I give him your number?"

"Sure, why not?" I responded.

Matt Hart and I talked on the phone a couple of hours later. He seemed nice, smart and relatively funny. Also, Matt was a pilot for Southwest Airlines and that was pretty appealing. We set up a dinner date for Saturday night, and strangely enough I was semi-psyched. Finally, a Matt I may actually hit it off with.

That night when Laura got home from work, I asked, "Do you know a guy named Matt Hart?"

My sister gasped. "I think so. Is he a pilot?"

"Yeah!"

"Yes, I know him."

"I'm being set up with him."

Another gasp. "*Do not* go out with that guy!"

"Why?"

"Is he divorced now?" she asked.

"Apparently."

"A couple years ago, when he was still married, his wife was a patient of mine."

"So?"

"He hit on me! He asked me if I wanted to have quote 'a no-strings attached affair.'"

"Really?"

"Stay away from that guy!"

I texted Matt Hart two minutes later and told him I had to cancel the date. After all, why even begin a relationship with someone you already know cheated on their spouse? Matt Hart was a waste of my time and energy, and he wasn't even worth one evening of my life. Sure, I was ignoring his side of the story, and maybe I was being a little bit closed-minded. That being said, once a cheater, always a cheater. Plus, I had been through enough loser Matts for one lifetime.

"As little faith as I have in the male species right now," I told Alice when she called to say hi from London, "I haven't lost hope that Mr. Wonderful is out there somewhere."

"He is!" she replied, her voice filled with its usual upbeat cheerfulness, "but his name definitely is not Matt!"

The next night, Tim McMillon arrived in town and Izzie was having a sleepover with her grandparents. As for myself on this particular night, I finally had a chance to catch up on work, a.k.a. make salsa, clean up the house, and maybe even watch a movie. I did none of those things, however. Instead, I headed over to *Sandy's Ski Shop*'s huge sidewalk sale. Isabelle had been asking me for a *North Face* fleece since the prior winter, and I felt like if the jacket was on sale, this would be a good opportunity to get it for her.

I found myself in a long line at the register, not just with one *North Face* jacket in hand, but with three. One for Izzie, one for Laura, and one for myself. The good news was that they were twenty percent off.

"Cute coats," I heard someone say.

I turned around and a very nice-looking guy was standing behind me with a black *Columbia* fleece in his hand. He was bald, but had nice eyes and a fit body.

"Yes," I responded with a shy smile.

"I'm buying this for my son," he said, holding up the fleece, "He's turning sixteen tomorrow."

"That's nice." I smiled politely and suddenly it dawned on me that I was being hit on.

The two of us made small talk for a couple minutes and I found myself intrigued. He seemed pleasant and very harmless. But he was sexy, in a quiet way. Then the bomb dropped. The guy extended his free hand. "My name's Matt, Matt Millstein."

Suddenly I burst out laughing, so hard that the guy began to chuckle nervously.

"What's so funny?" he asked.

"Nothing," I said, "I'm a little crazy." I shook his hand, "Don't pay any attention to me."

"Have you eaten dinner yet?" he asked, "Would you like to grab a bite?"

"Right now?"

"Sure, if you're free."

"It just so happens, I am free, Matt," I said, semi-playfully, "but I have to be honest with you. I can't go out with you because your name is Matt, and I have really bad luck with that name."

"Now that's one I haven't heard before."

"I wish I was lying, but I'm not. In the last week, I've been out with four Matts, actually only three. I never even made it past the initial phone conversation with the fourth one. All of them have been nightmares!"

"If that's the only reason," Matt replied with a smile, "then you need to give the fifth Matt a chance. I promise I'm a nice guy. You can call my ex-wife. She even likes me."

"I don't know, Matt," I said playfully, "I'm on the fence with this. Give me one really good reason I should go out with you."

"Okay let me think…" he said, pretending to be stressed.

I was thoroughly entertained and said to him, "Make it good, Matt. Your name is really hurting you and time's running out."

"I've got it!" he exclaimed.

"Shoot."

"Have you ever seen <u>The Hangover</u>? People tell me I resemble Bradley Cooper." Matt pointed to his head and finished, "Especially when I had hair."

Within twenty minutes, Matt Millstein and I were seated in a booth at a steakhouse having dinner. As I gazed lovingly at him across the table, I kept trying to figure out how I'd missed the resemblance. Matt M, the best Matt ever, really did resemble Bradley Cooper. It was something in his eyes, his facial expression.

But aside from my sick fantasy that I was having dinner with my celebrity crush, our date was heading in a good direction. Matt was engaging and funny, in a quirky kind of way. And he was nice. The conversation was going well. I told Matt all about my business and he got a huge kick out of my *Hotter than Bradley Cooper* salsa.

Matt then told me about his career. He was a lawyer who specialized in helping victims of insurance company fraud.

"Wait a minute," I said, suddenly realizing I had read about him in the papers, and that he'd won dozens of cases over the past few years, "You're sort of famous."

He smiled shyly and nodded, confirming I had the right guy. Matt wasn't obnoxious about his wealth and success. He was actually very understated and modest. And I liked that.

The two of us also talked about being single parents and about dating. I found we had had lots in common, and by the end of dinner I realized that even with his major red flag, his name, this was a great, great guy.

During coffee, I took a deep breath and then I said, "Listen, Matt, I was thinking of asking you to come back to my place, but I recently had kind of a bad experience, so I'm hesitant."

"What happened?"

"Matt number three thought that me asking him over meant that I wanted to sleep with him."

"Oh," said Matt with an assuring smile, "Well, if we go back to your place, I'm good with not fooling around. Maybe just a little kissing."

"That sounds fun, Bradley," I flirted.

"And maybe a little weed?"

What? Did I just hear right? I asked myself. Did he just say weed?

"Are you up for it?" he asked, "I've got a couple of doobies in the car." He smiled, "Good stuff."

I sat there frozen for a minute or so, till Matt realized he'd said the wrong thing. "Or not..." he said with a nervous chuckle.

"Do you smoke pot a lot?" I asked him.

"Yeah, actually I do. I take it you're not into getting baked."

The room was spinning. Matt, a seemingly great guy, who really did resemble Bradley Cooper was in actuality a stoner. I'm not claiming to be Miss Perfect, and I'm not saying I never smoked pot in my life, however, I had a strong suspicion that Matt wasn't just an occasional pot user. Therefore, as much of a bummer as it was, I had to immediately end my short-lived relationship with Matt the lawyer, the lawyer in whom dozens of innocent victims put their trust in daily, the lawyer who did good by day and got high by night. Another disappointing Matt experience. When would it end?!

I handled my exit with class and grace. I grabbed my purse, kissed Matt on the cheek, thanked him for dinner and told him I wasn't up for getting involved with a smoker of any type of tobacco, regardless of whether it was legal or not.

He responded by telling me that even though I was a little bit too "goody-two-shoes" for him, he thought I was a great girl.

"Hope to see you around," I lied as I parted ways with him and headed to my car.

"You too, Emma!" he replied, lying as well, I think.

Good-bye Bradley Cooper! I said to myself. Then I promised myself I would absolutely never ever ever again, in my entire life, go out with another person named Matt.

And then, just as I was about ten feet away from him, Matt called out my name.

I cringed. He came running toward me. What could he possibly want? I wondered. Wasn't he in a hurry to go get stoned?

"I think this fell out of your purse," he exclaimed. He then proceeded to hand me my photo of Den0507. "Why are you carrying around a picture of Denny Fitzpatrick?" he asked.

Chapter 29

The second I got home I ran upstairs and changed into my PJ's, giggling as I thought about the look of shock I must have had on my face when I realized Matt, the stoner, knew *Den0507*, or I should say, Denny Fitzpatrick. Fitzpatrick. Obviously not Jewish. Did I care, though? I thought about it. Sam was Jewish, and that was a good thing, but what about Alan? Jewish. Hurt my sister. My father. Jewish. Hurt my mother. And every one of the five Matts were of the Jewish faith, so there you have it. Matt one was boring, Matt two was sleeping with two women and still getting set up on blind dates, Matt three was a borderline rapist (although he was only half-Jewish), Matt four was an adulterer and Matt five was a pothead. To say I was slightly turned off by men who'd had Bar Mitzvahs was putting it mildly. If Denny Fitzpatrick was a devout Catholic who received the holy communion three times a day, that was going to work for me at this point.

I got online, pulled up the white pages, punched in "Willow Ridge" and then "Fitzpatrick, Dennis."

"Fitzpatrick...Fitzpatrick..." I whispered to myself as I waited for the address and phone number to pop up. Two seconds later, when I saw Denny's address, I gasped.

"437 Butterfly Lane?" I shouted to myself. Den0507, Dennis J. Fitzpatrick was practically my neighbor! He literally lived no more than two miles from my house. How could he and I never have crossed paths except for one time outside of Walgreens?

I took a deep breath, sat cross-legged on the floor and dialed his number. Boy, I was nervous. What was I going to say? I decided to wing it and not rehearse anything, which was a horrible idea because when I heard him answer, "Hello?" I froze.

"Hello?" he repeated himself.

"Hi," I said slowly, "Is this Denny?"

"Yeah, it is. Who's this?" he responded in a very friendly tone.

I loved his voice instantly. It was a very high, raspy Irish voice that sounded a lot like the voice of Ed Burns.

"My name is Emma Bloom. I live in your neighborhood and..." Now I started stuttering and semi-giggling like a teen-ager. "Well, this is kind of difficult...and embarrassing...but I saw your picture on Match dot com and I read your profile...and...well...I just...I thought maybe...oh God...this is horrifying. You know what? Let's just forget it."

I was about to hang up when Denny interrupted. "Wait a minute!" he said with a chuckle, "So you want to get together? Is that what you're trying to say?"

I exhaled for the first time in over thirty seconds. "Yes, thank you."

"So you saw me on Match...so why not contact me through that?"

"Actually, I'm not a member on that site. It's kind of complicated." I wasn't ready to tell Denny that I carried around his picture and showed it to at least three dozen people.

"It's okay, don't worry about it. You'll tell me another time. So, where do you live?" Denny asked, beginning a conversation that would last for over an hour. We started with our addresses, and then chatted about divorce, my daughter, his kids, my salsa business, his mortgage business, our lives as single parents, and the fact that we'd never seen each other before (I decided not to tell him about Walgreen's yet).

"Would you like to get together this week?" he asked me, "maybe Wednesday night?"

"Okay, sure."

"Should I pick you up or would you feel more comfortable meeting somewhere?"

"Let's meet," I answered. Judging by all of my recent experiences, providing my own transportation was a must.

198

"Okay. I'll call you Wednesday and we'll figure out where and what time."

I told him that was perfect, and then we exchanged cell numbers.

"Great!" he said happily in his high, borderline Irish brogue.

"Hey, Denny?" I said right before we hung up, "I hope you don't think I'm psycho or desperate or anything."

"Please..." was all he said.

"Thanks. What's 0-5-0-7 by the way?" Silently I prayed, "Please don't say my height...please don't say my height..."

"My birthday."

"Great!" I said as I exhaled, "See you soon."

"Good-night," answered the lover of salsa and <u>The Hangover</u> in his sexy, Irish voice. Now I couldn't wait to see him in person (again).

When I hung up the phone, I literally screamed. I let out a high-pitched shriek of joy.

"What's going on in here?" I heard my sister ask.

She had obviously just walked in, and I was thrilled to share my news, so I went running to my entryway shouting, "Oh my God! You'll never believe it! I have a date with..." I stopped in my tracks when I saw she was not alone. Standing there with her: Tim McMillon.

"Oh...hi," I said, giggling.

"Emma, this is Tim," said Laura.

We shook hands. "So great to meet you!" I gushed, trying to get a read on my sister. She looked happy and I surmised the date was going well.

"Should we have a drink?" Laura asked both Tim and I, "I want to hear the reason for the scream I just heard."

"Sure," Tim and I answered at the same time.

I glanced at my sister's date for a split second. He had an attractive face and seemed kind. I was thrilled.

We made our way into the kitchen and while Tim opened a bottle of Pinot, I got some black bean salsa out of the fridge and some chips from the pantry.

The three of us sat at the kitchen table eating and drinking, and when Tim commented on the salsa, Laura told him all about my business. He was very complimentary, and told me he had a lot of respect for both my sister and I professionally. I liked this guy more and more as the minutes ticked by. As I watched Laura beam, I thought to myself, 'finally...'

I told them all about my night, how it had begun at *Sandy's Ski shop* and how I had ended up at dinner with Matt, the pothead, and how he was the one who identified Den0507, the hottie I now had a date with Wednesday night.

I could tell Laura was happy for me. We exchanged smiles at one point and things seemed perfect. The way Tim and Laura were acting with each other was so natural, not forced, like most first dates. Tim told us about his job, about his divorce, and about his kids. By the end of the hour, I was doing cartwheels in my head over this guy. Finally, Laura had struck gold. I couldn't find anything even remotely wrong with Tim McMillon.

"Show Tim *Den0507's* profile," Laura requested.

I was headed toward my computer when Tim made a suggestion. "Here, just use my *iphone.*" He picked up his phone and logged on to match dot com.

I quickly searched the tiny screen, and within ten seconds, Den's picture and profile popped up. I showed it to Tim.

"Nice," he said, nodding at the phone and then reaching over to the bottle of Pinot to give himself another pour.

"Let me show you..." said my sister, taking the phone out of my hand, "Den's interests..." She scrolled down with her finger, looking for the information to show Tim. "It says here somewhere that his favorite food is salsa and ch..." Laura suddenly stopped talking and scrolling, and froze.

"Chips," I finished for her, "salsa and chips."

She remained frozen, and her facial expression had just gone from happy and relaxed, to shock and dismay.

"What is it?" I asked.

"Are you okay?" asked Tim.

Laura looked at Tim, her eyes glossy. "You just got a text. It's from Lexie. Let me read it to you."

Tim went to grab his phone out of her hand, but Laura pulled away and read the message. "Honey, we're out of milk. Want me to go shopping tomorrow before you get back?"

I'm pretty sure I gasped. As for Tim, he took his fingers and ran them through his hair, a total sign he knew he was in deep shit.

"Are you living with someone?" Laura asked.

"Hmm…" Tim began, obviously wondering how he was going to weasel his way out of the mess.

"Sure seems that way," my sister continued.

"Listen, I'm going to go upstairs and leave you guys alone to talk." I disappeared as quickly as I could, and then, although I hate to admit this, I stood at the top of the stairs and eavesdropped. The only way I can rationalize listening to their conversation is that I knew, not only wouldn't Laura mind, she'd actually want me to hear what went down after I left.

"Lexie's my girlfriend," said Tim, "She doesn't officially live with me, although she really wants to."

"Are you kidding me?" said Laura with a fake, bitter laugh.

"Look, I really like you," I heard him urge, "I wouldn't be here if I didn't."

"You're missing the point, Tim. I don't really like *you*! You're pathetic. You're visiting a woman in another city while your girlfriend is hanging out in your house. Please, get out of my face. I can't look at you."

As I stood and listened, I was so proud of my sister. Her voice was relatively calm when she booted Tim, the snake. She didn't seem by any means, hysterical or upset. She was firm and matter-of-fact when she spoke.

The next thing I heard was my front door open. "I don't want to hear from you again," Laura said, "I'm sure you can understand that."

"I'm so sorry," said Tim, "I mean it."

Laura's voice softened when she answered. "It's all right. Comparatively speaking, you're the best of the three men I've been involved with since I got separated, which is pathetically sad and isn't saying much."

"But it's something," Tim said in a hopeful voice.

"If you knew the other guys, you wouldn't be too thrilled," she responded. Then I heard the door slam shut, and I heard Laura let out a huge laugh.

"Did you hear?" she shouted to me.

I started laughing and came down the stairs, and the two of us howled for a long time. What had just happened really was quite hilarious.

"My cheeks hurt from laughing," Laura said after awhile.

"Mine, too. That whole scene was something out of a movie, wasn't it?"

Laura wasn't too sad or upset that night, but right before she went to bed she did ask me if I would ask Denny if he had any single friends. Her request was both depressing and uplifting to me. I was so sad that my poor sister had again been burned, however, she seemed to be learning that the flaws in these men were entirely their shortcomings, and in no way, shape or form had anything to do with her. Laura was gaining a new self-confidence that was truly evident in her demeanor now. And I loved it. It was as if she'd finally realized that being smart and successful didn't mean she had a deficiency in the looks department. She knew now that she had both inner and outer beauty. It was wonderful to see how she'd grown in this regard.

I kissed her good-night, sent her to bed, and then checked my company website while I waited for Izzie to get home. The second my e-mails came up, I noticed one from *Winchester Foods*. My heart skipped a beat, as I instantly thought about one of the company's tens of thousands of employees, Preston Christiansen from the Information Systems department.

I opened the message. It wasn't from Preston, and there was no connection to him. The e-mail was from Philip Warren. I had no idea who he was.

"Ms. Bloom," it read, "I am contacting you because *Winchester* is interested in acquiring *Solo Chicka's Salsa.*"

I gasped and continued reading.

"Please call me to discuss this opportunity at your convenience. I'm at 847-555-9888. Thank you. I look forward to hearing from you. Sincerely, Phil Warren, Executive Vice-president, *Winchester* snacks division."

I sat there almost unable to move. *Winchester Foods* wanted to buy me out?! This was overwhelmingly astonishing. I ran up to Laura's room and told her about the e-mail. She screamed. "Do you understand what's happening here? You're going to make a ton of money!"

"Really?"

"Emma, *Winchester Foods* is going to buy your business!" She jumped out of bed and began jumping up and down and hugging me.

"Oh my God!" I exclaimed, "You're right!"

Right then, I ran to the stereo, got out a Bruce Springsteen CD, put it in the player, and put on *Born to Run*. I started singing and Laura joined in and played air guitar.

Not that the lyrics of the song pertained to my situation in any way, shape, or form, but there was something majorly appealing about blaring out my favorite Springsteen song during a moment when I couldn't have felt better. I could honestly never remember experiencing such self-worth in all my life.

Winchester wanted my company! *Winchester* actually found value and importance in what I had to offer, and they came to me!

We sang loudly, *"Together, Wendy we can live with the sadness...I'll love you with all the madness in my soul...Oh, someday girl I don't know when...we're gonna get to that place we really want to go and we'll walk in the sun, but till then tramps like us...baby we were born to run..."*

And as I blasted out the lyrics, I thought about how great life was all of a sudden. I had so many good things happening, and so much love around me. I wasn't sure if I'd love Den0507 with "all the madness in my soul," but I was certain I was going to have a fabulous date with him on Wednesday night. And I truly loved, and had the love of my parents and Laura, and Izzie, an incredibly amazing little girl who loved me unconditionally, whether I sold my company to *Winchester* or not.

As far as all the madness in my soul, I was beginning to realize that it was reserved for someone. It was reserved for the person who'd wiped my bloody knees, the one who was beyond easy to talk to, whose body was next to mine on a towel at the beach, and whose hairy chest I wanted to reach out and touch that day.

Luke was in my soul now. I had to admit it. Being in his house, crying in his arms, eating pizza with him at his big wood kitchen table, it felt like we belonged with each other. There was something very right about the two of us. Then again, Luke was in a marriage. So, was this wishful thinking? Or was my gut declaring that Luke and I were somehow going to be together?

I wasn't sure, but I did know one thing for certain. It took until now, when I had this amazing news to share, to realize that it wasn't as exciting if I couldn't tell my friend Luke about it. Hearing the news that *Winchester* wanted to buy *Solo Chicka's Salsa* was like being given the sweetest, richest, most delicious cake on earth, with a piece missing. The piece was Luke Sullivan.

Chapter 30

At 8:15 on Wednesday night, I walked into *Green Grass*, an elegant, yet trendy hot spot a couple of suburbs north of Willow Ridge. I was wearing my two best friends, my *Rock & Republic* jeans and my *Christian Dior* smoky eye shadow, a free gift with purchase that gave me eyes as sexy as Angelina Jolie.

Sitting at the bar with his back to the door was my date, Den0507, sipping a beer. Nervousness enveloped me. After all, I had seen Denny's picture, and I had even seen him in person briefly, but he had no idea what *I* looked like. What if there was no attraction on his part? Would I sense that immediately? I wondered. I took a deep breath and then I tapped my date on the shoulder. He turned around.

"Hi, Denny," I said with a shy smile.

Not to be conceited, but Denny was pleased by what he saw. I was sure of it, judging by the smile on his face. He almost seemed relieved, pleasantly surprised.

He stood up and extended his hand. "Nice to meet you, finally," he said in his adorable, high, Irish voice that I was now beginning to get to know. He was wearing a light sweater that was kind of tight and it was showing off his muscular biceps. I wondered for a split second why on earth no girl had grabbed this guy!

"Want to sit down and have a drink before dinner?" he asked.

"Sure," I smiled.

Three sips into my first glass of wine, Denny declared, "Okay, so I need to know how you found me. If you're not on the site, how did you get my name and number?"

I proceeded to explain very honestly about how I was looking for guys for my sister on the computer, and how I came across his picture. Then I told him about how I saw him walking out of *Walgreens* one day.

"Oh my God, I think I remember that," he said, almost shouting, his high-pitched raspy voice making the volume go up even more, "I knew I knew you from somewhere!"

"So you remember?" I asked.

"I do. You gave me this weird look."

"I did not."

"Yeah, you did."

Denny and I were now chuckling and arguing like we'd known each other for years. "So, how did you figure out my name and phone number?" he asked.

I smiled.

"Tell me," he urged.

I looked at him, hoping my gray eye shadow would detract from the redness now taking over my cheeks. "Actually, I printed out your picture and carried it around with me, and I asked everyone I came in contact with if they knew you." Then I pulled out the picture from my little hand bag and handed it to my date.

Denny took it and then burst out laughing.

"So like how many people saw this picture?" he asked.

"Forty or fifty?"

"Wow," he smiled. Then, he looked right into my eyes. "I'm so flattered by what you did. I think it's amazingly cool and so gutsy. Very impressive."

A grin instantly burst onto my face. "Thanks."

"So, who recognized me? Who told you my name?"

"It was Matt Millstein."

"Oh yeah...great guy. He's a client of mine. He buys a lot of real estate."

"And a lot of pot."

Denny laughed. "He *does* like to smoke."

"I met Matt at *Sandy's Ski Shop* and went out to dinner with him," I said, "He's a really nice person. I'm just not into smoking."

"I understand."

We ended up getting a table a little while later and then proceeded to have a three hour dinner at the posh French Asian fusion restaurant. I did all the ordering, as Denny confessed he had "no clue what half this stuff was" and that he had only chosen this place to impress me.

Denny was so open and honest. I loved the way he found humor in the fact that he had a hard childhood and came from a hard-working blue-collar family. "They're all really good people," he joked about his siblings, "but each of them is a pain in the ass in his or her own special way."

As I sat there force-feeding Denny a piece of my seared Ahi Tuna with baby bok choy (after he confessed he had never eaten raw fish before), I had to admit I was having a great time, even though we came from such different worlds. Denny was so rough around the edges, but not in a bad way. He was thick-skinned and tough, and it didn't surprise me when he told me he had been a professional boxer in his younger days. It seemed like Denny had led sort of a tough life, his family of ten always struggling for money and doing what they could to get by and survive, hence the boxing career.

Yet, there was a refined part of Denny too. He had put himself through college and had settled into a successful mortgage business. He didn't seem bitter about having to work so hard for everything. That was refreshing to me. Denny seemed optimistic and upbeat.

It was the way he spoke of his children and ex-wife, however, that started my real interest in Dennis James Fitzpatrick, the Second. When Denny spoke about his two kids, who were eight and four, his whole face lit up and his eyes became bright and very alive. It was lovely to see a man who loved his children like he did.

As far as his ex, he said to me at one point, "Stephanie's not a bad person, she's just a person with a lot of problems." What a completely refreshing description of someone's ex-wife! There was no bitterness in Denny, not even a trace, unless he was superb at hiding it, which I thought was highly unlikely. Denny was pure, simple in a way, his aura full of goodness and kindness. Being around Denny was soothing and I felt like I could just exhale and say, "Ahh…"

As we finished our meal with white chocolate cheesecake and coffee, Denny began telling me about how he would bribe his little girl with candy to get her to sing to him. "Wait! I actually recorded it!" he exclaimed, taking out his cell phone and showing me a thirty second video of his four year-old singing *Oh, Suzanna*. Denny's voice could be heard in the background, helping his daughter with some of the words.

"You seem like a really great dad," I said, my heart almost hurting from how sweet he was.

"I try," he said.

It was a no-brainer that Denny ended up on my couch after the date. We must have kissed for four hours straight. Mr. Sullivan crept his way into my mind as he did every time I was in the presence of another man, but tonight I found myself dismissing him pretty quickly. I kept my distance from Luke tonight, and let myself enjoy a guy who I was actually spending time with, versus my running partner who compared our relationship to a Tootsie Pop. Why part of me felt like I was cheating on him, I'll never know. I had a suspicion, though, that if Luke knew I was presently lip locked with Denny, he'd be really jealous.

Denny and I kissed for so long that my lips were actually getting chapped. I had no interest in ceasing this very fun activity, though, one because it felt great, but mostly because I knew I was with a good, good man. Was I sure he was my soul mate? No, but I liked him, and that was all I cared about right now.

Denny and I didn't just kiss all night. We talked too. He seemed very interested in me and my life, and asked a lot of questions about Isabelle and *Solo Chicka's Salsa*. I was more than proud to tell him about both my daughter, and the fact that I might be selling my business to *Winchester Foods*.

At 4:00 a.m., we both realized it was probably a good idea for Denny to go home. We had kissed a year's worth of kisses, all while managing to keep our clothes on, except for a brief moment where Denny lifted up my shirt a little bit to get a glimpse of my belly button.

"Why do you want to see it?" I asked him.

"I just want to check it out. Is that cool?"

"Okay."

When Denny saw my belly button, he didn't say anything. He just sort of studied it, while tracing it with his finger. Now I was getting nervous. "Is there something wrong with my belly button?" I asked him.

He continued to examine it and still didn't utter a word.

"If you don't say something I'm going to assume it's weird looking."

"It's cute," he said with a smile.

The next day, as I was walking out of one of my client's stores, I received a text. "I had a great time with you and your cute belly button."

My smile was so big I almost had to hide it. What a cutie. I texted back, "I had fun too Den0507. Thanks for exceeding my expectations. U r adorable in real life."

My second date with Denny turned out to be that night! Around 7:00, still exhausted from the night before and the four hours of sleep I'd gotten, I got a call.

"I know this sounds crazy," he said, "but I don't have my kids tonight, and if you can get your sister to babysit, I was thinking, without sounding completely perverted, maybe you could come over and I could play with your belly button for a little while."

"Hmm..." I said playfully, "I guess we could do that. As long as you know my belly button is the only thing you'll be playing with."

"Oh, then that's okay. I think I'll pass."

"Denny!" I shouted with a giggle.

"Just kidding," he said, "Come over. How do you like your pizza?"

"Let me put Isabelle to sleep first and then I'll be over," I told him, "Cheese, pepperoni and mushroom."

The second I hung up, I heard, "Let me guess. You're going out with Mr. Belly Button again?"

"Is that wrong?" I asked Laura.

"No," she smiled, "It's great!"

I put Izzie to bed around 8:30, and then made a mad dash to fix myself up for my new guy. I put on light make-up, old jeans and a tight pink Juicy t-shirt that accented the belly button of which I was now *very* proud.

When Denny answered his door, he didn't say hello. Instead, he grabbed me and kissed me. We must have kissed in the doorway for fifteen minutes before I even walked fully into the house.

Then the two of us sat at his little kitchen table, eating pizza out of the box and gulping down water out of huge water bottles. While we ate, Denny told me about why he got divorced. He explained that he and his wife had problems, "like everyone else," but that he thought it was pretty normal and that they would work through them. "When she told me she wanted to separate, it was like someone pulled the rug out. I was completely shocked. And devastated, obviously."

"I'm so sorry," I sympathized.

Denny asked me about Sam, and I told him what happened. I didn't get into details, and I didn't tell him about the fight we had on the night of Sam's death, but I was honest about the fact that Sam and I weren't getting along in the days prior to his death.

"Wow, I'm so sorry," Denny replied, "That must be really hard."

"Yes, it is," I said, "It was very confusing for a long time, but I'm learning to accept things."

"You sound like you have a really good therapist."

I smiled. "Their names are Helene, Laura, and Alice." I left out Luke.

Denny took my hand and led me into his family room and onto his couch. The first thing he did was pick up my t-shirt and touch my belly button.

"Do not sleep with him, Emma!" I told myself, "You don't know him!"

"I don't know you!" I exclaimed, quickly sitting up and pushing his hand off of my innie umbilicus. "Did you know that your belly button is technically the scar left from separating from your mother at birth?"

"So?"

"So," I said as I pulled down my tight tee, "You don't even know my mother, and here you are with your hands all over my belly button that was once attached to her."

"What are you trying to say?"

I stood up. "I'm trying to tell you that I'm not ready for this. I'm not ready for sex and lust and naked bodies."

"Okay," Denny said softly. He sat me back down and put his arm around me. "I'm sorry."

"I'm really sorry, Denny. I just want to kiss. I don't want to get into a physical thing yet."

"Don't worry," he said softly, "I'll wait."

I looked into his eyes, this seemingly good, decent man, whose divorce was an enigma to me. "How could a woman leave a guy like this?" I asked myself. I couldn't imagine Denny Fitzpatrick doing anything that was so bad that it warranted a permanent separation. I wondered if I would ever find out for myself.

Denny took me in his arms and kissed me for a long time, and I realized right then how much the human body, just like it needs food and water, needs strong arms to cover it every now and again. And it was strange. I felt Luke begin to drift away from me. Maybe it was because I had just made a conscious decision to let him go, or maybe I was really connecting with someone else. I wasn't sure, but at this moment, I decided to give in, let Luke live his life with his family, and allow myself to focus on someone who was unattached, someone who was mentally available, and someone who really seemed to want a relationship with me. Maybe in life, timing was much more powerful than love.

Chapter 31

The next morning, Izzie went to school, Laura went to work, and the second the house was empty, I picked up the phone and called Philip Warren (who I'd been playing phone tag with for almost a week) to discuss the potential sale of *Solo Chicka's Salsa*.

Surprisingly, he answered his phone and we ended up having a long conversation. At times, my mind drifted to one of Phillip's co-workers. I wondered how old Phil would react if I told him about my steamy relationship with a certain information systems guy over there. Yes, there were ten thousand *Winchester* employees working in Phil's branch alone, but still, there was a chance he knew Preston. Unlikely, but possible.

It was difficult not to think about Preston while talking to someone from his company, but when Phil began throwing out numbers in regards to what he thought *Solo Chicka's Salsa* was worth, I quickly stopped obsessing over the womanizer who had dropped off the face of the earth.

"How did you come across my company?" I asked Phil.

He explained that one of the executives from *Winchester* had noticed my salsa in a store and had told Phil about the opportunity.

"After several hours of research," Phil said, "I came to the conclusion that it makes financial sense and could increase profitability of *Winchester's* Mexican snack division."

Phil and I set up a meeting for two weeks from the following day, and the second I hung up, Denny called.

"I miss you," he said.

"You just saw me twelve hours ago."

"I still miss you," he repeated.

"Me too," I said with a smile. What an endearing person he was, open and honest, and unafraid to admit his feelings. "This is so easy," I told myself. "No complications, no guessing games, and most importantly, no ex-wives coming back into the picture."

Denny and I began seeing each other over the next couple of weeks, every chance we got. Quick lunches, dinner dates when Laura or my parents could babysit, phone conversations that lasted for hours, and the ultimate, a late-night visit from my guy, simply for a good night kiss and nothing else.

It was a Tuesday night around 10:30, and I was just finishing up a batch of my latest concoction, Blueberry Patch salsa, when I got a text from Denny. "I'm stopping by for two minutes. Is that okay?"

"Sure," I responded.

My sister, who was helping me with the dishes was ecstatic. A few minutes later, we heard a light knock on the door. I opened it.

"Hi," said Denny with a huge grin, "I came to kiss you good-night."

"Uh...this is my sister," I said quickly, in an effort to show him we were not alone.

Denny extended a handshake as he made his way into the house. "Nice to meet you. Can I kiss you goodnight, too?" he joked.

Laura grinned, "Want to sit down and have some chips and salsa?"

Denny accepted the offer and the three of us ended up chatting for an hour or so, until Laura said she was going to bed.

Denny left shortly after. "Sleep well, sweet girl," he said, after a long goodnight kiss in the doorway. I stood there smiling while I watched him walk to his car.

I think it was at that moment that I decided I was ready to give myself to Denny, this adorable guy who had just made a special trip to my house to kiss my lips without any agenda or other motives attached. I didn't mean just physically giving myself to him, although that was part of it. But I wanted to give Denny all I could emotionally, as well. It was time. Time to take a chance again.

Once in bed, I texted Denny, "I'd like to make dinner for you on Saturday night. What do you think?"

"Love the idea. Mmmwwwaaahhh..." he responded.

So that was my plan. Isabelle and Laura would stay at my parent's house, and I would make my kind-hearted new boyfriend an amazing dinner. And for dessert, he would have me.

I was even beginning to think I would introduce Izzie to Denny fairly soon. And that was a big deal because I had it in my mind that I didn't want my child to be exposed to a long line of dates and boyfriends. Any man I would potentially introduce her to would probably be a man who would be in my life for a very long time, perhaps for forever.

Obviously none of the Matts fit that description, and introducing Preston to Izzie had never been seriously considered, except for the brief period when I thought I may be giving birth to his child. Strangely enough, my gut had always told me that Luke would be the first man in my life to meet my daughter. It was time, however, to tell my gut to go shove it, and move on with my life. Yes, Denny Fitzpatrick would meet Isabelle. And although it would probably be difficult for her to see her mother with someone else, she would like Denny. I was sure of it. Who wouldn't?

By the time Saturday came around, I was feeling nervous, but good about turning up the volume a notch on the Denny relationship. This was a big step for me, but I felt ready. I began marinating my flank steak at 8:30 in the morning, and while the meat was successfully soaking I took Izzie to an indoor swimming pool and water park in the area. While she slid down the tube slide for the hundredth time, I couldn't stop thinking about how it was going to feel to make love with Denny.

We had certainly waited long enough. Lots of dates, lunches, dinners, visits to each other's houses, and all we had done was kiss. Taking things to a new level physically was probably going to change everything, and would hopefully draw us even closer than we were. These thoughts were both joyous and scary.

I got a text from Alice. "Good luck tonight! Just have fun and enjoy yourself." Then I got a text from Laura. "Stop by *Walgreens* and buy condoms. That was from Mom too."

I dropped off Izzie at my parent's house, and then I went home to tend to my meat. When I pulled into the driveway, I noticed a bag sitting outside my front door. I went into the house through the garage and immediately ran to the door to see what it was. Inside the bag was a big white box with a pink bow around it. There was no writing and no card on the box.

I took it inside and put it on the kitchen table, and then I opened it. Immediately, I began to giggle. Inside the box, wrapped in tissue paper was a big huge box of Tootsie Pop lollipops. I realized instantly, there was only one person who would send these to me. I was equally elated and angry at the same time. Only Luke would have this kind of timing. Only Luke would send me a gift on the exact day I had a major milestone occurring. Just like he showed up to rescue me at the jogging path just hours before my first date with Preston, Luke was showing up now, only this time in the form of hard candy. Why was he always putting himself inside my heart just when I felt I was on the brink of true happiness with someone else? It was outrageously disturbing. And exciting.

A card was taped to the box. "Emma," it read, "If you're up for it, I'd like to start taking some licks. Luke."

I stood there with my jaw on the ground, shocked for a second at the notion that Luke was pursuing me. I realized that things with his wife must be over, and this was his way of telling me that. His timing, however, couldn't have been worse.

What about Denny? What about the man who had made our relationship from day one effortless, fun and worry-free? Wasn't he the obvious choice? I found myself furious. How dare Luke confuse me! Just because he and his wife decided to call it quits (again), I was supposed to drop everything?

I put the lollipop box down and then I took a seat at the kitchen table and I sat there for a moment, angry and wanting to cry. Why was I so upset? Was it relief that Luke had finally come around? Or maybe I was frustrated. Deep down though, I knew exactly what was making me so upset. Guilt. I felt like a criminal who just did something majorly illegal. Why? Because sitting here staring at the box of Tootsie Pops in front of me, I was wishing it was Luke coming to my house tonight for flank steak.

"What's wrong with dating both of them?" Laura asked me. I had called over at my parents and requested she stop over. She was sitting at my kitchen table sucking on a cherry Tootsie Pop.

"I'm not really the kind of person who can do that," I responded, "You know...multiple dates with different guys. I'm a one guy at a time kind of girl."

"I wish I could tell you what to do," she said, "What does your heart say?"

"Luke, Luke, Luke! But the practical side is calling Denny."

"Well don't make any decisions tonight. I mean, just enjoy your dinner with Denny and see how things go."

At that moment I got a text. I looked at it in disbelief. It was from Preston. "I miss you," it read, "Will you be my Tootsie Pop? How many licks does it take to get to your center?"

Laura told me she would never have believed the coincidence of the Tootsie Pop analogy had I not shown her the actual text message on my phone. I agreed wholeheartedly. What were the odds that two men I knew would both compare me (on the same day, mind you) to a household name in lollipops?

"How do you feel?" Laura asked.

"Angry!" I exclaimed, "I never thought I'd hear from Preston again. I was hoping the next time I saw him would be in the hallway at *Winchester,* right after I make my million dollar deal! What gives him the right, after all this time, to sext me?"

"It seems like it's just his style. I'm sure he misses you."

I knew she was right, but I was infuriated by his fun, casual message. Didn't Preston owe me an apology for staying away for so long? Did he expect me to jump right back into bed with him after everything that happened?

Between Denny and Luke and Preston, my mind was racing. Three completely different guys. Three very different relationships. Each one unique. Three guys, each who meant such different things to me. To say I was confused was an understatement.

Chapter 32

Five minutes before Denny got to my house, my cell phone rang. I saw it was Luke calling, therefore there was no chance I was taking the call. I couldn't handle it right now, so I continued cutting up vegetables for the salad while I waited for him to leave a message. Two minutes later, I listened to it.

"Hi, Emma, it's Luke. Just calling to see if you got my gift." He chuckled at this point. Luke seemed nervous and it was kind of funny. "I wanted to see if you'd like to get together and go out and talk. Give me a call and let me know. Thanks. Have a great night."

Luke's message was so hard to hear. I wanted to call him back and tell him he had the worst timing in the world! I had felt so sure about Denny, and now, just because Luke dropped a hundred lollipops off at my door, I had doubt. Add to the mix the crazy text I'd gotten from Preston, and it was a recipe for mayhem.

I wasn't considering getting together with the sexter, but I did have the desire to call him and let him know how inappropriate his message was, how disappointed I was that he had so easily dismissed me after the miscarriage, and how he had no right to pop (no pun intended) back into my life and ask if he could lick me.

By the time Denny rang my doorbell, I was a bundle of nerves. When I answered the door, my dinner date attacked me with kisses. Had this been yesterday, or any time before I received the Costco size box of Tootsie Pops,

I'd have kissed him back, perhaps for hours. Who knew? Maybe we would have skipped dinner and gone right upstairs to officially turn our relationship into a love affair. But things were different now. Luke had complicated things. And I hated him for that. And loved him for the same reason.

Denny sensed my hesitation immediately. "What's wrong?" he asked me, "You seem jittery. Are you nervous I may not like your cooking?"

"No," I lied, "I'm fine. How about some wine?"

"Sure."

From that moment on, the entire night seemed forced. It was awkward, strange, and so completely different than the other ten times we'd been together. All our conversations dragged. Being with him was uncomfortable and weird. But I was taking credit for all of it. It was *my* issue.

After dinner, as I stood at the kitchen sink doing dishes, Denny grabbed my waist from behind me and turned me around. He began kissing me and I kissed him back, trying to return to the place I'd been with him for the past couple weeks. I couldn't, though. The same lips I'd been enjoying were now making me extremely uncomfortable, and I felt like the scum of the earth because poor Denny had no clue that this had nothing to do with him.

I wanted so badly to be able to turn on a switch in my core to make myself continue to fall for Denny. But it was just not happening. Being in his arms felt unbelievably wrong. The bottom line was, I couldn't stop thinking about Luke. It was as if he was standing here in the middle of my kitchen, telling me to send Denny out the door and go to him.

"What's wrong?" Denny asked me softly, "Please tell me."

I looked up at his kind face, tears instantly appearing in my eyes. "I don't know. I don't know what I'm doing."

"With me?" he asked softly, "Are you sick of me already?"

"No! I promise, that's not it."

"Then tell me. You can say anything and I'll listen, and try to help you."

"I can't talk about it. I'm sorry."

He backed away. "Well then, what should we do? Should I go?"

I looked at him sadly and said, "Maybe."

Denny left, and I felt both relief and panic at the same time. On one hand, I was experiencing unbelievable reprieve. I needed to gain a clear perspective on exactly how I felt, and that was impossible to do with Denny around. I needed to be alone. The flipside was, I had just let an amazing guy walk out my door. Would I regret it? I wasn't sure, but the fact that I was taking that risk spoke volumes in and of itself.

And maybe all this had nothing to do with Luke. Maybe I wasn't ready for anybody, although the thought of running over to Luke's house and into his arms was extremely appealing at this moment. I did no such thing, though. Instead, I finished cleaning up and headed upstairs.

After tossing and turning in bed for about twenty minutes, I made a phone call completely on impulse.

"Hi, Preston," I said when he answered his cell.

"Hi!" he exclaimed.

"I got your text."

"I figured." Now there was silence, neither of us knowing what to say next. Preston finally spoke again. "The thing is, the reason I texted you is, I'm not done yet."

"What does that mean?" I asked, my voice rising to the point of anger, "You're not done sleeping with me yet?"

"It's more than that. I miss you."

"Then why did you stay away for so long?"

"Because that's me. I was upset about what happened and I needed time to think."

"You hurt me."

"I'm sorry," he said, "Are you really mad at me?"

"Yes, I'm really mad at you." Lying under the covers in the dark, I realized I was only half-serious, and that our conversation was becoming light-hearted and fun. Hearing Preston's voice made any issues I had with him fade rapidly. After all, he wasn't evil. He was just being himself: closed off, non-committal and confrontation-fearing.

"Being mad at me could be a good thing," he said with a chuckle.

"How so?"

"Ever hear of hate sex?"

"What?"

"You heard me. Would you have hate sex with me?" he said with a laugh, "It would be fun."

And there it was. The bold man was still the bold man. Preston Christiansen, the same person who told me the first time I met him that he wanted to see me naked, now wanted me to take my animosity toward him, all my hostile feelings and dislike for the way he handled things, and channel it into physical pleasure. And sickeningly enough, the thought of doing that was somewhat exciting.

How did he have such power over me? Preston had this strong ability to turn me into someone I didn't know. I mean, I was thinking of jumping into bed with a guy I wanted to scream at for hurting me. I should have been appalled by his suggestion, yet it made more sense than anything, only because this was Preston. And nothing with this man or this relationship was ever normal. It never had been, not even from the start.

"When can you get here?" I found myself asking.

"Twenty minutes," he answered, "See you then?"

"Okay." We hung up and then I froze. What had I just done?! Preston Christiansen, the man who with one look could melt me, was coming over to my house in twenty minutes for nothing more than sex. The man who went away so suddenly, and who caused my entire body to physically ache for months from withdrawal, would be here, in my house, and in my bed, minutes from now.

I got up, went to my dresser drawer and pulled out the sexiest underwear I owned, a red lace push-up bra and matching thong undies. Then I put on a Michael Stars t-shirt and some old Lucky Brand jeans. And then it dawned on me. What was the point of worrying about a good outfit? My clothes were going to be off in the first sixty seconds the guy was in the door.

The same logic applied to makeup. I put on a little face powder, a touch of blush, mascara and lip gloss. With a splash of *Chanel Coco Mademoiselle,* I was ready for date number two. Actually, it wasn't even a date. It was sex, plain and simple. And that thought took my breath away and sickened me at the exact same time.

In the few minutes before I knew Preston would be at my place, I sat at the kitchen table drinking a glass of leftover wine from my dinner with Denny, the man I'd planned on sleeping with tonight, but instead let go home. Denny was the man who offered the closest thing to a normal, healthy relationship. He was safe. He was kind. He loved me and I knew it. But I realized right then that if I had Luke on my brain the entire time he was here, and if I was letting Preston come over for dessert, I clearly did not feel the same way.

I heard a light knock at the door. My heart pounded. I got up and answered the door, and when I saw him standing there with his beautiful dark skin, his olive brown eyes, his rock hard body and strong arms, I practically dove into him. I grabbed his face and began hungrily kissing him. Preston always had and could still bring out inhibition and sexual impulses I never knew existed within me.

He kissed me back, making his way into the house. Then he picked me up and took me upstairs. My lips and my mouth and my tongue could not get enough of him, his familiar smell, his full lips, and his dark, soft hair. Why had I waited so long? I wondered. How could I have gone all this time, denying myself the pleasure that awakened me so intensely?

"Tell me how much you hate me," he whispered, as he put me down on the bed.

"I hate you, Preston," I whispered back, "I hate you so much!" I was giggling, but a part of me really did hate him. I hated him for cowering out of a hard situation. I hated him for staying away. I hated him for having such a perfect physique. Most of all, though, I hated him for making me lose control every time he so much as touched my skin.

"Show me how much you hate me," he said softly, leaning over me.

I responded by pulling off his shirt and unzipping his jeans.

"You don't hate me," he whispered, while looking right into my eyes.

"I could never hate you," I whispered.

We kissed and kissed and now my clothes came off. And the hunger was ever present. I was ready to explode.

"God, I missed you, Baby," he whispered.

When I heard the word baby, my heart sank. I froze. I felt disgusted. This was wrong. Preston on top of me was wrong. Preston in my bed was wrong. Preston in my house was wrong. Preston in my life was wrong!

I pushed him off of me. "Stop!" I exclaimed, out of breath.

"What is it?" he asked me.

I got up and quickly put my shirt back on. "I can't do this. I made a mistake asking you over here."

"Really?" he asked.

I went to him and held his face. "I adore you," I said sadly, "But what we had is over. It's so over."

"Are you sure?"

I nodded my head sadly. "I wish I didn't feel this way. I wish we could go back to the days when everything with us seemed perfect. When things were untainted. We can't, though."

"Are you sure? I mean, this attraction we have...I know you feel it too."

"Of course, I do. But it's not enough for me. I want more."

Preston took a deep breath, as if he was thinking, and then asked, "How much more?"

"I want you around, and we both know that's never going to happen."

He didn't say anything right away, I think because he knew I was right. He looked really sad, though. He stood up and then said, "I really care for you, as much as I'm capable of caring for anyone."

"I know," I smiled.

I walked him to the door. We hugged, made a fake pact to keep in touch, and said good-bye. It was strange. There had been so few words exchanged between us. He was here, and then we undressed each other, and then we got dressed. And that was it. I hadn't even told him that his company might be buying mine! I would have liked to have shared that news with him, but I forgot. My mind was too focused on the hard body I so desperately wanted on mine, and then didn't.

The entire way up to bed (for the second time) I was smiling. What had just occurred was pretty funny. But I will say, once under my thick fluffy covers alone again, my grin disappeared. I was truly sad because as I did every night now, I'd have to fall asleep thinking about how much I wanted Luke next to me.

Chapter 33

Patty's Pizza and *The Noodle Shop* were the two restaurant choices I gave Isabelle for dinner the following night. I could have heated up leftover flank steak at home, but I had no desire to be reminded of the bizarre previous evening. Plus, Izzie doesn't eat steak.

"How about McDonald's?" she asked cheerfully.

"That wasn't one of the choices."

"I have a great idea. Let's go to *Casa de Michael!*"

"Sure," I smiled, "I wouldn't mind tacos. Let's do it."

Half an hour later, we were at the hostess stand in the Mexican restaurant, waiting to be seated. I couldn't help but smile as I looked around the empty bar, remembering the night I told off Dan, went off on Luke, and fortuitously met Alice.

"Mommy, can I get lemonade?" Isabelle asked.

"Sure."

We waited some more.

"Can we get guacamole, Mommy?" she asked me.

A voice I would know anywhere, and a voice that was so familiar I sometimes heard it in my sleep responded, "What do you think, Mommy? Guacamole?"

I turned around. Standing there was Luke with his two boys, one of them deeply engrossed in a Nintendo DS.

"Hi," I said with a nervous smile. My heart was pounding. "Hi, guys!" I said to his kids.

"This is Max and this is Andrew." He tapped his son on the shoulder, "Hey," he scolded, "Look up and say hello."

"Hi," said Andrew. He immediately looked back down at his game and continued to play.

Luke's boys were little miniature versions of Luke, and as I studied their cute faces, I had this urge to hug the crap out of them for some bizarre, unknown reason.

A moment later, Luke knelt down and said to my daughter, "What's your name?"

"Izzie," she replied shyly, burying her face in my waist.

"So, what are you doing here?" I asked Luke, feeling stupid, because wouldn't his answer be "having dinner?"

"Having tacos?" he replied with a smile.

Just then, the hostess appeared and said to me, "Your table is ready."

I was just about to say good-bye to the Sullivan's when Luke blurted out, "Emma, do you want to have dinner together?"

"No, Mommy!" Izzie whispered loudly.

I pretty much wanted to crawl into a hole at this point.

"Isabelle!" I scolded, "That's not nice."

"It's okay," Luke said to her, "I'm a really nice guy, actually. Who's that on your shirt?"

"iCarly," she responded, guardedly.

"Oh...I've seen that show." Then he whispered, "My boys don't like to admit it, but they really like *iCarly*."

"Dad, come on," said Max.

Andrew looked up from his DS. "Yeah, Dad, what are you doing to us?"

"See?" Luke announced, "They're really sensitive about it."

Izzie giggled.

"So, what do you think?" he asked her, "Want to have dinner with us?"

"Can I sit next to you, Mommy?"

"Sure," I smiled.

"We're just going to get one table for five," Luke said to the hostess.

"Okay, sure," she smiled, "right this way."

Luke motioned to me to walk in front of him, and while I headed toward the table, Izzie followed closely behind me, holding my leg the entire time.

The meal got off to an awkward start when Isabelle asked me where the mommy was. Ironically, I was kind of wondering the same question. Although, I figured since Luke was wooing me with lollipops, the writing was pretty much on the wall.

Luke winked at me and then answered, "She's having dinner with her friends tonight."

Andrew looked up. "My parents are getting divorced."

"I'm sorry," I answered.

"My daddy died," Isabelle said to them, causing both boys to get these looks of shock on their faces that were so pronounced it was almost comical.

"Finally, a conversation that won over DS," said Luke.

All I could do was burst out laughing, and from that moment on, everyone began to relax.

While we ate, Izzie colored and listened, and Luke's boys talked and joked about all the teachers in their school. Miss Stellenberger had just announced to the class that she was getting married and had showed them all her diamond ring, Mrs. Kastle's last day was next week. She was having a baby. And Mr. Stone, the gym teacher was dating Miss Handleman, the music teacher, who in Max's opinion was pretty but had bad breath.

As for Mr. Sullivan and I, we had our own conversation going, and when I told him about *Winchester,* his whole face lit up, and it made me feel really good about myself.

"That's great!" he said, "Aren't you psyched?"

"Yeah," I giggled, "But it hasn't happened yet."

"It will," he said with a big grin, "And you should feel really proud of yourself. Do you know the odds for something like that to happen? This is really something." He looked right into my eyes and finished, "You're amazing."

The fact that Luke was so impressed with me took my self-esteem to a new level, and I realized right then how much I valued and craved his respect. And now I knew I had it. At that moment I gave him a big grin, and all I wanted to do was run into his arms and kiss his lips. Hard. I literally wanted to attack the guy. Not just for sex, though. I wanted *him*! All of him. The whole package. And I knew he could see that in my eyes.

Both of us realized, however that the kids, especially Isabelle, were aware of every word exchanged between us, regardless of how great the scoop was at Hoover Elementary School. And I was glad about that because I knew I was safe, and that there wouldn't be any discussions about our relationship, or Denny, or Luke's ex-wife, or the Tootsie Pop delivery.

I did want Luke to know I got the lollipops, though, so I said softly, "By the way, thank you for the Tootsie Pops."

Isabelle's head immediately shot up from the kid's menu she was coloring. "Did *you* give us those?"

"Yes," Luke answered with a nervous chuckle.

"Why?"

At this moment I noticed that Max and Andrew were now staring at Luke, waiting for him to answer.

Luke looked at me. I held my breath. Then he looked at Izzie and responded with a smile, "Just because."

All the kids looked confused but satisfied with his response. I looked at Luke and he winked at me.

Suddenly, everything felt so perfect. My daughter, his kids, me and him, all having dinner together. We weren't a family, yet there was a certain comfort level that seemed natural and easy. Right then, I had the strangest thought. Very recently, I had been thinking about how I didn't want to introduce Izzie to anyone I was dating unless he was significant. At that time, I had predicted Denny would be the first, and perhaps the only boyfriend she would ever meet. I had ignored my gut instinct that Luke would be the one.

So tonight, sitting here having Mexican food with Luke and his kids, I realized that even though we weren't a couple, not even dating, in fact, Luke had ultimately turned out to be the first man who meant something to me, *and* the first person I'd brought around my child, without even meaning to. This wasn't the way I had planned them to meet, yet a twist of fate had brought us all together. The irony was unbelievable. Maybe this was a sign. Maybe Luke and I really had a chance.

"What are you thinking about?" he asked me quietly.

I answered with a grin, and then I pulled out my Blackberry and texted him, "Let's talk later. Can I call you after I put her to bed?"

I heard Luke's phone bling. Instantly he pulled it out of his pocket and read my text. Then he looked up at me and said, "Sure." He looked happy at this moment.

When the check came, Luke insisted on paying.

"Thank you, Luke," I said, "it was a nice night."

"Yes," he smiled, "It was."

During the short car ride home, my daughter asked, "Mommy, who were those people?"

"Um…friends."

"Where did you meet them?"

I was sensing that my six year old daughter detected something going on between Luke and me. "Well, I met Max and Andrew's dad a few months ago on the jogging path, and now we're friends."

"Is Luke your boyfriend, Mommy?"

"No!" I answered defensively.

"I like John and Andrew."

"I'm glad, sweetie."

"Mommy…"

"Yes?"

"Are you ever going to get married again?"

"Hmm," I said thoughtfully, "I don't really know. If I do, it won't be for a long, long time."

"Would you ever marry Luke?"

"Oh honey, I don't know. He's a good man, but he's just a friend for now." For now, I thought, as I continued driving, my insides aching, thinking about how much I needed and wanted to talk to him.

Just as I was pulling into the driveway, Izzie asked, "Hey, Mommy?"

"Yeah?"

"Is it okay if I talk about Daddy?"

I put the car in park and turned around to look at her in the back seat. "Of course it is! Why are you asking me that?"

Izzie burst into tears.

"What's wrong?" I asked as I shut the ignition off and got into the back seat with her.

Through tears, she said, "I'm afraid we're going to forget about him."

I hugged Izzie so tight to the point I hoped I wasn't hurting her. "Listen to me. Your dad is your dad. No one will ever take his place, do you understand that?"

"Yeah."

"He loved you and we can talk about him every day if you want. In fact, I love talking about him."

"Really?"

"Yes, Izzie." I realized right then that I wasn't lying to my daughter. I did enjoy talking about Sam, because I knew Isabelle needed that.

I put her to bed shortly after we got home, and lying there in her cute, little nightgown, she asked for a bedtime story.

"I have the perfect one," I began, "Once upon a time there was a boy and a girl. Their names were Emma and Sam..." And then I told Izzie the story of how her father and I met in the stands of a Bears game. "It was a freezing cold night and the Bears were playing the Steelers..."

This would become one of many stories I would tell Izzie about her father and me. She never got tired of hearing them, and I never got tired of telling her things about the father she'd never come to know on her own. It was tragic, but beautiful.

When Izzie was asleep, I went to call Luke, but something stopped me. I decided I had another call to make first.

"Hello?" Denny answered.

"Hi, it's me."

"How are you?" he asked curtly.

"I'm okay." I took a deep breath. "I'm so sorry about last night."

"It's alright. Are you feeling better?"

"The thing is...I really like you..."

"But..." he said. It was obvious Denny was guarded. He also seemed a little hostile, but I couldn't blame him.

"But...I don't think I can see you anymore. I'm so sorry."

There was a long period of silence, the kind where everyone's holding their breath, anticipating what's going to happen next and who is going to be the first to say something. I've always been told that the first one who speaks loses.

"So, that's it?" Denny asked, "It's over?" His voice began to rise. "We just had an amazing few weeks together and now you're just dumping me?"

"I'm not dumping you, Denny," I said, "I just don't feel right about the relationship anymore. It's nothing you did. You are wonderful and I really, really enjoy being with you. I just don't think I can give you what you want."

Now Denny softened and even made a little joke out of it, I think in an attempt to lighten things up. "I'm so bummed!"

I laughed softly. "Me, too. You are an amazing guy."

"I really like you, Emma. Are you sure?"

"Yes, I'm sure. It just doesn't feel right. I'm sorry!"

"Well, at least you're honest. Hey, Emma?"

"Yeah?"

"I think we have a great thing. Please call me if you change your mind."

"Okay, thanks. And thank you for being so understanding and sweet about this. I'm really sorry if I'm hurting you."

"Hey," he said in his cute Irish voice I adored so much, "I had a great time. I don't regret it at all."

"Stay in touch?"

"You got it."

"Bye, Denny."

"Bye, Emma."

I hung up the phone relieved beyond belief and sad at the same time. I was losing a friend. But I was doing what I had to do.

The next call I made was to Alice. I wanted to talk to her before my big meeting with Phil Warren, which was taking place the next morning. I needed her to prep me, both emotionally and professionally. There was no one better than Alice to psych me up and tell me what to say.

We spent an hour on the phone, talking for the first ten minutes about her new girlfriend and my old boyfriend, *Den0507.*

"He sounds like such a great guy. You should feel good about that."

"I do."

When we started talking about *Winchester,* she was (as always) full of energy, coaching me on what questions to ask, and how to negotiate without offending anyone.

After saying good-bye to the beautiful woman who never failed to put me on a high far better than any drug, I went to my closet and picked out the suit I would wear to my meeting. I chose a light pink dress with a matching jacket.

Finally, it was time to call Luke. I went to his name in my address book, but just as I was about to hit the call button, I changed my mind. I was just too drained to talk to Luke right now. I decided to text instead. "Thank you again for dinner. We had a really nice time. Is there any way we could talk tomorrow? I'm really tired."

"Sure," Luke texted back, "Are u okay?"

"Yes."

I wasn't really okay, though. In the past twenty-four hours, I'd had a bad date with Denny, I'd come extremely close to having hate sex with Preston, I'd eaten a family dinner with Luke, and I'd broken up with Denny, a man I felt extremely guilty for hurting, not to mention that all of this was going on just before what was probably the biggest professional day of my life.

Oddly enough, I found myself thinking about Sam. My husband was the last man, perhaps the *only* man in my life that I'd ever really loved. That love had been taken away from me in an instant. But the worst part of it all was that I wasn't sure I loved him at the time of his death. And because of the guilt I felt by admitting that, I wondered if I had the guts to really love someone again.

I realized now that I'd enjoyed Preston so much because there was never any threat of love. Although I didn't admit it to myself at the time, I had known all along in my heart that Preston and I would never say those three words to each other, and that made things safe. And looking back, that factor was as attractive to me as Preston's rock hard abs.

I thought about all of the Matts I went out with, and to Denny again. When I threw myself into the dating scene, I was, like anyone else, looking for love. That's what I thought at the time. Now, in retrospect, not only was I *not* looking for something serious, I was avoiding it, and was desperately hiding from it, much like my daughter at three years old had hidden from me when it was time to take a bath. In other words, I wanted to find someone to love, and yet I sabotaged myself in the worst way.

And then of course, there was Luke. From the day I'd met him he was unavailable, still attached to someone else. Even though I didn't know that at the time, maybe I knew it subconsciously, and maybe it pleased me because it was easier to be in an imaginary relationship than experiencing a real one. It was possible that Luke still being involved with his ex was the root of the attraction.

It was so clear to me now. I had pretended to want love, but had chosen men who for one reason or another didn't want a relationship. It let me off the hook. I was running from commitment just as much as Preston was, if not more. Just in a different way. And truthfully, I had more respect for Preston, because at least he admitted it to himself.

So now, Luke was now ready to start something with me. He was, in essence, calling my bluff. I had never really planned for this. He wasn't supposed to come around. But it was happening. And it was scarier than The Blair Witch Project. How could I be sure that he was really serious? Just because he sent over a few lollipops did that mean he wanted to be in a relationship with me? And if he did, was I capable of that?

For now, though, I had to put all my men on the backburner and think about *Winchester Foods.* That's what mattered most right now. The last thing I remember before dozing off was deciding if I should wear nude or black pumps.

Chapter 34

"Hi, my name is Emma Bloom," I said to the sixth floor receptionist at *Winchester* headquarters, "I'm here to see Philip Warren."

"Yes, Ms. Bloom," she answered, "Have a seat. I'll let him know you're here."

"Thanks," I said. Then I turned around, sat on a nearby sofa, and began leafing through *Time* magazine, looking up every time I heard someone walk by. I wondered if Preston worked on this floor. What if he happened to walk by? My heart began to pound and I really needed Mr. Warren to hurry up and get me out of the reception area.

"Ms. Bloom?" I heard. I looked up. Standing there was a nice looking older man who reminded me of Gene Hackman. "I'm Phil Warren," he said with a smile. We shook hands.

"Please, call me Emma," I said.

"Sure."

Phil took me back to his office, which turned out to be a huge corner space with wall-to-wall windows, a big oak desk, and a separate seating area. Two women were seated on the couch, and another guy was in a nearby chair. All of them stood up when Phil and I entered the room. That's when I knew something huge was going down. All these people were here for me!

Each one introduced him or herself, every one of them a Vice-President of something. And after shaking hands with all of them, Phil told me to have a seat, and motioned to the chair next to the other guy. Then he sat on the couch, next to the women. A secretary appeared and asked me if I wanted coffee or water or anything to drink.

"No, thank you," I said, my voice shaking, "I'm fine." Right then, I noticed about a dozen jars of my salsa placed on the coffee table in front of me. Phil noticed me noticing.

"I bought those from a little boutique in the area," he said.

"Oh," I smiled."

"You have quite a business," one of the female executives named Margaret Paulson said.

"Thank you."

Phil and his entourage spent the next several minutes asking me questions about the business, like what motivated me to start it, to what had I contributed its success, what I felt the drawbacks were, what the biggest challenges were, and my favorite, why I named a salsa after Bradley Cooper.

I answered as professionally as I possibly could, but I was honest, too, and I could tell I was winning them over, just like I could tell when I was about to make a sale.

"I think I'm ready to get to the point," said Phil. He looked at all the other V.P.s. "Don't you think so?" All three of them nodded. I held my breath.

"Mitch has done a lot of research on the salsa industry," Phil began, motioning to the guy in the chair, "and we feel there is clearly a market for what we're calling 'Gift-packaged Gourmet Salsa.'"

The other woman, whose name was Claudia Barnes added, "We've also done some research on you and your background. We know you have extensive sales and marketing experience."

Margaret finished, "And based on what we've seen you do with *Solo Chicka's Salsa,* we think you would be a very valuable asset to *Winchester.*"

Now my jaw was on the ground. "Are you offering me a job?" I asked.

Phil leaned in and handed me a thick folder. "Have a look at this. We'd like you to join *Winchester* as a part-time consultant for our Marketing and Consumer promotions department in our Mexican snacks division. We would start you at sixty-five thousand dollars a year."

Mitch added, "We would also like to buy your company for two-hundred forty-five thousand."

I'm pretty sure I gasped, because they all had huge grins on their faces now. "I...don't know what to say," I exclaimed, "I'm so flattered by this. And so grateful!"

"Well, we're grateful to you, Emma," said Phil, "We think we can make a lot of money from what you've created. Congratulations on a job well done!"

We spent the next few minutes going through my offer in more detail, and then Phil told me to take a few days and think about it. Before leaving, I shook everyone's hands. Claudia Barnes walked me out, and when we reached the elevators she turned to me and said, "It was a pleasure meeting you, Emma. I hope you'll join us here at *Winchester.*"

"Thank you again, Claudia."

We shook hands. I pressed the elevator button and watched Claudia walk away. When she was a few feet away, she turned around and said with a huge grin, "By the way, I love Bradley Cooper, too!"

I got in the car and literally screamed. While driving home, I called Laura and left a message, saying that I needed to talk to her. I then did the same with my mother, my father and Alice. Where was everyone?!

There was one other person who I was dying to call. I wanted to share my news with him. I knew he would be so happy for me, and I knew he'd be proud of me, too. I couldn't bring myself to do it, though, because I was scared. The next conversation he and I were going to have was going to involve the Tootsie Pops and our future. And I was terrified of that. Everything was going so well. I was on top of the world. I had a new job, a new career, new money. Did I really need to risk my happiness by getting into another relationship?

That night, I ended up having a dinner party. With a little help from *Casa de Michael,* or I should say, *all* the help from *Casa de Michael,* I fed my mom, my dad, Laura, myself and Izzie. I also invited Alice. Everyone seemed quite enamored with my beautiful, smart friend, and Laura monopolized her time for most of the evening.

When I announced the sale of my business and my job offer, my mother let out a huge scream. My dad told me he was proud of me, Laura hugged me so tight it actually hurt, and Alice simply smiled and gave me a wink, as if to say she knew all along that things would turn out this way.

Isabelle then did something I will never forget. She walked up to me and in a very businesslike way, she shook my hand. "Emma, I'm very proud of you," she said.

I couldn't help but laugh. "Thank you, Isabelle."

"Mom, you rock!" Then she hugged me tight.

At the end of the night, when Izzie was in bed and my parents had left, I said good-bye to Alice.

"How did I get so lucky to cross paths with you?" I asked her.

"I think your sister likes me," Alice joked. Then she handed me an envelope. "Open this later."

I gave her a hug. "Thank you."

Alice blew me a kiss and left.

When I walked into the kitchen, I found Laura at the sink doing some dishes.

"I thought you went to bed," I said.

She exclaimed, "I loved Alice."

"Isn't she the best?"

Laura smiled. "Yes, she is."

"Are you okay?" I asked.

"Yeah," she replied unconvincingly.

We sat down at the kitchen table. "What is it?"

"Well, the thing is…"

"What? Please tell me."

Laura's eyes filled with tears. "Alan and I reached a settlement. I guess he and Maggie found another place, so he's giving me the house. I can move back in anytime after Monday."

"Laura, that's great! Aren't you happy?"

A tear rolled down my sister's cheek when she answered, "Yes, I am. But I'm going to miss you."

We hugged for a long time, and my heart was actually aching. I was so happy for Laura because I knew it made sense for her to go home. That being said, I would miss my goodie-two-shoes, judgmental, polar opposite sister more than anything in the world. I was one way, she was the other. I had an opinion on something, hers was always different. I was the wild, fun, ditzy sister. She was the giving, selfless, serious, smart one. We drove each other crazy. But we truly were best friends.

Through these tough times and through living together, Laura and I had learned to see things through each other's eyes. We'd realized that having such vastly different viewpoints on things can be healthy, and we learned to take each other's points of view as valuable gifts, not judging so much, but appreciating a different outlook. And I felt so fortunate for that.

"Good night, Laura," I said when my sister decided to head upstairs to bed, "I'll miss saying that to you in person."

She smiled at me. "Me, too. Thanks for being my best friend."

"Same to you."

"You coming up?"

"In a minute."

Once Laura went upstairs, I opened the envelope Alice gave me. To my surprise, inside were several cut-up pieces of paper with writing on them. I smiled as I dumped the contents onto the kitchen table. 'Leave it to Alice to write me a letter and cut it up into a puzzle,' I thought, turning all the pieces right-side-up.

It took me a minute to put it together.

"*Dear Emma*," it began, "*I want to let you know that I am truly happy for you. What you have done professionally is amazing and well deserved. I respect and admire you a great deal. Your life has been like this letter, a puzzle, and you've had to figure out how to put the pieces together. From the looks of things, you've accomplished that and more. You now have everything you want: your health, a healthy, wonderful child, a nice home, a great family, and a wonderful career. And you can take credit for all of it because you bought into putting the past behind, thinking positively, working hard, and doing the right things. But there's a piece missing in your puzzle. Go out and get him, Emma.*"

On the verge of tears, I read the last line. "*He's your free gift with purchase.*" The letter was signed, "*I love you, Alice.*"

"Go out and get him, Emma. He's your free gift with purchase," I read out loud, tears welling in my eyes.

At that moment, I thought to myself, "What am I waiting for?" I could actually feel my fear of romantic love leave my body, with exhilaration and self-empowerment taking their place. I was like a sky diver at twenty thousand feet, waiting to jump, and focusing on the beauty of the blue sky rather than the trepidation of how high up I was. What I had to do next was very clear.

Chapter 35

It was cold and windy and the sky was dark. Rain would inevitably be coming down soon. There was no question about that. And here I stood, shivering at the entrance of the jogging path at 5:55 in the morning, waiting for a certain runner, who I knew was here every morning at 6:00.

Suddenly I heard a dog barking. I turned and looked. There was Lucky. And Luke. They were walking toward me. I took a deep breath. Luke let his dog's leash go and Lucky ran to me, continuing to bark and wag her tail while showering me with licks.

"Hi!" I greeted my good pooch friend, bending down to return her warm reception. Then I looked up at her owner, who was now standing in front of us. "Hi," I smiled.

"What are you doing here?" Luke asked me. He motioned to my jeans and added, "You're not here to run, I see."

I stood up. "No. I'm not here to run."

"Then what is it?" he asked, "Are you okay?"

There was so much to say. I wanted to tell Luke how sorry I was that I hadn't called him. I wanted to tell him that I loved the fact that he sent me a box of Tootsie Pops. I wanted to let him know that I understood his decision to try to work things out with his wife. I wanted to tell him that the day I spent at the beach with him was in my top five of my all-time favorite days in life. I wanted to tell him that when he rescued me from my fall and put band-aids on my scraped up knees, he wasn't just rescuing me physically.

I wanted to tell him that he'd rescued me. Period. And now, I wanted to rescue him. I wanted to tell him all of those things, but I didn't. I said only one thing.

I looked him right in the eyes and with the bold courage I learned from Preston, I declared, "Luke, I want you to kiss me."

Without any hesitation whatsoever, he leaned in and obliged. His lips and his touch felt so natural and so comfortable, and it was like I'd been in his arms a million times before. At that moment, I felt my entire core transform instantly from cautious and reserved to gutsy and unabashed. I was now a girl who wasn't afraid to put the past behind her and go after what she thought could be her future.

A few moments later, Luke pulled away from me and said with a chuckle, "How was that?"

"It was good," I smiled.

"Emma..." He put his head down for a second and then looked up at me. Softly, he continued, "You're like the girl I've known since I was three. You're the girl who lived next door, the girl who I always felt was mine." He took my hands and kissed them, and then he finished, "I feel like you're mine. Is it wrong to say that?"

"No," I whispered, fighting back tears, "Nothing's ever felt more right."

"Uhibuk," he said softly.

Tears sprung up instantly. "What?"

"You heard me. I've been brushing up on my Arabic."

I smiled and whispered, "Uhibuk," which means I love you in Arabic.

Luke put his lips on mine and began kissing me again in the middle of the Willow Ridge jogging path with the wind blowing brutally and Lucky seeking shelter in between us. And as we stood there embraced, I realized something. Alice helped me see it, and so did Laura and my mother, and Preston, and Denny, and even all the Matts.

People with a past, people with baggage if you will, are still capable of finding love again, and the difference between those who do and those who don't is pretty simple. The ones who end up happy are the ones who put the bitterness and the anger bags down, the ones who stop thinking like a victim and find the guts to go out and grab the life they want, the life they feel they deserve. And not only do they hold onto, but they cherish the pieces of significance that give their lives true meaning.

In the arms of the man I loved, I now realized I possessed more self-worth then I'd probably ever had in my life. Grace, acceptance and gratitude were part of my mantra. But most importantly, I was carrying the most precious piece of baggage on earth: my daughter. And at this moment, I felt like I had more free gifts than I'd ever dreamed possible.

Epilogue

One month later...

At *Stella's,* the little wine bar where I'd had my first drink with Alice months earlier, four couples plus my daughter sat at a big round table, eating and drinking, and celebrating my birthday. The crowd included my new boyfriend, Luke Sullivan, my almost nauseatingly in love parents, and Alice and her new girlfriend, a tall, thin, nice looking blonde woman who wrote children's books for a living. Laura was also there with her date, a man she'd gone out with a few times, who seemed like a great guy, other than the fact that his name was Matt.

"How did you guys meet?" Alice asked her during dinner.

"Well," she gushed, "Alan got our TV in the settlement, so I went shopping for a new one."

"I sold her a fifty inch flat screen," Matt said proudly, putting his arm around my sister.

"He was my free gift with purchase!" Laura joked.

Just after we finished eating, I looked up and noticed a couple seated at the bar, not far away. My heart skipped a beat when I recognized the guy's big sculpted shoulders and gorgeous dark skin. Preston Christiansen, the man who had given me memories that could still cause the hair on my arms to stand up, was sitting no more than twenty feet away.

To my initial dismay, his date was gorgeous. And young. Her long blonde hair and perfect body, complete with fake (but beautiful) boobs caused a tinge of envy in me. I smiled to myself as I realized that Preston was with the person he was supposed to be with right now and so was I. My incredibly strong, smart and sexy older guy was by my side. His arm was around my chair and he was in a conversation with Alice about her job. Everything seemed as it should be.

Still, I felt I needed a little closure, perhaps one more conversation with the womanizer who affected me so deeply. So when I saw him get up to go to the bathroom, I decided to follow him in hopes of stealing a minute of private conversation. Although a very high school-ish move, I stood inside the women's bathroom, holding the door open just a crack and waiting for my old boyfriend to come out of the men's room. I hadn't spoken to him or seen him since the night we were about to have sex and then didn't.

The second I saw him walk out of the men's room, I pushed the women's room door open and feigned surprise. "Preston?"

He turned around, his face lighting up the second he saw it was me. The expression of happiness was so genuine, I instinctively threw my arms around him. "Hi!" I exclaimed, hugging him tight.

He chuckled, "How are you?"

I pulled back and said, "I'm good, how are you?"

His smile was so perfect. "Good." He then said, "You look great, Baby," almost causing me to go into cardiac arrest from overstimulation of the heart muscle.

"You do too."

"Who are you here with?" he asked.

"My family and..." I hesitated, "my boyfriend."

"You have a boyfriend?"

"Yeah," I answered with a shy smile.

"I'm happy for you."

"Preston, listen..." I said, "Can I say something to you?"

"Sure."

"The thing is..."

"Tell me," he urged.

I took a deep breath and blurted out, "The thing is, I think I wanted you to fall in love with me."

Preston gave me a smile that melted me like push up pops in ninety degree weather and then said, "How do you know I didn't?"

"Because I know you."

"The truth is," he said sadly, "I'm not sure if I know how to love somebody."

I looked at him, and surprisingly I felt sorry for him. He truly was afraid of commitment and love. The good news was, Preston knew himself, and I felt in my heart that when he was ready to help himself deal with his fear of commitment, he would do just that. And I strongly suspected that one day, this man, beautiful both on the outside and in, would eventually find love. And just like me, it would be on his terms, when he was ready.

The sex fiend suddenly switched gears and smiled playfully at me. "You know, if you're interested, we could sneak into the bathroom and finish what we never finished at *Donatella's*."

"We're finished, Preston," I said with a sad smile, "And I'm sad about that in a way. But I would never, ever change a thing with you. You were sweet and kind and sexy, and you made me feel amazing." I kissed his cheek softly. "Thank you."

Preston gave me a wide grin, "So, your salsa business is really a success, I hear."

All of a sudden, something clicked, and it dawned on me. Maybe the fact that I'd sold my company and landed a great job wasn't a coincidence. The story suddenly became very clear. "Oh my God," I said to him, "You did it, didn't you? You're responsible for my buyout and my job at *Winchester*."

"No. *You* did it," Preston said with a grin, "All I did was hear from Stacy and John McGowan that you started a salsa business. I knew how good your salsa was, so I bought a few jars and put them on Phil Warren's desk."

"Oh my God! You made all of this happen for me!"

"*You* made it happen, Emma. *You*."

I threw my arms around him. "Thank you!"

Through laughter, he answered, "No problem."

"Will you come meet everyone and have a drink with us?" I asked him.

"Sure. Let me get my date."

I arrived back at the table and pulled up two chairs, feeling the strange looks from all my cliquey friends and family. Up walked Preston and his Gwyneth Paltrow looking girlfriend. "Everyone," I announced, "this is Preston Christiansen."

I was thoroughly entertained as I watched the man who I once desired to the point of being unable to function shake hands with everyone. Laura was hilarious, bubbly and nervous and very inquisitive, Alice was not surprisingly kind, and so were my parents. When Preston shook hands with Izzie and said, "Nice to see you again," Izzie's face lit up and she looked at me and said, "What's *he* doing here?" Everyone laughed.

It was perhaps Luke's reaction to meeting Preston that was the funniest. I had never seen Luke jealous. He was jittery, self-conscious, and territorial, making sure his arm was around me constantly.

I would tell Luke later in the night, when we were alone, that there was nothing to feel threatened by when it came to Preston. Yes, he was gorgeous and sexy, and girls had a way of gasping at the sight of the guy, but I had a place in my heart for Preston and it was far, far away from the spot where Luke sat. Preston was my past, Luke my future.

A few minutes later, I heard a cell phone ring. "Someone's phone is ringing," I announced.

"It's yours," said Laura. Once again, my sister had changed my ring tone. "Money, money, money, money...money..." It was the theme song from *The Apprentice*. Everyone started laughing and when I said hello I was still giggling.

"Hi, is this Emma?" a familiar voice asked.

"Yes it is. Who's this?"

"This is Bradley Cooper."

"Ha ha...come on, who is this?"

"This is really Bradley, Bradley Cooper."

I gasped and the entire table became silent. I knew right then I was speaking to my ultimate celebrity crush. "Hi," I said.

"Hi," said Bradley with a chuckle, "I was calling to tell you that I had a chance to taste your *Hotter than Bradley Cooper* salsa, and I really enjoyed it."

"Thanks!" I gushed. Then I mouthed to my sister, "Bradley Cooper."

"Oh my God!" she gasped. Then she told everyone at the table and they all just sat there, gazing at me.

"Phil wanted me to call you and let you know I just signed a deal with *Winchester* to endorse your salsa and put my signature on the jar."

"Really?"

"Yes."

"Well, thank you so much!"

"You're welcome. I'll look forward to meeting you next time I'm in Chicago," he said.

"Yes, me too!"

After I said good-bye to Bradley, everyone at the table started laughing and talking about Bradley Cooper and his movies. We were interrupted by a couple of waiters who came out of kitchen singing happy birthday to me and carrying a cake with a few lit candles on it.

While they sang to me, I looked around the table at all my loved ones. There was Izzie, my beautiful angel, who was so brave, dealing with life without a father. She had a look of excitement on her face that only a child gets in response to a cake with lit candles on it. Then there were my happy parents, two amazing people who had dealt with and survived infidelity. And my sweet, sweet sister, who by being my roommate had offered the beauty of seeing things from a different perspective. I giggled, thinking about the fact that she had actually picked up the guy who sold her a TV. And Alice, the woman who I'd kissed, and the woman who with one look could inspire me to no end. She looked so beautiful. I wasn't sure if she would ever know how much she helped me in life.

Then there was Preston, the gorgeous heartthrob, who had redefined me sexually, gotten me pregnant, fell off the face of the earth, and then turned my business into a gold mine. He had ultimately served a purpose in my life that was truly unexpected.

And Luke, of course, the man who I'd met while lying on the ground after I'd just fallen on my face. The man who'd physically and mentally picked me up and helped me heal by offering his friendship initially, and then his love. For all these wonderful people surrounding me, I felt blessed beyond belief.

"Make a wish," shouted Izzie.

I looked up and with tears in my eyes I announced, "But I already have everything I want."

I looked back at my daughter, and then I looked down at the burning candles, closed my eyes, and thought of the perfect wish. I wished for Isabelle to be as lucky as I was, in giving and receiving love, and I wished that she would find as much joy out of life as she possibly could, just like I had. Then I drew in a big, deep breath, and blew out my candles.

The End

Enjoy these Great Salsa Recipes!!!

Black Bean Watermelon Salsa

Provided by: Linda Anderson

Four cups diced watermelon
One cup chopped Vidalia onion
One clove minced garlic
One tsp. chopped jalapeño pepper
½ cup chopped cilantro
Two cans black beans (drained)

Mix together and chill in fridge for two hours

Pineapple Mango Salsa

Provided by: Lynn Bruno

2 large ripe mangoes, cored and diced
1 firm avocado, pitted and diced (overly ripe avocado won't stand up)
1 medium cucumber, peeled, seeded and diced
1 red bell pepper, seeded and diced
1 jalapeño pepper, seeded and diced (optional)
½ of a ripened pineapple, peeled, cored, and diced
1 small red onion, diced
1 small bunch of cilantro leaves, chopped
salt and pepper to taste

Dressing:
¼ to ½ cup olive oil 2-4 tbsp. white wine or cider vinegar
juice of 1 lime
1 tsp honey

Combine all diced items in a bowl and toss to combine. Add a bit of fresh ground pepper and sea salt to the mix to taste. Wisk dressing ingredients in a small bowl, or combine them in a sealed jar and shake until mixed. Pour dressing over fruit/vegetables and toss to combine. Add more salt and pepper to taste. Let sit for ½ hour for flavors to meld together. Enjoy over fish, chicken, pork, or all by itself!

Kiwi Strawberry Peach Salsa

Provided by: Stephanie Hodges

1 peach ~ peeled, pitted, and diced into small pieces
1 kiwi ~ peeled and diced into small pieces
6 strawberries ~ diced into small pieces
1 jalapeno pepper ~ seeded and diced into small pieces (use as much as you'd like. I use sometimes use 2. You can use 1/2 if you don't like it too spicy)
1 tablespoon lime juice
1 green onion ~ diced into small pieces
2 tablespoons chopped fresh cilantro or parsley
1 pinch salt

Mix all ingredients together. The longer it sits, the better the flavors come together. I try to make it a day or two in advance, but I've also made it and used it right away.

Cranberry Salsa

Provided by: Pauline Levy

12 oz package fresh cranberries, stems removed
2 finely diced large celery stalks
1 diced small white onion
1 jalapeño pepper, seeded and minced (may substitute banana pepper)
¼ cup chopped, fresh cilantro (more if you prefer)
½ tsp kosher or sea salt
1/2 cup sugar
3 tbsp fresh lime juice

Process cranberries in food processor until coarsely chopped. Transfer cranberries to medium bowl and then add remaining ingredients. Stir well. Transfer to serving bowl. Cover and refrigerate until ready to serve. For spicier salsa, include seeds from jalapeño.

Fresh Salsa: Always Healthy!

Provided by: Missy Vacala

(Use organic ingredients if possible)
1 ½ cup tomatoes, diced
2 tbsp finely diced white onion
2 tbsp finely chopped red bell pepper
2 tbsp finely chopped yellow bell pepper
1 tbsp fresh chopped or 1tsp dried cilantro
1 tsp fresh lime juice
1 jalapeno pepper, seeds and white ribs removed, minced
1 tsp minced, sautéed or pressed garlic
1/8 tsp minced or powdered ginger
Sea salt to taste

Combine all ingredients thoroughly in a bowl and refrigerate until ready to serve. If you'd prefer, season with a dash of onion powder, garlic powder, cayenne, turmeric powder, celery seeds or cumin, whatever you like! I add the sea salt just before eating, since it draws out the tomato juices.

(For corn salsa, add ½ cup corn kernels cut off the cob. For mango salsa, add ½ cup diced mango. For pineapple salsa, add ½ cup diced pineapple. For avocado salsa, add ¾ cup diced avocado)

Bean Salsa

Provided by: Ruby Kang

Bean salsa
1 can navy beans
1 can black beans
1 can corn
1 can petite diced tomatoes
1/2 medium sweet onion diced small
1 orange sweet bell pepper diced
1 bunch cilantro roughly chopped

Envelope of Good Seasonings salad dressing mixed as directed on packet. Drain and rinse beans, drain corn and tomatoes. Add all ingredients in large bowl and mix together. Serve as a side dish or with tortilla chips as a dip.

Mango Salsa

Provided by: Susan Palkovic

Ingredients:

2 ripe mangos, peeled & chopped
1 medium red onion chopped
1/4 c fresh cilantro leaves
4 fresh jalapenos chopped
1 Lime juiced, (about 2 tbsp.)with rind grated
dash of salt

Mix together and let chill for at least an hour.

Made in the USA
Charleston, SC
20 March 2013